NIGHTHAWK BLUES

About the Author

Peter Guralnick was born in Boston and has published widely on a variety of subjects over the last twenty years.

His first book, *Feel Like Going Home: Portraits in Blues and Rock 'n' Roll*, was published in 1971. Its sequel: *Lost Highway: Journeys and Arrivals of American Musicians*, was published in 1979. *A Listener's Guide to the Blues* was published in 1982, and *Sweet Soul Music: Rhythm and Blues and the Southern Dream of Freedom* was published in 1986.

Guralnick has just begun work on a full-scale biography of Elvis Presley, tentatively titled "Last Train to Memphis: The Rise of Elvis Presley."

He has free-lanced for numerous magazines and periodicals, including *Rolling Stone*, *The Village Voice*, *The New York Times*, *Country Music*, *Living Blues*, and *The Boston Phoenix*. He contributed six chapters to the *Rolling Stone Illustrated History of Rock 'n' Roll*, including the ones on Elvis, Ray Charles, Fats Domino, and B. B. King.

He has written a good deal of fiction, both published and unpublished, but to date *Nighthawk Blues* is his only published novel. He has recently completed the second draft of a new novel, tentatively called "Democracy."

NIGHTHAWK BLUES

a novel by PETER GURALNICK

THUNDER'S MOUTH PRESS

NEW YORK

Published in the United States by
Thunder's Mouth Press
93–99 Greene Street, New York, N.Y. 10012
Cover design by Marcia Salo
Grateful acknowledgment is made to the New York State Council on the Arts and
the National Endowment for the Arts for financial assistance with the publication
of this work.
Permission to reprint lyrics from the following songs is gratefully acknowledged:
"Don't Deceive Me" by Chuck Willis © 1954 by Tideland Music Corp.; "How
Long, How Long Blues" words and music by Leroy Carr © copyright 1929 by
MCA Music, a division of MCA Inc., N.Y., N.Y., Copyright renewed. All rights re-
served.

Library of Congress Cataloging-in-Publication Data

Guralnick, Peter.
    Nighthawk blues : a novel / by Peter Guralnick.
      p. cm.—(Contemporary fiction series)
    ISBN 0-938410-64-4 (pbk.) : $9.95
    I. Title. II. Series.
    [PS3557.U7N5 1988]
    813'.54—dc19
                                      88-9750
                                      CIP

Manufactured in the United States of America
Distributed by Consortium Book Sales
213 E. 4th Street
St. Paul, Minnesota 55101
612-221-9035

FOR ALEXANDRA

Now you's a dirty mistreater
Robber and a cheater
Slip you in the Dozens
Your pappy is your cousin
Your mama do the Lordy Lord . . .

—"Dirty Mother for You"

NIGHTHAWK BLUES

Prologue

WRECK
ON THE HIGHWAY

As USUAL they were arguing—it was always about money or women or something that had happened in the dim forgotten past, and half the time it was a combination of all three. Hawk was driving, his hands gripped tight around the wheel. Teenochie sat next to him, stiff and erect, a derby perched lightly atop his shaven head. Wheatstraw kept one hand on the doorhandle, and every so often the door itself flew open, prompting cries of "What you doing, you crazy fool, you want to get us all killed?" and a squealing of car brakes.

"What you talking about?" Hawk's voice boomed out unmodulated, filling the automobile as if it were a concert stage. "I been knowing that gal for fifty-two years, and she be doing tricks when I met her. That gal got a cock that's made of whalebone, and your dick better be made of rubber if you want to last the time with her. One time she get a whole orchestra in the

3

studio, and she do 'em all, sometimes two at a time. That's why they call her Ma Grinder. She-it." He chuckled to himself. "That gal keep all the nickels she ever made, she have more money than Rockefeller ever seen."

Wheatstraw giggled, and the door nearly flew open again. He gave his Woody Woodpecker laugh and fished a battered harmonica out of his suitcoat pocket.

"Yeah, yeah, but still and all, she wasn't no whore," Teenochie protested. "She made some good records—"

"Shoot. Just because she whispered sweet nothings in your ear fifty-two years ago!" Hawk rolled down the window and spat contemptuously. "You think every pussy you get has got your name written all over it. You get them little old white gals come up to you at the colleges, say, Mr. Teenochie, play me some blues, and right away you be thinking they gonna suck your dick. Shoot. You couldn't use none of that pussy no more anyway. You better off with a goat."

"A goat!" said Teenochie indignantly.

"Yeah, just like that 3-in-1 oil, with a goat you can suck, fuck, or buck, then when you get tired of that you can cook it and eat it up—man, that's where you really getting your money's worth."

Hawk guffawed heavily. Teenochie sent daggers of resentment with a lopsided, gold-toothed grin. Wheatstraw ran his lips over the mouth harp, closed his eyes, and dreamed of Arkansas.

"You think they give you a good count?" said Teenochie, taking a long pull from his bottle and pointedly recapping it without offering Hawk a drink.

Hawk nodded. "Don't make no matter. They got it worked out between them."

"Who? That kid and Jerry?"

Hawk just grunted.

"Well, Jerry ain't so bad, man. Not like some of them managers I had. At least the cat is trying."

"She-it, I wish he try a little harder and just get out of my life," said Hawk. "I get along fine before I ever knowed that boy, and I get along fine after he be long gone. Sometimes he act like he don't even think I been out here before, but I been out here for sixty years, before I knowed him, before I knowed you—"

"I don't like playing in no college gyms," Teenochie cut in, not wanting to hear any more of what Hawk had to say, not wanting to put up with any more of Hawk's emphatic opinions. Ever since they had been out on the road, for nearly a month now, he had had to listen to Hawk's stories, he had had to endure seeing Hawk get the credit which, if there were any justice in the world, would go to Teenochie Slim, he had had to suffer Hawk's impatient correction and practical jokes—and he older than Hawk himself and practically having given him his start in the business! He had pleaded with the boy, he had told Jerry that Teenochie Slim was a solo act, but the boy wouldn't listen, evidently Hawk had taken the boy in, too. He said, "Hawk and I are friends, we've worked together for a long time now." Friends! That motherfucker wouldn't know the meaning of the word "friendship." Well, that was all right, Teenochie thought. He would get his own back in the end. He always did. He twiddled with the radio dial, but the radio, of course, didn't work. "Sound of the piano get lost in them gyms," he said. "Boy didn't have it miked properly tonight."

"Hunh!"

"You asleep or awake? I can't never tell, cause your eyes be open all the time. You still awake?"

5

"I must be awake. I can still hear your yammering."

"And another thing. I don't see why you got to go on last all the time. Just as many peoples there to see me as there is to see you. It make more sense, I think, if I be out there playing piano behind you, then I just stays out there and does my little number at the end."

"That's all right," said Hawk imperturbably. "We just call up the boy and tell him. You know, you stomping all over me tonight anyway—I don't think I want to hear no more piano when I be playing."

"What you talking about, I be stomping all over you? I couldn't hardly hear myself, your git-tar was turned up so loud. Hey, where you going? You wandering all over that center line."

Hawk said nothing. Wheatstraw woke up and started playing his mouth harp, a sad, lonely, achingly astringent blues that seemed curiously at odds with the franchise-cluttered highway. "That's pretty," said Hawk, nodding his head. "Play some more." Wheatstraw, who scarcely needed encouragement in the first place, beamed. "Yeah, it be better to play than to talk," he said, in a statement that pretty much summed up his personal philosophy. It was then that Teenochie saw the truck. They seemed to be heading straight for it. "Hey, Hawk, hey, Hawk," he said, not worried at first, thinking it was just another game Hawk was playing. When he looked over, Hawk was still gripping the wheel, still staring fixedly ahead, but seemingly not seeing anything. "Hey, wake up, you crazy motherfucker," Teenochie screamed. "Don't you be doing me this way." Wheatstraw just kept on playing.

I

RHYTHM ROCKIN'
BOOGIE

JERRY was in the middle of an uncharacteristic sequence of conference calls—shifting phones from ear to ear, trying to act casual, as if it were really he who was negotiating another big-time deal instead of that improbable impostor who had taken over his true klutzy self—when his secretary, a high-school dropout in blue jeans and pigtails, sailed in oblivious and tapped him on the shoulder. He stared at her, looked out the window, listened to what Sid and the lawyer each had to say, watched the kids run through Harvard Square and the traffic jostle noiselessly along. He raised his hand—no interruptions, he said with a gesture, knowing that Stephie wouldn't take that kind of ceremony, she would just give him shit about it afterward. Over in the corner was a bar, though Jerry never drank alone and rarely had people in. The big-screen color TV had a game show on; the women were exclaiming silently over a new, all-purpose, all-in-one ap-

7

pliance which, if you believed all the claims made for it, could only help implement Thoreau's advice to simplify, simplify; the MC cooed with his patent-leather hair and stay-press soul. . . .

"It's Hawk," Stephie said loudly.

"Look, could you, I'm sorry, could you hold for a minute, look, why don't you guys just, uh, talk to each other, I just, something just—What?" he said to Stephie, knowing full well what she had just said.

"It's Hawk on the other line."

"So?" He stared at her blankly.

"He's calling from the hospital," Stephie said.

This was ridiculous, he was thirty-six years old, he might in some quarters even be considered a success, he didn't have to apologize to anyone. . . .

"Look. I'll call him back."

"He doesn't sound so good," she said. She dabbed at her eye. Did Stephie, too, have feelings that extended beyond the next Springsteen concert? Oh, shit. Why did Hawk always have to be his problem? Truly sometimes he wished he had never met —but then, of course, he would never have met Lori, whose contract he was in the midst of renegotiating. In fact everything that had happened in the last ten years, good or bad, was in some way connected with Hawk. He wished he were married. He should long ago have come to some resolution—

"Look, gentlemen, something's come up." He sensed the consternation at the other end. Did they think he was getting smart? Did they think he was getting cute in his old age? What was there to get cute about? Lori hadn't really made any money for the company, 120,000 units on her last album, sure, but what was that compared to her potential? And there was no way she could live up to her potential if she wouldn't guarantee a minimum of personal appearances, if she wouldn't promise to follow up the next album with a full-blown personal tour. And that she wouldn't do under any circumstances. She insisted on seeing her music as art, not commerce, making the records the way she wanted, when she wanted, and with whom she wanted. He'd be lucky if he could get front money of $50,000 for re-signing, and this was for an artist who everyone agreed could be a monster. Which was the only reason they still wanted to hang onto her. They didn't want to let him go, but he was firm. Who knew? Maybe this would jack up the price another $25,000.

"Yeah?" he said, jabbing the button on the phone console.

Hawk's voice sounded whispery and far away. The familiar hoarse rasp was barely audible.

"Something happened, boss."

Jerry was annoyed. What the fuck did he have to call him boss for? He knew how it irritated him. It made him look like an asshole. He supposed that was why Hawk did it. Hawk thought he was an asshole. After all he had done for Hawk, practically lifting him out of the gutter—well, out of the Sunset Cafe in Yola, Mississippi, which wasn't far from it. A ludicrous fate for this man who was virtually a legend in his own time, a source, an inspiration, an unreconstructed—Jerry was embarrassed at the rhetorical flourishes even his imagination conjured up after all the similar flights of fancy he had served to the world, both before and after meeting their subject—genius. "Nigger," Hawk corrected him in mournful, dolorous tones. "You know, boss, I ain't nobody's angel child, just another nigger baby trying to get along in the world."

"An accident," said the voice on the line. "We just about made Indianapolis."

Jerry began to get worried. Maybe he shouldn't have sent

them out alone. Three septuagenarians in one of Hawk's interchangeable twenty-year-old piles of junk on wheels. The Blues Express, his idea—they should be playing Notre Dame tonight.

"What kind of an accident?" Jerry's voice rose in concern.

"How many kinds of accidents is there? Ain't never heard of a good accident myself. Wheatstraw gone."

"Wheatstraw's dead?"

"Yeah, that simpleminded fool done gone to his reward. He couldn't hardly talk, but he could play."

Jerry thought he must have come in in the middle of some bizarre joke. "He's not dead?"

"Went flying right through the fucking windshield. I saw him. Man, I know. He looked like some big bird just about to take off. I say, Hey there, motherfucker, you think you can fly, so that's what you mean when you sing about that old flying crow?" Jerry thought he must be losing his mind. Was Hawk chuckling softly under his breath? "He didn't never do nobody no harm, he were just simpleminded from a kid on up. I told you, man, I didn't never want to do this tour. Didn't want to be no blues legend."

Little beads of sweat stood out on Jerry's forehead. Wheatstraw dead. Hawk was right, it was his fault. Hawk hadn't wanted it. Hawk hadn't wanted the tour in the first place. But Jerry had seen it as the opportunity for one last payday. In the ten years that he and Hawk had been associated, trends and styles had several times changed, and the wave of nostalgia which had unearthed the great blues singers in their sixties and seventies had now passed on to something else, bookings were fewer and farther between, and old black men were no longer fashionable on campus. Jerry didn't tell Hawk any of this, but he had conceived of this tour as a kind of farewell appearance on campuses across the country and promoted it as such. Three old black men. The Screamin' Nighthawk. Alex Wheatstraw. T&O "Teenochie" Slim, the piano player.

"How about Slim?"

Hawk mumbled something.

"What?"

"Ain't nothing wrong with Mr. T&O Slim that a gag in the mouth wouldn't cure. Man, what you send me out with that sorry-ass motherfucker for? Always getting fucked up by them pretty young things. Oh, Mr. Slim, would you teach me how to tickle them ivories? Tell me about the time Mr. Lester Melrose brung you up to Chicago so's you could make your classic sides with Big Bill and Tampa. Tampa, shit, can't even tie his own shoelaces, and Slim couldn't never keep his yap shut, dawn to dusk, drunk or sober, whether he knowed what he was talking about or not, he always be shooting off about something—"

Oh shit. Oh shit. He was going to have to go out to Indianapolis, he knew he was, he was going to have to straighten out this whole mess—

"Well, look, how do you feel? Do you think you can hang on for a little while? I'm kind of tied up here right now, but I can catch a plane later tonight or tomorrow morning."

The voice on the other end audibly weakened. "Well, you know, boss, I ain't doing all that good, really, but I'm sure I'll be fine. Why don't you just stay where you are, I don't require nothing, ain't no need to call Mattie, I don't suppose. They say it must have been some kind of shock, but I'm coming along real good now. Won't be no time, boss, before I can get around on my own, you know."

Jerry had visions of old black men reproaching him in his sleep. It wasn't his fault. It wasn't his responsibility. "Look, I'll be out," he said. "You just tell the doctors or whoever that I'll be out, I'll straighten it all out—"

There was only a satisfied silence at the other end.

He hurried to get ready, called the airport, shaved around his beard and drooping mustache, observing himself all the while with soft self-pitying brown eyes. He packed a light suitcase, called back CBS, and then explained to Stephie what was going on. He gave her careful instructions to close the office at five, put the phone on answering service, and not bother to show up until he got in touch with her in a few days. He called the wire services and tried to think of anything else there was to do, and when he couldn't then he made the call.

She was in New Orleans for no good reason. She had gone down there with her bass player, who was black, fifty-two years old, a junkie, a physical wreck, and had played with every prominent New Orleans musician for the last forty years. By sheer chance he got her after only a couple of calls at some old jazzman's house. He didn't have to explain, he knew he wouldn't; that quality of passionate intensity that seemed so at odds with her flat self-conscious speech patterns came into play almost before he got the words out. It was the same quality that transformed her singing voice into a graceful, soaring, instinctive instrument that seemingly had little to do with plan or intention. Was there anything she could do? She'd fly out right away. She would, of course, pay for Wheatstraw's funeral, at least help out, she insisted, when he mumbled that wasn't necessary. Here were some numbers where she could be reached. How was Hawk? Jerry answered all the questions slowly, patiently, all the while seething inside. There was never a word, of course, not a single word, about her discoverer and mentor—how he was, how he was bearing up under the strain, how terrible it must be for him. She was, after all, his discovery; if she had the talent he was the only one with the willingness to advance it, to promote it, to indulge it, to put up with her absurd middle-class guilt, the lack of necessity behind her art. Her public should give him a medal, they honestly should, because without him—oh, it was absurd on the face of it, he was just distorting the reality. It was Hawk, not Jerry, who had first heard that something in her voice, it was Lori herself who had sought and captured Sid's attention. Still, if it hadn't been for him, she might still be in ethnomusicology getting her Ph.D. somewhere, playing timid bottleneck behind some decrepit old bluesman the local Blues Appreciation Society had brought to town, beautiful, deferential, effacing herself and her talent. Her pictures surrounded him mockingly, each click of the camera undeniably capturing some aspect of her appeal but somehow leaving the inner self untouched. Her eyes calm, still, playful, her lips pursed in an oddly self-satisfied smile, her blond hair whipped around her face no doubt by one of those vigorous blushing denials, elusive, teasing, inviting, sensual, the whole obscured by each of the parts, the whole somehow untranslatable—

He knew now what he should have done. He should have hidden her talent from her, he should have denied it when others spotted it, never even hinted that it might exist. But that hadn't been an option. That had never been an option. She would have realized, someone else would have told her, and then he would have lost her anyway. He hung up the phone bitterly. "What do you say?" he said to himself, not for the first time. "What do you say?"

At the airport he was as confused as ever by the dizzying rush, the isolating bustle. They were just thousands of strangers gathered under one roof. And yet somehow, as he always did, as he always would, of course, he got through. On the plane he ordered a double Scotch and then another, settled back, sailed into the sunset, and closed his eyes for a brief troubled dream before the rude shock of landing jarred him awake. At the claims area he hung around waiting for his bag, eyeing the black porters, black taxi drivers, black maintenance men, middle-aged and elderly, any one of whom for all he knew might be another Screamin' Nighthawk, another castoff from another life who might be sought out and lionized by a community of whose existence he could be only dimly aware, while he was himself insignificant and anonymous within his own community. God help him.

At the hospital they gave him a hard time, because it was after visiting hours. It didn't seem to make much difference that he had come all this way, nor were they interested in who the Screamin' Nighthawk was. What they were interested in, of course, was who was going to pay the bill. Indianapolis had enough indigents of its own, thank you, said the admitting nurse, taking down the scanty information that Jerry was able to provide—born December 27, 1902, 1900, 1899? Given name: T.R. Jefferson. Social security number? Jerry almost wished he had brought clippings, but it wouldn't have meant shit. Name. Rank. Serial number. Date of birth. Mother's maiden name. Father's occupation. Maybe these people had it right. Maybe that was all that counted, these statistics, facts, an orderly life's progression, the very factors whose absence had made it so impossible to locate Hawk for a period of nearly twenty years.

At last he cornered a young, mustached doctor. Briefly he explained the situation. The doctor introduced him to another doctor, portly, middle-aged, his white hospital gown wrinkled and stained. The old man led him to the elevator, which was stuck somewhere between the fifth and sixth floors, explaining between emphysematous puffs just what had happened and what was likely to happen. It was just as Hawk had said. An automobile accident, Wheatstraw like a big black crow sailing through the windshield. Teenochie had escaped unharmed. Teenochie in fact had escaped altogether, vanishing into the early-morning squalor of Indianapolis, where no doubt he had a friend, knew a woman, was acquainted with a bar where thirty-five years before he had passed through and no doubt thirty-five years hence he would expect to pass through again. And what about Hawk?

"Mr., uh, Jefferson is doing about as well as can be expected," said the doctor as the elevator doors finally opened and a stretcher with a covered-up body on it was wheeled out. "He is, after all, not a young man. He's subjected his body to a considerable amount of abuse. From what he says, I gather he must be in his seventies, he has sustained a number of coronary attacks already—"

Jerry expressed surprise.

"Oh yes, there's no doubt about that. There's some evidence of ventricular damage, cholesterol level is high, blood sugar is elevated, too, and of course he suffered a small shock."

"Shock?" Jerry remembered Hawk saying something like this, but he thought Hawk said it had been quite a *shock*.

"Yes. Mr. Jefferson suffered a slight shock, a cerebral incident —in fact that's probably what caused the accident, though it's difficult to be sure. For a period of time he lost control of his functions, which is not uncommon, and until a short while ago he was unable to move his left side—"

"You mean he's paralyzed?"

"The feeling seems to be coming back. I'm quite sure he'll have nearly full use in no time. With the proper therapy we'll probably even get him back to strumming on the guitar. But, of course, there can be no question of his continuing as an entertainer. The shock should be taken as a warning, really. The effects will probably wear off, but it's a signal, it can't be ignored. The next one could leave him paralyzed or worse—and there's bound to be a next one, unless he radically changes the way he lives. I don't know how much of this Mr. Jefferson can take in, but I hope you can appreciate the seriousness of his condition. There can't be any thought of performing. His diet, medication, drinking will all have to be strictly regulated." He paused, stared openly into Jerry's eyes, as if he doubted that Jerry was even listening to what he was saying.

Jerry glared back at him. He could have been a doctor, he supposed. Except he hadn't wanted to be a doctor. Cold-hearted motherfuckers—he might have made his parents happy.

"Do you think he'll be all right?" said Jerry miserably.

"Well, frankly, I just don't know," said the doctor. "It's always hard to tell with this kind of case. You know, these people really don't take very good care of themselves."

He shrugged, and for a moment Jerry bristled once again with the kind of indignation he rarely felt these days. *Take in . . . these people!* Hawk had never been a lush—what did these assholes mean? Didn't they realize they were in the presence of a great American poet, proud spokesman for a proud people who had had to reinvent language and experience for themselves as strangers in a strange land? His heart wasn't in it, though. His heart hadn't been in it for a long time. Let the chickens come home to roost, let everyone suffer under his own self-perpetuating delusions.

"You know, we had to put Mr. Jefferson in restraints. He insisted that he had to leave the hospital, that he had to make an engagement—"

"He did," said Jerry helplessly. "He had a concert at Notre Dame tonight."

"Ah, well, perhaps if you could speak to him—"

Jerry nodded, not so much in agreement as out of exhaustion. This man didn't understand, he couldn't understand, how could anyone understand if they didn't know Hawk? You could talk for a minute, or you could talk for an hour, you could talk until you were blue in the face and think you were making progress, but Hawk would never do anything other than precisely what he intended all along. He was the most self-centered man Jerry had ever met, and by that Jerry didn't mean the most selfish or least generous. He could show real warmth and generosity of spirit on occasion. But he was the most self-oriented, self-righteous, self-assured son of a bitch that Jerry ever hoped to encounter. He was the Screamin' Nighthawk, and that, Jerry thought, might turn out to be his eternal misfortune. He was a man who had built a self-conception around a legend, and it was the legend that he felt obliged to live up to, holding himself erect even if he was doubled over inside, referring to himself so often in song and speech as a marauding bird of prey that it almost seemed as if he had come to believe it, expending every last ounce of energy so long as he had a public of even one to impress with his vitality. From the day he had made those great early records for a furniture company that manufactured phonograph records in Grafton, Wisconsin, from the moment his caricatured face had appeared in Paramount advertisements with the legend "You think you've heard the blues? Well, you haven't heard anything yet, until you've heard this Mississippi native moan, cry, shout and, yes, scream the blues," he was hooked, stuck forever on his own publicity notices. And even as his voice had thickened over the years and that eerie high-pitched edge had modulated into a thick-toned growl, even though today's seamed and weatherworn face bore little resemblance to that of the bright-eyed young man who had physically had to be held back to keep him from rushing time in those early days, though the guitar he now carried was a patched facsimile of the new Gibson he held in the picture, he was still the Screamin' Nighthawk and he still roared out the words of the song with conviction.

I'm the screamin' nighthawk, baby,
And I hunts both night and day
When I gets my claws in you, baby,
You gonna scream and holler hooray . . .

"The Screaming Nighthawk is in your town," the tattered poster read. "He will entertain you and sing the blues. When this Hawk screams and plays his golden guitar, the whole town is going to run for cover. Come and see the Screaming Nighthawk on _____ at _____." That was his calling card, and that was his life. . . .

There was a television set on low, a beeper sounded, Jerry looked straight down the long stinking corridor into the crowded ward where one man lay with his foot up in the air, another groaned. "I think I'll go in and see him now."

Hawk was furious. His thick beetling brows knit in concentration. His squat heavy body was wrapped in hospital swaddling clothes. The long scar on his cheek burned with indignation. His eyes were yellow with fury. "I want to get out of here, boss," he croaked. "I told these sorry-ass motherfuckers, I got to get out of here."

Jerry didn't know what to say. The room was filled with sick old men. Helpless men. Sad old rummies with tears running down their cheeks. Dying men. In their midst Hawk didn't look all that different, unless you studied the anger in his eyes, the veins popping out on either side of his forehead. It would make a good picture, Jerry thought. If he'd just thought to bring his camera—maybe he'd pick one up, send it out on the wires, get some free play—oh shit, what was the matter with him?

"So how you doing? Boy, you really gave me a scare," Jerry said, looking for conversational cheer. Hawk didn't say anything, just glared. "They treating you all right? Oh man, what happened to Teenochie?"

"They treating me like a piece of dogshit," Hawk said at last.

"You know, I talked to the doctor. He says you're going to be out of here in no time, seemed like a nice guy, wanted"—Jerry didn't know why he had to say this—"me to send him one of your records."

Nothing.

"I said I would."

Hawk didn't even lift an eyebrow. "They tied me down."

"Well, they were worried about you."

"Tied me up like some damned baboon didn't even know enough to scratch his own ass. They taken all my clothes. They won't give me my guitar, bother me with all their damnfool questions, they keeping me here against my will, ain't that against the law even for niggers?"

Jerry scrutinized him surreptitiously. With his right hand he gestured forcefully; his left lay down at his side. Was it imagination, or was the expression on his face slightly lopsided with the left side frozen in a lifeless grin? It would be a helluva way for it to come to an end, in a fleabitten urban hospital—

"You know, Lori wanted to fly up to be with you, she's down in New Orleans now with Coot."

"Yeah, Coot." Hawk chuckled.

"I told her to wait a few days."

Hawk's face softened. "Yeah. It be better in a few days. How she doing anyway? Her and old Coot?" Hawk slapped the white sheet with his right hand. "Oh man, I known Coot since he was a little kid and we passed through New Orleans with Silas Green. He better be taking good care of that gal."

Hawk had always had a soft spot in his heart for Lori, Jerry didn't really know why. It was as if he had reserved some special space for her which he would grant to no other individual or musician. Jerry remembered the reporter from *Newsweek* who had badgered Hawk for a quote on the Rolling Stones after they had recorded one of his songs and made a big show of presenting the first royalty check, even though truthfully there was no way of proving that Hawk had written the song. "They're nice boys," Hawk said diplomatically, thinking no doubt of $10,000 in the bank and maybe more to come. "But are they blues musicians?" the *Newsweek* reporter persisted. "I mean, have they suffered enough, have they paid their dues, can a white person ever really sing the blues?" Hawk glowered at him and said nothing. The reporter was a bright kid, had long tangled red hair, and had indulged Jerry in an hour of reminiscence for a one-sentence quote to lead the article. "I mean, I know that Muddy says that whites can play the blues, but they can't ever sing the blues—" Hawk passed a big paw over his close-cropped head. "That's dogshit," he said. "You listen to Lori Peebles if you want to hear a white girl got soul." "But what about the Rolling Stones?" the reporter implored. "There ain't no way," said Hawk, "they could cause a nigger whore to even wiggle her ass." Thus ending the discussion, ending the interview, ending the checks, and eliminating the possibility of any tour with the Rolling Stones. "I don't know what it is," Hawk said whenever he was asked to explain it. "That girl must got memory pain. Cause she singing about experiences she could only have had in another life. Can't nobody tell me that that girl ain't singing from the heart." To which Jerry, though he had doubts about reincarnation, was forced to agree.

The other inmates of the room glanced over from time to time but were scared off by Hawk's unblinking gaze. His eyes, Jerry thought, burned yellow. He wondered if Hawk was going to die. "Naw, I ain't gonna die, motherfucker," Hawk said in strange good humor. "You know, Crow Jane think she too beautiful to die, but I'm just too mean. You see that motherfucker, Teenochie, you tell him he just better make sure to deliver me the money that he stole. Cause if he counting on I'm gonna kick, he better start running now, I don't get that money. You know, I give him his chance back in '29. He fucked up then, and he's fucking up now. Probably gambling my money away in a game right now. I told you he wasn't nobody to be trusted all along, I knowed it then and I knowed it now." And with that Hawk fell off to sleep.

>>><<<

Jerry checked into a hotel near the hospital and right away started making calls. When his ear started to ache from the phone, he flicked on the TV and watched a few minutes of a situation comedy about the '50s that wasn't anything like the way he remembered it. Then wearily he got up and went looking for the desk clerk to see if he could get any kind of a line on Teenochie.

The clerk, an old white-haired man who was watching the same program on his own TV, a little portable, didn't seem to understand what he was talking about at first. "Oh yes," he said with weary enthusiasm, "we have some wonderful nightspots in Indianapolis." He started running down a list of glittery-sounding clubs and show bars. Jerry shook his head. "I'm looking for a colored place, a little bar maybe, where they have a piano, feature old-fashioned music."

"You looking for a girl, mister?" said the old man, his glance flickering back to the youthful images on TV. "Now I don't know about that sort of thing—"

Jerry didn't have much better luck explaining himself to the taxi driver, who was black. He was looking for the black part of town, the old Naptown, he tried. Taxi driver nodded. He wasn't looking for a girl, he was looking for a place, maybe it was somebody's house, the kind of a place that had a jukebox, an old piano, maybe featured live entertainment two or three times a week, not soul music, not disco, blues music. The driver just looked inscrutable. He nodded his head and pointed the cab in a certain direction and drove for what seemed like hours, as Jerry got his first extended glimpse of Indianapolis. They drove and drove as neighborhoods deteriorated, vacant lots and boarded-up buildings replaced crumbling row houses and factory sites, white faces disappeared, and Jerry had the impression more and more that they were making their way into a trackless jungle from which the very idea of retreat was foreclosed. Finally the cab came to a halt. The meter read $14.80, and Jerry gave the driver a twenty-dollar bill. "Don't know if this is what you want, mister," said the cab driver. "These last couple of blocks, they got quite a few of the old joints. Used to be a whole lot of music in Naptown. Music, women, seem like the music bring out the women, sometimes they was so many you could shake a stick at 'em, but it ain't like that now. Don't know if you going to find what you looking for here." Jerry nodded, tried to keep his teeth from chattering. He had, he reminded himself, been in lots of jungles. He thanked the driver and watched forlornly as the cab sped off.

The first bar that he tried he didn't even get in the door. It was called Duke's, and there was a woman with an ill-fitting black wig behind a scarred Plexiglass partition who shook her head ominously as Jerry edged down the stairs. Not a word was spoken, but Jerry didn't hear any music either, so he just turned around and went back up the stairs. He didn't fare much better with the second or third joint either. There was just the noisy crush of people, laughing, chattering, slapping hands, having a good time. Then he heard it. From down the street, across a little alley, he heard the unmistakable sound of a piano, of *the* piano— the walking bass and right-hand triplets, the eerie dissonance and unsynchronized rhythms, the sense of stepping back into another time which had first struck him the very day he had discovered Hawk. Above the door in hand-painted letters it said "Johnny Twist's Hurricane Lounge." There was a rope across the entrance held loosely at one end by a big man whose one good eye gleamed sadly in the dim light. The cover charge was a quarter, and Jerry reached into his pocket to pay it. Without a word the man let the rope trail on the floor, and Jerry stepped carefully over it.

Inside it looked like a bombed-out site from some forgotten

era in Indianapolis' undocumented history. Once his eyes became accustomed to the murky light Jerry could make out the dangerous bulge of the walls, the precarious slope of a floor which had to be negotiated carefully to begin with due to the crater-sized holes with which it was pitted, and the upturned wooden crates which substituted precariously for tables. The stale smell of sweat and urine filled the room. Over to the left was a bar and to the right a small bandstand of misshapen boards raised a foot or so off the floor. There, sitting dignified at the battered upright in a silk vest, red suspenders, and his habitual derby hat, was Teenochie.

As he looked around, Jerry became aware that every eye in the room was on him. This didn't surprise him, as he himself could hardly understand what wayward impulse had brought him here. As he stood uncertainly, unsure of what to do next, a small man with a dapper mustache and a wicked glint in his eye came up behind him and touched his elbow. Jerry jumped at his touch. The man just smiled. "Allow me," he said with a flourish, "to show you to your seat."

"Oh no," said Jerry, flushed and acutely aware of the perilousness of his situation. "I didn't, I mean—"

"No, no, please—" The man's wide white muttonchop sideburns gleamed in the darkness.

Teenochie sang, "How long, baby, how long, must I keep my watch in pawn?" The piano rolled out its swelling, out-of-tune melody, supple bodies shivered and swayed in place, there was the constant sound of boisterous good times as men and women shouted over and in response to the music.

The little man showed Jerry to a table which sat by itself in a corner. Jerry thanked the gentleman and sat down. "Please allow me to buy you a drink," said the man. Jerry didn't feel like a drink but didn't feel like saying so either.

"Well, sure, thanks," he said gingerly.

"Well, if I could holler like a mountain jack, I'd go up on the mountain and call my baby back. . . . For how long, how long, baby, how long?" Teenochie looked drunk. He flung his great shaved head back and roared out the words. He was, he had proudly proclaimed to Jerry the first time they met, the oldest living blues singer in North America. Jerry didn't know if that was true or not, but it was close enough. Huge, hulking, slightly menacing, and in the end almost foolish.

Of course, Jerry hadn't known it at the time he was putting the package together. When he told Hawk, he got what he took to be Hawk's perpetual scowl, no more, no less. "You know him, don't you?" he said to Hawk.

Hawk nodded. "Sixty years I been knowing him. Don' like him no better now than the day we met. It was in a fancy house him and me was playing back in the turpentine camps, wasn't nothing but a funky old whorehouse. Course he don't like to be reminded of that, but that's why I call him a barrelhouse man, sporting man, he play and the whores jump, that's what it was all about."

Jerry never found out just what it was that Teenochie had done wrong in Hawk's eyes. Probably made the mistake of trying to steal a girl away from Hawk. Or he had insisted on soloing while Hawk was singing. Jerry didn't know, he just couldn't imagine what it had been like for them then. All he saw now were two cantankerous old men. What about the young Screamin' Nighthawk? What about Teenochie, when he had hair on his head? Their tales of those times were legion—the pimps and whores and mobsters that they had known, Honey Man, the numbers boss of Mobile who had taken a fancy to Hawk and employed him for almost two years, seeing men get cut and shot and blown away, almost nightly by their account, doing hard time at Parchman and Angola. Jerry no longer knew what he believed was true. But it was certainly, undeniably true that Hawk and Teenochie hated each other's guts, they had scarcely even spoken from the time that they had started on the tour, using Wheatstraw—good-hearted, simpleminded, now-dead Wheatstraw—as their hapless go-between, grunting commands and instructions in a guttural language that Wheatstraw alone could make sense of. By the time Jerry realized just how tense the situation really was, there was nothing he could do about it anyway. The tour was booked, it was a natural, Jerry just hoped that one of them didn't get killed. And now one of them had. Only it wasn't either Hawk or Slim.

"What are you drinking?" said the old man amiably, staring at Jerry as if he were an archaeological exhibit.

"Oh, I don't know," said Jerry with another nervous flutter. "I'll tell you what, let me buy you a drink."

The old man would hear none of it, though. "You our guest," he said in honest surprise. "I mean, I'm happy to make your acquaintance, man. I'm glad to make your acquaintance." He pumped Jerry's hand again.

Well, I'm going, going away, baby
And I won't be back till fall
I'm going, going away, baby,
And I won't be back till fall
If I find me a good gal
Then I won't be back at all.
Well, Tee-na, tee, na na . . .

26

Teenochie was singing his theme song, that must mean his set was just about over. Jerry looked at his watch. It was after eleven-thirty. They would probably be going on all night if he knew Teenochie. He had a drink set up on the piano. Jerry was always warning him about his diabetes, but he insisted, "Sugar ain't got nothing to do with drinking," and so far he had not been proved wrong.

The mike was pushed away from the piano. His big voice boomed through the tiny room, dispensing with amplification, cutting through all the smoke and clatter and noisy conversation. Teenochie would sing as long as there was one person to listen. He would pay to sing if he had to, just to have the opportunity to get up in front of a crowd and be somebody. Away from his piano he was an almost contemptible old man, sneaking, suspicious, always plotting for some obscure advantage, a mean drunk. He had no friends that Jerry could discover. Other blues singers distrusted him, and since his wife had died he seemed to wander more and more, visiting college campuses or run-down little bars, singing in back-country juke joints if he could find them or in any tenement apartment that still had a piano. Like Hawk, like Wheatstraw, like all the ones that were left, the last of a dying breed.

"What I wonder," said the old man, "is what brings a gentleman of your persuasion to these parts."

Jerry stared self-consciously, but there was no hostility in his expression, there was no sarcasm in his voice. "I mean," said the old man, "it isn't often that we see a gentleman of your light complexion down here."

Jerry touched his springy hair. Did the old man think he was really black, did he think Jerry was trying to pass—that was crazy, he supposed it was a compliment of sorts. "Well, you see,

I'm a friend of Teenochie's, I'm a booking agent who represents him and a number of other blues singers. I guess I've always loved the blues—"

"Oh, I see," said the old man helpfully. "Well, I wonder what it is that draws a member of the Caucasian race to this sort of music. I mean, do you like Tom Jones?" Jerry shook his head. Teenochie was playing a fast boogie, taking an encore in the face of a smattering of applause. Couples were dancing in the narrow aisle which led to the gents' and ladies', big padded women and small angular men, big-legged ladies scrunching down in tiny skirts which showed off their tree-trunk thighs, bright splashes of color and movement in the otherwise dark room. The bartender gazed on imperturbably. Over at a table by the bandstand a woman picked up a bottle and shattered it noisily on the table, going after another woman in a shocking-pink suit with the broken bottleneck. Chairs and tables were knocked over, but she was quickly restrained, her wig the only casualty of the struggle as it rested askew on her head, revealing the close-cropped nappy hair underneath. Slivers of glass gleamed wickedly on the floor. "Because it seems to me if I were of the Caucasian race," said the man with no seeming hostility, "I don't think I would go any further than that. Do you ever watch that Tom Jones on television? Now he's somebody that seem to me to have a lot of what we call natural *soul*, do you know what I'm talking about?" Jerry nodded helplessly. "Personally speaking, he's my favorite."

> *Now when I say jump*
> *You jump*
> *And when I say stop, you stop!*
> *Stop!*
> *Now don't you bip another bop . . .*

"Well, I like Tom Jones, too," Jerry said, sweating and wishing that he were invisible or at the very least could take on the proper protective coloration for his surroundings. Then Teenochie spotted him. He leaned back from the piano, keeping up a steady rolling left hand while trilling with his right. "Hey, man," he said with a big grin, waving expansively as he slowed the tempo down and made the typical bandstand announcement. "Well, I see by the old clock on the wall that old Slim's got to pause for a cause. But I'll be back, jack, to party hearty for you and your party, because the blues never die, if you don't dig that you gotta have a hole in your soul. Ain't that right, people? Ain't that right?" His big shit-eating grin never diminished even in the absence of any kind of response; the dancers just kept on grinding away, the drinkers kept on drinking and the talkers talking, seemingly oblivious of this slice of history which Jerry transported from college campus to college campus to teach a new generation something about the blues.

"Aw, put it in the alley, Mr. Slim," said Teenochie, half standing over the piano and moving his torso in a slow grind that had prompted one reviewer to write, "Jerry Lee Lewis must have learned at the feet of the great Teenochie Slim." "And while I got y'all's attention," said Slim, "I just want to introduce a friend of mine in the audience, my personal manager and an international promoter, he gonna send me to Europe next, ain't you, boss man, this here is Mr. Jerry Lipschitz. I want you to give him a nice hand, which is what he deserve, because this cat has paid his dues, if you can dig what I'm saying. This cat have put old Teenochie Slim back in business. So put your hands together, please, and let's hear a nice round of applause for Mister Jerry."

Jerry turned beet-red and only gradually worked up the nerve to take his eyes off the floor. It seemed as if only the old man he was sitting with had paid the slightest bit of attention to what Teenochie was talking about; he alone in the entire room was patting his hands together and beaming at Jerry proprietarily. "Ain't that nice," he said proudly. "That's nice. You almost a celebrity, like Tom Jones."

Teenochie joined him at the table. Off the bandstand he was an old man once again; the entertainer's grin which creased his face from ear to ear was replaced by the crazy expression, sly and a litle bemused, as if he were always peering beyond you toward some jackstropper no one else could see, that Jerry had come to know so well. He had put his coat on, and still he seemed chilly. The bright-red suspenders caught the light every now and then, like the gold tooth in his mouth. Teenochie had brought his drink with him, but he didn't need it, really; he was already as drunk as he could be. "So how you doin', how you doin', man?" he said, pumping Jerry's hand over and over again. Jerry looked at him balefully. Someone had plugged in the jukebox, and the sounds that filled the club were the sounds of twenty years ago —Elmore James, Muddy Waters, Howlin' Wolf, all acquaintances, all students at one time or another of the Hawk.

"How's Hawk?" Teenochie said, as if jogged by an unpleasant memory. A slight sneer which was probably intended to convey sympathy crossed his face.

Jerry nodded. "All right. He's all right."

"Wasn't all right last time I seen him," Teenochie said half to himself. "That motherfucker couldn't even wipe his own ass. He couldn't move nothing." Teenochie's face tried to assume a doleful countenance, but there was no way of hiding the almost spiteful satisfaction he obviously felt at surviving his long-time tormentor. "Doctors say he gonna be all right?"

"They didn't know," said Jerry. Then, thinking better of
it, he added, "They're pretty sure he will be."

"Oh yeah?" Slim cocked a doubting eye. "Oh yeah? You
could've fooled me, man, I thought he was done right there.
Man, he was acting crazy. I been telling him since the beginning
of this tour, Let me do some of the driving. Why don't you turn
over the wheel to Wheatstraw?—God bless the dead. But you
know that stubborn-ass old man, him and that damn machine of
his, ain't no use in talking to him about nothing. Never was. Vida
Mae say to me from the first, What you want to ride with that
damned old fool for? He ain't got nothing you ain't got, you hear
what I'm talking about, man? And he treat me like I'm some kind
of country clown, when *he* the one that the times passed by.
Many's the time that these white boys and girls come out and say
to me, What you carrying that poor old man for, seem like to
me you should have been out on your own. And I says, Yes, sir,
yes, sir, I just does what the man tell me to. Ain't no sense in it.
Wasn't no sense from the beginning. Midnight, Mississippi,
where we first met. Shoot, man, he couldn't play nothing with
me then, can't play with me now, never could make the proper
changes, you dig what I'm saying, Jack? And he getting old,
too. Had to get the white boys to tune his guitar for him. Sorry-
ass old nigger with his sorry-ass old guitar. I'm telling you, man,
I could make it better on my own. You know, if the truth be
told, most of these boys and girls, they don't know nothing about
no Screamin' Nighthawk, man, they coming out to see me,
Teenochie Slim, I been in the public eye for sixty-three years
now, ever since my daddy set me down at the piano out in back
of his still. Shoot, that's why the young people come out to see
me, cause I got a colorful record, and I knows how to present

myself to the public nice. They don't care nothing about no sorry, no-account old man, can't even tie his own shoelaces, can't even wipe his own asshole, that ain't even had the experience entertaining the public—do you know when my daddy hired him he wasn't but eighteen years old and hadn't even been off the *farm*, that's how green he was, and my daddy, he say, Why don't you try playing with Slim here? And it was a joke, man, the people just up and laughed, it was so pitiful. You put me out by myself, man, you ain't gonna be sorry. I give you a bigger cut, bigger piece of the action besides, what you say about that?"

Jerry nodded wearily. He had heard this monologue many times before. Everyone had. That was why no one wanted to see Teenochie, he had just been added as an afterthought. Oh, they liked him at first; and sometimes his interviews showed up well, as he made up one story after another, mixing fact and fantasy, past and present, until you had no idea where one began and the other left off. But he overdid it. He tried too hard. And he insisted that everyone love him when he had no love in his heart, except, possibly, for his often-invoked and dear departed wife, Vida Mae, who entered nearly every conversation with advice she couldn't have given for the simple reason that she had been dead for ten years and had, according to Hawk, kept Slim so pussywhipped that he didn't dare look at, let alone speak to, another woman, while all the while she was popping it to every musician that Slim brought home for a meal or to board overnight.

"What happened?" said Jerry.

"It was a truck," said Slim, snapped back into a factual account. "I seen it a mile along. Wheatstraw seen it. I thought Hawk seen it. He driving along just like he always is—" Slim put his hands to grip an imaginary steering wheel as if he was going to choke it. He peered over the wheel the way Hawk always did, with the intentness of a man who regarded everything in his path as a potential enemy. "He hugging the center line just like he always do, not giving an inch to nobody. We getting closer and closer. Then Wheatstraw, that simpleminded fool, he start in to hollering. And I kind of give Hawk a little nudge, but he naturally don't even blink, just keep that wheel heading straight. Truck go off the side of the road. Scarcely even touched us. What caused the commotion I still can't figure out. Hawk just keep right on going. And when the road curve he keep on going straight. Next thing I know there's a whole lot of people around us and steam coming off'n the hood and a big hole in the windshield where that nigger go sailing through." Teenochie shook his head. "He getting too old. I mean, he ain't in full command of all his faculties. You know for yourself for a fact Nighthawk was always strange. But he getting stranger and stranger. Won't talk to nobody. Getting angry over nothing. Sometimes I wakes up in the middle of the night, catch him just standing by the bed staring at me whilst I'm asleep. I say, What you looking at, fool? But he don't answer nothing. Not one word. Just look at me like I'm crazy when you and I both know he the one that crazy—"

"He says you took his wallet."

Teenochie stared at him shrewdly, as if to determine whether this was surmise or accusation. "Yeah, I got his wallet, sure," he said with some reflection. "You know, man, I was holding it for safekeeping. Hawk, he don't trust no doctors."

"Yeah, well, he wants it back."

"Oh sure, sure, man, I mean I ain't got it on me—"

Jerry just stared at him balefully. "I mean, I could get it, no problem." He reached into his jacket pocket and drew out a

33

fat bulging purse of cracked leather, a relic of God knew how many years and miles ago. "It slipped my mind, man," Slim said sheepishly. "Well, I guess it's about time for me to get back to work." Teenochie rubbed his hands together briskly, as if to restore the circulation.

Jerry glanced at the wallet. "Is all the money there?"

Teenochie clasped his hands behind his back and rocked back and forth nervously. From his great height he looked to Jerry like a giant bird of prey. "Well, I had expenses. But naturally I only took what I won off him."

"What you won?"

"In pitty-pat."

Jerry just wanted to get out of here. "How much did you win?"

A broad smile crossed Teenochie's face; he knew he had him beat. "One hundred and twenty-four dollars."

Jerry nodded. He would replace the money himself. It wasn't worth the argument.

"Now you give some thought to that little proposition we discussed," Teenochie called after him, as Jerry made his way to the door. From the outside he could hear the sounds of Teenochie's piano and then his strong shouting voice. He made his way carefully along rutted streets thick with menace until he came to a lighted intersection and miraculously found a cab.

Back in his hotel he replaced the money. With what he had added, there was more than $1,500 in the wallet. Hawk didn't believe in checks—they were nothing but pieces of paper, he said —and he didn't believe in banks either. He was, as Teenochie said correctly, a stubborn-ass old man. Everything that he owned, everything that he was or had been, the whole story of his life, was in that wallet. Booking agents long since dead, recording contracts he had signed in the '30s, royalty statements for $0.98, $1.24, from Victor, Columbia, Decca Records. A faded handbill that showed Hawk as a young man with just the date and the venue to be filled in. The priceless memorabilia of a lifetime— Hawk didn't see it that way, undoubtedly. Still, the money was an irrelevance, even Hawk recognized that; if there had been no money at all, he still would have fought Slim to the death for what was in that wallet.

It contained in addition to the foregoing: business cards, yellowed clippings, publicity stills, scattered reviews, telephone numbers, several well-worn passports, scrawled-out addresses, copyright notices, an occasional telegram or letter. It was the sum of something—a life well spent? A life that was spent. Nothing odd about that. The only odd thing about it, Jerry thought, was that Hawk couldn't read. Not a word. He was not only functionally but totally (with the exception of being able to sign his name) illiterate.

"How did you get into the army, then?" Jerry asked him one night. Hawk responded with a wave of his hand. He had been in the army for nearly four years during the war and right after, even traveled to Japan with a quartermaster unit attached to the Ninety-third Infantry, never ceasing to sing and play his battered guitar. Hawk himself must have been in his forties then, but that didn't seem to matter either. Jerry had learned he could be whatever age he chose to be with no birth certificate to contradict him. It was hard to imagine him entertaining for his boss, Colonel Shaw, but Hawk claimed it was no different from playing for Honey Man. "Singing 'You Are My Sunshine,' 'Sunny Side of the Street,' all that kind of racket. Didn't mean nothing

35

to me; that was what *they* wanted to hear. Matter of fact, it just about give me a nervous breakdown, but I didn't care nothing about that neither."

Well, Hawk had negotiated the army just as he had negotiated his sixty years of cross-country travels, Jerry supposed, somehow or other managing to cope with a system which could never have imagined it might have to contend with Hawk someday. For sixty years—well, probably forty years since he had purchased his first flivver, before that it was just a matter of walking, hitchhiking, or riding the rails—Hawk had been engaged in a succession of never-ending journeys, crisscrossing the country endless times without ever once gaining the benefit of a legally acquired driver's license—or one acquired in any other way, for that matter.

Because he couldn't read the roadsigns he had never, so far as Jerry knew, ventured on to any of the newer interstates but instead clung to the old back-country roads that headed plunk for the middle of every little town that had grown up on the highway. "There's an old co'thouse on the corner," he would say, describing a turnoff that had to be made in St. Joseph, Missouri. Or he would identify a landmark in Modesto, California, as a used-car lot which had disappeared fifteen years ago and long since been replaced by a McDonald's. It was a never-ending source of wonder to Jerry, but he always managed to get where he was going, whether by instinct, telepathy, or some deep-seated race memory which preceded his present corporeal existence and would live on long after the flesh had decayed.

Perhaps it was the same causation which enabled Hawk to riffle through his wallet and always come up with just the paper or document he was looking for. A review, a contract, a letter from overseas, somehow Hawk always produced it. Then he would have to have someone read it to him, of course, and after savoring the memory or words of praise or just the fact that someone had taken the trouble to put down on paper what he knew without question to be his natural due, he would return it carefully to his wallet, not necessarily to the same place but always to some appropriate niche.

For the last few years Jerry had been working to get Hawk a valid driver's license in any state that would have him. He had even gotten Hawk enrolled in a Senior Citizen's Remedial Reading Enrichment Course when Hawk had settled down for a few months one spring in Chicago. Hawk had no patience with any of it, though. The alphabet meant nothing to him. "Ain't nothing but a bunch of ignorant old fools anyway," he complained to Jerry. So Jerry finally gave up and tried political influence, but he could never get Hawk to stay still long enough to establish a place of residence anywhere his political influence might extend. Once Jerry had tried to school Hawk himself, but he had quickly given it up as an impossible task, for Hawk—who could spend hours patching up an antique exhaust with baling wire, then see the whole thing fall apart a hundred yards up the street, and roll back under the car again with scarcely a murmur of complaint—would practically explode with frustration within moments of confronting these useless abstractions.

When Jerry thought of Hawk, he always had two images. One was of that big bulky form bearing down angrily upon him, furious over some imagined slight or insult or imposition upon his time or attention. The other image was of Hawk teaching Lori how to play the guitar, answering the questions of some innocent fan, usually female, with the same gentleness and patience that he showed working on one of his jalopies or patching together that homemade wreck of a guitar, which, Jerry

37

suspected, was held together with little more than Scotch tape at this point. Everything that Hawk owned was ready to fall apart, and yet it all had a stability and permanence to it—nothing had changed since Jerry first met Hawk more than ten years ago—that made Jerry feel as if it would go on forever. Until this, Jerry thought, removing his clothes, not even able to remember anymore where the day had begun. He turned out the light, feeling weary in every bone of his body and reminded once again that he was not the one who was cut out for traveling. Then he fell into a fitful sleep.

WHEN HE got to the hospital in the morning, Hawk already had a visitor. He was sitting up in bed, leaning on one elbow, conversing in unintelligible grunts confirmed by vigorous nods of the head. The visitor was a frail-looking, white-haired old lady whose expression seemed to be fixed in a kind and understanding smile and who was dressed as if she had just come from church. She wore rhinestone-studded glasses which glinted merrily when she tilted her head, a pink pillbox hat, and a worn gray suit that hung loosely on her body. Though she and Hawk maintained their animated conversation, even close up Jerry still couldn't make out a word of it. Hawk nodded curtly at him when he handed back the wallet. His color was still bad, but he looked better than he had the day before. Jerry stood uncomfortably to one side, not sure if he was supposed to politely ignore this colloquy, as discretion dictated, or step right in and introduce himself. Either way he knew Hawk would find fault.

Finally the woman stood up to go. "Now you remember what I tole you," said Hawk in a voice that was closer to his booming rasp than the hoarse whisper in which he had conversed yesterday.

The woman nodded. "Pleased to make your acquaintance," she said as she edged past Jerry, smiling with grandmotherly tenderness all the while.

"You seen Slim," Hawk said flatly.

Jerry nodded. Hawk patted the wallet, not even looking at it but picking through it with gnarled black fingers which touched the cracked leather as if they were greeting a long-lost friend. "He know he better keep his distance."

Jerry stared at the man in the hospital bed, the Screamin' Nighthawk, and for the first time felt sorry for him. Why should Teenochie fear this weak, helpless old man? "Boy from the newspaper come by to see if he could do an interview. I ask him, You gonna pay me what I usually get? He say, How much is that? I told him he better talk to my manager." Hawk chortled to himself.

"You didn't feel like talking?" said Jerry for want of anything better to say.

"I didn't feel like talking for *nothing*," Hawk hissed meaningfully. "What I want to do that for? I done talked enough for free. Make some poor sucker rich off my words. Shoot. When you gonna get that book on me, make us some *money*? I give you enough of that old-time shit can't nobody else remember nothing about and don't nobody care, you could've written three books by now. Shit, you probably just waiting for me to kick, so you can cash in all the chips."

Jerry shook his head, murmuring denials. Lori had transcribed the many painful hours of interviews. For three years he had carried the book around in his head. He didn't see any better way to sell it now than he had then. No one cared about this old man's memories anymore. When they were riding the crest of the blues wave, *Rolling Stone* had expressed interest in excerpting a chapter, but he had not been quick enough and they had not been serious enough, and now it was San Francisco and Summers of Love they were nostalgic for.

"Hey, we gotta go see about getting you out of this hospital bed," he said unconvincingly to Hawk.

Hawk smiled a strangely twisted smile. "I be out of here before you wish it," he said cryptically.

"Is there anything I can get for you?"

"Yeah," said Hawk, laughing. "Get me a young woman. I got me a old woman already."

SHIT, it ain't like he thinks it is. It ain't like none of them imagine. They think it was all hard times and suffering, they think you lived like some kind of animal, like some kind of beast of burden that sleeped in the fields. Shoot, it wasn't nothing like that, we had good times, man, *good times*. Oh man, the way they got it, must have been born with a whiskey bottle in your hand instead of sucking on the titty like everybody else. Just imagination—what do they know? I think it'd disappoint 'em if I told them the truth. I didn't touch whiskey till I was sixteen years old, three years after I was first married, after I taken Mattie away from Ol' Man Mose that they got on record, they call him the Father of the Mississippi Bottleneck Style, shoot he wasn't nothing but a mean old drunk, used to beat up on a young wife, left her with marks she couldn't never erase, across them titties, her thighs was pretty well striped, too. Wasn't nothing but a thirteen-year-old kid, but I was growed. Working in the fields beside her so she could support that raggedy-ass funky-butt old nigger, he couldn't have been no more

than thirty-five back then, but I thought he was as old as the
hills, couldn't never imagine that I'd make it up in age that way
myself. That nigger had it soft, just lay up in the bed all day,
stay out all night long playing them old country reels and eagle
rocks—people'd slow drag to them and buzzard lope and turkey
trot, it used to be a regular mess when you get out on the dance
floor, dirt packed tight as your fist, Mose's big feet stomping
away, she-it. Now they say to me, these young suckers, Well,
you musta been right at the cat's feet, picking up them pointers,
learning all them techniques, growing up like you did on the
same plantation as Ol' Man Mose. Oh man, it musta been your
lucky day. It was my lucky day all right, but ain't nothing to do
with that motherfucker's *music*. Well, you know, I may have
gone to the balls, but it was just to make sure that lying old man
was occupied for the evening. Then I snuck back across the field,
just as fast as I can, couldn't hardly wait to get in the door before I got my britches undone. And Mattie, the first Mattie, she
was a delicate little thing, high yaller, nice skin, nice hair, people
couldn't understand what she be doing with a coal-black nigger
like me, man she was all over me hugging and kissing and
squeezing, sometimes we couldn't wait to get in the bed. When
he come home the next morning, you could hear him coming
across the fields, most of the time he so drunk he got someone
bearing him up. A lot of times he come home with his guitar
cracked in two. Sometimes he have less money than what he
started with. If he drunk enough he just fall on the bed. But
sometimes he come home mean. That was why she start pestering at me to take her away. I was just a little bitty kid scared to
do anything without Mr. Charlie's say-so. I was living at home
then, my stepfather pushed me just the oncet, and I wouldn't
stand for that, I stood up to him and Mama, she say, You leave

him be, Cholly. You leave him be. And we went to the country frolics and picnics, from the time I was a little bitty kid, and everybody was just so nice. Just country people laughing and joking and having a good time, didn't know who was president and didn't care, never heard nothing about the condition the country was in, just drinking that corn and eating that country ham and sweet potatoes, and Miz McAlister sent over some of her canned goods and peach pie. And the little girls, little pickaninnies, looking so nice and neat with their hair all done up in pigtails. I wonder how many little pickaninnies got their cherry popped in the bushes while the fiddle music was playing. And Mose, him standing up there in front of all them people and singing about "So cold in China, birds can't hardly sing"—that was his song, sure was, even though he never recorded it. And at that time—I mean before Mattie, and even then afterwards, shit I got to be honest, no sense fooling yourself—I just naturally fell in love with that man and his whole style of guitar playing. Oh yeah, Mose a motherfucker all right, but ooh-wee could he sing. When he open up, I mean when he rare back and really let go, you could hear him, that sound must have carried for miles across the fields, people be hearing that sound for miles around and they wonder what is that old lonesome ghost come messing around my house? Charm the birds right out of the trees—you think there is any birds in China? She-it. My manager say, Someday you can go over there and find out. It probably just a fable like all them old-time sayings. Wasn't nobody back in those days got much beyond his own home town. Plowing. Partying. Courting. Raising a family. Just Ol' Man Mose, and he was a big man because of it. But I were thinking about Mattie, wasn't I? Mattie, the first Mattie, tightest pussy I ever had. She didn't care which way you did it, it was all equal to her. It was great for a kid just starting out. May be dead now, may be feeble, just two old people, we's past it now. What? Who's that? Come on, quit your foolishness, man. What you thinking about? It's the medicine that they give you. You know you ain't done yet. Are you still here, man? Shoot, I thought you gone a long time ago. But you know it's hard when you get to be seventy-seven years old. It gets hard, man, just to be making it. . . .

WHEN JERRY CAME BACK in the afternoon, Hawk was sitting up in bed, soundlessly fingering his guitar. How it had suddenly materialized Jerry didn't know, but he could imagine the fuss that Hawk must have kicked up to obtain it. The other men in the room scarcely paid any attention, occasionally lifting their heads from one comatose study or another. Sitting beside Hawk was the same woman who had been there in the morning.

"I see you got your guitar," said Jerry. Hawk's forehead knit intently.

"He couldn't live without that guitar," said the woman in a voice that most resembled a croak. She nodded sociably at Jerry. "That's the truth. I know."

Jerry in his turn nodded. "Where'd you find it?" he said, trying not to stare at Hawk's fingers as they clumsily struggled with the strings. His left hand, his chording hand, was still virtually immobile, he could barely clench and unclench the fingers, as he struggled vainly to make a chord.

"Oh, I knowed where it was all right," she said. "Roosevelt told me how to get it, and I—"

Hawk glared at her. Roosevelt! thought Jerry. He had never heard anyone but Mattie call Hawk by any part of his Christian name. Theodore Roosevelt Jefferson, one of a generation of children named for the Rough Rider, born shortly after the

43

charge up San Juan Hill. "Named for two presidents," Hawk always said. "And my mother didn't even know about one of them. That was because I was the seventh son, born on the seventh day, I ain't gonna say what month, but you can figure that out for yourself. I guess that's why I'm blessed with second sight." Which was a lot of shit, even discounting the second sight, because Hawk was no more likely to be a seventh son than Jerry was himself, and Jerry had only a sister. Plus he was born in December, "just around Christmastime, the first real snowfall my mama ever seed," he liked to recollect sometimes to other interviewers when it suited his purpose.

"Have you known Hawk long?"

"Oh my, yes," she said, pursing her lips.

"Oh," said Jerry, waiting to see if anything else would be forthcoming. "Well, Hawk and I go back a ways ourselves. But I've been listening to his music all my life—well, for twenty years anyway—"

"Isn't that nice?"

Hawk glared some more. He didn't like people talking about him in his presence, or behind his back either for that matter. Well, fuck Hawk, if he wouldn't say anything for himself. "You need anything?"

"Sherry," said Hawk.

Jerry had a momentary twinge—was this a dying man's last request?—but he resolved to remain firm. "Come on, Hawk, you know I can't do that. These people'd bust me for sure if I started bringing in liquor. Since when have you started drinking sherry, anyway?"

Hawk looked at him disgustedly. "Sherry," he repeated with greater emphasis this time.

Jerry was perplexed. He didn't want to push the issue. "He

44

want ice cream," said the woman in her cracking voice. "Sherry ice cream."

"Oh sure," Jerry said with some relief. "Cherry ice cream." Hawk nodded.

When he came back, Hawk was strumming a little more audibly, bent grimly over the guitar while the woman hummed patiently along to his laborious accompaniment in a cracked and tuneless voice. Hawk gobbled the ice cream down. "I needs the sherry for my throat," he explained between spoonfuls. It reminded Jerry of their earliest meetings, all the unnecessary misunderstandings (were they willful on Hawk's part, or his own?) in their long and complex association.

"Oh sure," he said, as if it were the most natural thing in the world—which it was. "No problem."

Everyone else in the ward was staring at them. A nurse started over but then thought better of it. She had probably approached Hawk once already. Hawk licked his lips and picked up the guitar again. This time the chord resounded throughout the room. His fingers still stumbled over the strings and he hit a lot of wrong notes, but he and the woman began to sing "Jesus Wears the Starry Crown," softly at first, then with increasing volume, as Hawk's guttural voice swelled from a whisper and took on the conviction of the song. Jerry was both moved and embarrassed. He wished, as he had so many times in his life, that he could retreat to the status of unobserved observer or at the very least surround them with a soundproof glass booth. It was touching, but the other patients were not so much moved as startled. One sat up straight and started to reach for the nurse's buzzer. Another turned over and groaned.

"Will you stop that caterwauling?" said the drawn, bald-headed white man in the bed beside Hawk's. Hawk just glared

45

at him, looking through him, not even so much as acknowledging his presence. The man pulled the cord for the nurse, yanking at it angrily until he pulled it free from the wall. The old woman's wavering cries formed an antiphonal wail behind Hawk's gruff lead.

"Jesus, Jee-zus, Jesus is coming soon . . ."

Jerry tried to attract Hawk's attention, getting up from his chair, pointing at their apopletic neighbor, touching his finger to his lips. At last he touched Hawk's sleeve timorously. Hawk stopped singing as if he had been shot and stared at Jerry as the old lady kept on heedless for a couple of bars. "Maybe we can find a room," said Jerry pleadingly. "I mean, there are other people who are sick, you know, and maybe they don't necessarily appreciate the music. Hawk, they're going to throw us out of here if you don't stop."

"Well, maybe that wouldn't be such a bad idea," said Hawk meaningfully. "Maybe they just kick my old black ass out of here now, set my things out on the street, I'll tell you something, man, that would suit me just fine."

The nurse never came, though, the other patients subsided, and Hawk set his guitar down. Later the woman left and Hawk said he was tired. Or at least he grunted when Jerry tried to talk to him about what the doctor had said, about how he would have to take it easy for a while. Hawk just lay there staring inscrutably off into the distance, his hooded eyes mean and hard as a snake's.

"Who was your lady friend anyway?" Jerry said as he got up to go. "I thought you liked 'em younger than that."

"At my age it don't make much difference. At my age, in my condition—ain't that what the doctors say?"

"She an old friend?" Jerry persisted.

46

Hawk stared at him contemptuously. "That were Bertha Johnson."

"Bertha Johnson," said Jerry, humoring an old man. "You don't mean—" Then he realized that that was exactly what Hawk meant. This was Bertha "Cool Mama" Johnson, who sang "I take pigmeat to Sunday school," and who in a famous test pressing circulated among collectors had declared, "I got nipples on my titties big as your right thumb/ I got something between my legs make a dead man come!" Bertha Johnson, who had sung duets with Hawk in the '30s, played piano with such driving force that some thought it was Cripple Clarence Lofton, even though Lofton clearly could not have been in the studio on that day. "I didn't even know she was still alive."

"Well, now you do," said Hawk.

Jerry sat there, plainly waiting for more.

"Will you get away from me now, boy? You heared what the doctor said. I needs my sleep."

Back in the dreary hotel room Jerry couldn't help being depressed. He knew he wouldn't be able to stick around much longer. Bouncing back and forth between hospital and hotel. Eating up twenty dollars a day in taxi fare and tips alone. Hanging around the lounge bar with all the other middle-aged hookers, drinking, brooding, feeling sorry for himself. It wasn't fair. Hawk had always been perfectly capable of taking care of himself. He had never needed anyone like Jerry in his life before. He could probably still get along, hobbled perhaps, a little slowed down, but still as mean as ever. That was one voice. Another voice argued that anyone could have seen this day coming, Hawk had to get sick and old sometime, who was going to take care of him, protect him, if it wasn't his manager? Shit. It was the same relation-

47

ship they had had since day one, when Hawk grudgingly, amid threats and imprecations, at last accepted the help that Jerry proffered him—only it was never enough, and Jerry was never quite sure it was really helpful. He had never managed to overcome Hawk's initial suspiciousness nor even erase his own guilt. What was the strange bond that held them together? What, Jerry thought, for the thousandth or ten-thousandth time, had he unknowingly gotten himself into?

He looked at himself in the mirror. There was gray in his hair, gray in his beard. Was this what he really wanted to do? Shepherd a flock of illiterate old black men decrepit with age and whiskey, manage the career of a woman whose destiny he would all too willingly link with his but who had other ideas about her life? In college he had envisioned himself a media person, and for a brief moment he was—even if he was only writing sports and advertising copy for a series of limited-market television stations in the Midwest and Northeast. Précising local news, matching text to visuals, boiling down the details of games for a nation of games-watchers—not players, watchers. He was a voyeur then and a voyeur now, only then he was helping people to avoid reality. Now, he thought, he was trying to lead them toward it. For three years he had never missed a big game on TV, his Sundays were constructed around football, telling Lin as he sprawled in front of the screen that on this one day of rest he wasn't just wasting time puttering around, he was acquiring proficiency in his chosen profession. She didn't understand. She wanted children, he didn't. He didn't understand anymore. He still watched football for relaxation, but he couldn't believe it was the same person who inhabited his body, a smaller body, the same person Lin had walked out on in the middle of Rose Bowl, 1964. She had kids now, her husband, who was a computer analyst, seemed like a nice guy, he had had dinner with them once, a suburban ranch house in Reading, Massachusetts. The kids had thought his beard was funny. Lin asked him, when her husband went out of the room for a moment, if he was happy. "I'd feel better if I knew you were happy." He nodded. "I'm happy." "We were just too young—you know?" "Sure," he said. He supposed that was it. "I'm happy for you," she said. "The life you lead seems so—different."

Different? Different? He supposed she couldn't think of any other word. Sometimes he imagined himself Howard Cosell at the Super Bowl—there wasn't any Super Bowl then, nothing was super as far as he remembered it, super had come in with the Beatles, hadn't it, around that time, when John F. Kennedy was murdered. A super-tragedy. Another spectator sport, another media event, tragedy for the masses. Maybe. Sometimes he wished he could wish it all away, television, satellite broadcasts, telephones, go back to an age of local heroes, neighborhood celebrities like when you were a kid. Someone who, when he walked down the street, could elicit admiration for the way he carried himself, for the way he hit a baseball, for the way he had stood up to old Mr. Murphy, the principal. That was what Hawk had been when he first met him, a local legend, not an international celebrity, not even someone who made the newspapers, just someone who was recognized for what he was, what he did, a man who sprang from his surroundings and could blend back into them if need be, someone who knew who he was. That nobody could ever take away from Hawk, but, Jerry reflected, if anyone could be said to have tried, it was he, who, in calling attention to the very qualities which made Hawk what he was, had taken Hawk out of that self-same environment in which he was comfortable and made him into another Sunday-afternoon hero.

In a gloomy frame of mind he dialed the first number Lori had given him and was surprised when she actually answered. "Oh, I'm really glad you called," she said in that breathless, fresh tone of voice which promised so much and was as indiscriminately dispensed as her sexual favors. "How's Hawk?"

"Oh, he's all right," said Jerry. "Guess who was in to see him today."

"I don't know. Who?"

"Bertha Johnson," said Jerry flatly.

"Bertha Johnson? Oh wow, you've got to be kidding. Cool Mama Johnson? Oh shit, what was she like? I'll bet she was just smashing, this funky old lady, I mean this fantastically bawdy person who's really alive and upfront about things. What'd she look like? She was really a beautiful lady when she was younger, you can just tell. Wow, I'd really like to meet her. Oh shit, Jerry, I wish I was there with you. I just can't get away right now. There are things that are important to me here. I mean, if you say I should come I'll come, but in another few days everything'll be cool, and then I'm gonna fly up. It must be awful for you there all alone."

"It is."

"Oh, I'm really sorry. Do you want me to come up?"

"Yes, I do," he found himself saying. "But not for Hawk, for me."

She laughed her skittish little laugh. "Oh, Jerry, you know it can't be that way. I wish it could, but you know it can't."

"Why can't it?"

"Oh, you know—" Lori's voice trailed off. Whenever she got stuck, her voice diminished to the point of inaudibility. Sometimes, on stage, she would mumble to herself, it could go on for minutes sometimes, as her audience, which was always polite, well dressed, above all *sensitive,* sent out sympathetic vibes, never grew restless, never yelled "Boogie!" and shushed anyone who raised his own voice above a whisper, and applauded warmly whenever she got herself together enough to come back to the mike. It was uncanny, Jerry thought, the very incoherence and confusion which made her personal life such a disaster and would have wrecked anyone else professionally only endeared her all the more to her fans.

"Don't you understand, Jerry," she said at last, "we're just not that way."

What did she mean, we're just not that way? He was that way. He thought she was that way. Why shouldn't they together be that way? "I don't know," he said. "I wouldn't make any demands. I think you could be happy. It wouldn't have to be just me. I want to get married."

He could picture Lori's face, blond, pure, clear-eyed, soft but not easy. She might feel sorry for him, but she couldn't very well act surprised. Men were always throwing themselves at her. She accepted it with a curious kind of formality, a grave reserve that seemingly enabled her to put a distance between herself and these tributes to an allure which she firmly believed she did not possess. Maybe it was that distance which allowed her to approach a music which should by rights have been no more accessible to her than to Jerry, a music which she approached just as much from the outside, but sang, Hawk said, "from the inside out, just like a woman squeeze you."

"You know you're just feeling sorry for yourself," she said softly.

"I'm not," said Jerry. "I am. But it's not because of what you think. It's not because of me. It's not because of what's happening *inside* of me. It's because of what's actually happening—

that's what's shitty. Ah, I don't know, you're probably right."
He said this last with a tooth-grating effort. Then he told her
about Teenochie and what he had observed of Bertha Johnson,
and they had a good laugh. She promised to come up in a day,
two days at the most, he didn't believe a word of it. And be sure to
tell Hawk that she would be there, and she expected to pick some
guitar with him, he would like that, he had *always* liked Lori
and Lori alone. By the time they finished the conversation Jerry
had almost forgotten what a fool he had made of himself tonight. That was for Lori to remember.

II

DOWN
IN THE FLOOD

WHEN HE got to the hospital in the morning, Hawk was gone.
He walked into the ward carrying a cup of melting cherry
vanilla ice cream, which he had gone to some trouble to get at
ten A.M. The first thing he noticed was the empty bed.

For a moment he experienced panic. Tears started to form.
He looked wildly to right and left, as the grizzled old men stared
at him, and a nurse, matter-of-factly emptying a bedpan, eyed
him with cool contempt. Then he thought, no, Hawk couldn't
be dead, Hawk wouldn't give his enemies the satisfaction, and,
armed with this momentary reassurance, he asked the nurse if
she knew where Mr. Jefferson was. Perhaps he had been taken
somewhere for tests? She was a sullen-looking black girl with hair
fanned out in a dark aureole. Hawk probably would have joked
with her, made fun of her hair, coaxed a smile from her, sung

her a song. She said she didn't know anything about any Mr. Jefferson, she was just on duty herself, go ask the floor supervisor at the nurses' station. He did that, and she knew just as little.

He was becoming increasingly concerned and, perhaps to mask his concern to himself, increasingly indignant. "Well, I mean he couldn't just vanish into thin air. Someone must know what's happened to him." They tried to calm him down. He checked with the young resident who had introduced him to the older doctor, but Hawk had been there when he made his rounds early that morning.

"Sleeping with one eye open," the doctor said. "I took a reading, gave him a shot, he muttered something and went back to sleep. He couldn't get very far in his condition. He's probably somewhere wandering around the corridors looking for the john."

But he wasn't anywhere in the corridors. Nor in the men's rooms. Nor in the ladies' rooms (at Jerry's insistence they checked). Finally they found a maintenance man, idly pushing a broom, who claimed he had seen Hawk. He was a black man with a pencil-thin gray mustache, and his green janitor's uniform hung loosely on him.

"Oh sure. Hawk," he said good-naturedly with a wave. "I knowed him the moment I seed him. I seen him play when I was a kid. I would've knowed him anywhere. Course he wasn't walking so good. But I imagine that's just the whiskey or some such. And he still got that same old big guitar. And same old heap parked outside. Course it couldn't have been the same, least I don't think it could, but one just like it anyway. Don't know how Hawk gets them to run, he must talk to 'em or something. Ain't seen Miz Johnson neither in quite some time, man you wouldn't believe what them two sounded like down home."

Jerry nodded. The doctor was speechless with rage. "You mean you just watched them drive off?"

"He told me he was *dis*charged," said the old man in an indignant voice.

"At seven o'clock in the morning?"

"What I know about these things?" said the old man, fooling with his broom.

I should have known better, Jerry thought to himself as he walked rapidly down the long hallway, listening to the young doctor's lecture on the risk he was taking, the guilt he must feel, the hospital's freedom from legal or moral responsibility in this matter. He didn't stop jabbering until Jerry signed the release form and paid the bill. "You ever hear Hawk sing?" Jerry said to the young resident. The other man shook his head. "Well, then, you don't know anything, motherfucker."

He felt pretty good about that, but that was all he felt good about as he checked out of the hotel, thinking, wasn't it just like Hawk to do something like this, knowing that Jerry would be obliged to follow him, knowing that it would just make things harder on Jerry, doing it perhaps only to get his own back at this pimp dressed up in philanthropist's cloth, who had persuaded an old man to forsake a comfortable life-style merely to satisfy the world and give it one last glimpse of a so-called great art form. Great art, my ass. All it was was bile.

Not in any particular hurry, Jerry ate in the hotel coffee shop and rented a car at the Avis desk. He knew now where Hawk would be going. He didn't have to worry about finding him.

Whenever he was in trouble, Hawk liked to say, he always headed for Highway 61. 61 twisted in and out through all the little towns between St. Louis and the Delta and on up to Illinois. It wasn't the fastest way to get anywhere, but it was the way Hawk knew best, it was the road he had traveled with Robert Johnson, Big Joe Williams, and Sonny Boy Williamson (the first Sonny Boy Williamson) and Stump Porter, the midget piano player, and it was one of the ways Jerry had found him in Yola in the first place. "Highway 61 rolls right by my door," he had sung in the 1936 version of the song. "Get home this time, ain't gonna be rambling round no more." So he would be heading for St. Louis, which for Hawk was the center of the universe. From there you could head east, west, north, south, but St. Louis was the hub. Yola was his destination, Jerry knew, and St. Louis was where he would be pointing for.

Jerry finally spotted him a little outside of Terre Haute, an old two-tone Ford—'53, '54—just chugging along, hugging the middle of the road. Blue puffs of smoke billowed from the exhaust, and through the rear window you could see a solitary figure hunched forward, a Stetson clamped on its head, hands clenched tightly on the wheel. Jerry hung back for miles, watching nervously in his rearview mirror as cars, pickups, even a tractor edged out, leaned on their horns, and flew by. Hawk never noticed a thing. He kept up a steady twenty-five miles per hour, didn't so much as glance at the gesticulating drivers who passed him, and never looked in the rearview mirror for the simple reason that there was no rearview mirror. Nonetheless Jerry felt sure that Hawk knew that Jerry was following him. When Hawk finally pulled into a filling station, he gave the attendant brusque directions and limped over to the men's room without even giving Jerry a backward glance. That confirmed it as far as Jerry was concerned. He had his own tank filled, had the oil checked, the windshield washed, the battery checked, talked with the attendant about the misfortunes of the country (inflation, unemployment, lazy niggers), selected a stale candy bar from the automatic dispensing machine, while waiting for Hawk to emerge from the men's room. At last Hawk did, and he shuffled to the gas pump, his pants undone, his fly half-zipped. He gave the attendant the washroom key and brushed past Jerry without a word. After several fumbling attempts, he placed the key in the ignition and tried it a couple of times, coaxing spluttering, choking sounds from the engine until at last, against all probability, it actually caught. They watched the car chug off down the road. "Damn," said the service-station man to himself, and Jerry was forced to agree.

Jerry stayed behind him for the rest of the day. Through four more stops, at each of which he got two dollars' worth of gas, at the last of which he purchased three quarts of oil. At the second stop Jerry went back to the restroom himself. "Hey, look, Hawk, come on, this is crazy," he said through the open window, then watched it slam down and counted twenty minutes before Hawk finally emerged as disheveled as when he had gone in.

"You better get out of my way, boss," muttered Hawk, after he had paid the attendant from his nickel-plated change belt, which he unlocked with a key he wore tied around his neck.

"Aw, come on, Hawk, this doesn't make any—"

"I'm warning you," Hawk said in a low growl and flung the door open, just as Jerry managed to jump free.

At the third service station they had a restroom which could accommodate more than one person at a time, and Jerry urinated with relief, as Hawk locked himself in behind the saloon-type door. Underneath the door Jerry could see Hawk's pants lying deflated on the floor. "Look, Hawk, I understand what you're doing, I really do. I mean, I agree with you, I think you ought to go home, rest up, take it easy. There wasn't any reason to stick around that place. But you've got to understand, you're still a sick man. I mean, you can't just ignore the fact that you've been seriously ill. Look, why don't you just ride with me. I'll get you down to Yola, I'll get you down there a lot faster than you're going to make it yourself, we'll get you to a doctor, and we'll just see what happens, take it from there." Hawk farted and grunted with about equal force. The smell drove Jerry out.

At the next stop the black man in the red greasemonkey's suit seemed to recognize Hawk. He greeted him with a big wave as Hawk rolled up and laughed as the car shook for a good minute and a half after the ignition was shut off. Hawk slowly got out and hobbled over to the gas pump, resting on the right front fender and slapping hands with the shaven-headed man, who was grinning from ear to ear. Jerry stayed in the car while the men conversed, waiting to purchase gas himself. His tank was practically on empty, since he had passed up a purchase at the last station, not realizing that Hawk would go this long between stops. Hawk brought four dollars' worth this time, and he used the men's room only briefly, but Jerry couldn't seem to get the attendant's eye. Some kids drove up, and he filled their tank. A lady got a dime stuck in the pay phone, and the man went to see about that. For five or ten minutes he looked around under the hood of Hawk's car, doing God knows what. Then he busied himself with straightening out maps and bringing the calendar up to date in the glassed-in office. Finally Jerry could stand it no longer and leaned on the horn. The man barely glanced at him. "Ain't got no time now, ain't got no time," he said dismissively, as Hawk emerged from the station, and they laughed and chatted some more. Only after he had sent him on his way with a wave and a slap on the hood of the car did he finally acknowledge Jerry's presence.

"You do sell gas here, don't you?" said Jerry sarcastically. The man laughed.

"What do you want?" he said. Jerry asked him to fill it up with high-test. "Ain't got no high-test. Just ran out."

Jerry stared at him in disbelief. His head hurt. He was tired of nursemaiding, he was tired of Hawk, he was tired of all this shit.

"What are you talking about?" he exploded. "You expect me to believe this shit?"

The man shrugged. "Suit yourself, mister."

Jerry watched Hawk's dust. He looked down at the gas gauge and calculated that there had to be a gas station up the road somewhere. He switched on the ignition.

"Now you better stop bothering this man," said the attendant in a quiet voice.

Jerry looked up. The man was smiling, but his smile was chilly. "You got no call to be harassing this man. He ain't broke no laws. He ain't never did nobody no harm. Why don't you turn around and go back where you come from?"

Jerry felt like crying. "But I'm a friend of Hawk's," he vainly protested.

The man regarded him with scorn. "You ain't no friend of Hawk's," he said. "Hawk told me who you was. You ain't no friend of his. Now why can't you leave that old man alone? You gotta squeeze the last dollar out of him, you ain't got enough already—"

Jerry threw up his hands helplessly. To go without sleep. To put himself out for this ungrateful old man. To subject himself to abuse on top of everything else from this shaven-headed guardian. He was tempted right then and there to abandon the whole thing, to let Hawk go home and die any way he liked. Why not? In the end it would come to the same thing. No matter what he did there was no way he could influence Hawk's course of action. And Hawk, he was sure, would seek out an audience as long as there was breath in his body. But it had gone too far, he was in too deep to back out now. Somehow he felt his and Hawk's fates were forever linked, at least until one of them kicked. He waved to the attendant and moved on out into the passing stream.

At the last stop he confronted Hawk directly. He jumped out of his car and blocked the driver's door before Hawk even had a chance to get out. "Come on, Hawk," he pleaded, as the young kid with floppy blond hair gaped at them. "You know I'm gonna keep on following you no matter what you do. You know, in a way I think you're counting on that. You're not so stupid," Jerry said, and thinking about it made him even angrier. "I think you're just taking advantage of me. You know you're sick. You know you shouldn't be taking this kind of chance. And you're just counting on the fact that if anything happens I'm gonna be right there to pick up the pieces. Well, goddammit, you're right, I am going to be there. But it's not for you, you old buzzard. It's for me. You wouldn't even say a word of thanks. You can't even imagine what this is costing me." Visions of his office, in far-off Harvard Square, desolate, phone disconnected, covered with cobwebs, condemned, all danced in his head. "You're a selfish old man, and you don't give a shit about anyone but yourself."

Hawk stared at him disgustedly and spit. The gob landed approximately half an inch from Jerry's left foot. Then Hawk lifted himself out of the car, awkward, heavy, foul-smelling, a legend in his time, and stood practically toe-to-toe with his manager. "What you want from me, boy?" he said angrily, not even looking at Jerry. "Ain't you through sucking on your mama's titty?" With that he plodded off toward the men's room, his shoulders slumping, his left leg dragging, the attendant running after him. "Let my manager take care of it," Hawk rumbled without even turning around. A small victory, Jerry thought, as he gave the man a twenty-dollar bill and asked him to check under the hood of both cars.

They were still out in the country when it started to get dark. Jerry wondered if they were just going to keep going straight through the night when he realized that the old heap in front of him had slowed to a virtual halt and that Hawk was peering over the wheel with more than his usual intentness. Behind them traffic had backed up for what seemed like miles, and the driver next in line behind Jerry started honking impatiently. Jerry shrugged without any hope of sparing himself embarrassment. He didn't know if this was Hawk's way of getting back or if the old man was simply oblivious to the chorus of horns which had started up.

Hawk turned off on a dirt path that didn't even deserve to be called a road, between a closed-down gas station and a boarded-up old clapboard house. Jerry hesitated slightly before following him, wondering for an absurd moment if Hawk might still be capable of springing some kind of improbable trap. The road, if it was a road, had obviously not been used in years, and to say that it was full of potholes would be giving it credit for an initial intention which it scarcely seemed to possess. Jerry lurched along behind the old black-and-tan Ford, for what seemed like miles in a time span that could have been hours, following the curve of the road overgrown with bushes until finally they came to what looked like a long-ago-abandoned dump, a clutter of rusting metal objects, rotting lace-up boots, tin cans, broken glass, a pile of brush, and a muddy stagnant pool of water. Beside it ran a rusted railroad track whose bed had become a garden of weeds, with half the ties twisted and broken and all the orangy color of rust. Off to one side was a railroad car, open to the elements, its door long since disappeared. Jerry watched in disbelief as Hawk climbed out of the car and with both hands scooped up some of the brackish water, tilting his head back and letting out a long sigh of appreciation as if it were fresh spring water that he was drinking. He splashed some on his face and then went to work gathering together the few sticks that were lying about, throwing on the remnants of what once must have been a chair, squatting down and coaxing a fire from this unlikely collection of combustibles. At last it caught and Hawk hunched over it for a few minutes, rubbing his hands in front of the fire until he was evidently warm, then hoisted himself up and swung back to the car, rummaging around without apparent success, then at last seeming to find what he was looking for. Jerry just waited—for what, he wasn't sure. There they were in the middle of nowhere, surrounded by ghosts of a past he had never known, and he was waiting for an invitation! Hawk limped back to the fire, where he pulled a saucepan from under his coat and started in to work. Soon something was frying away, whatever it was the smell soon filled the air, and for all of his distaste, for the scene and Hawk's presence in it, Jerry grew hungrier and hungrier as he watched the old man add ingredients to the sizzling repast. At last when it was ready Hawk removed the pan from the fire and set to work on his meal, patiently picking at it piece by piece, licking his fingers scrupulously as he finished each separate portion. Jerry kept thinking that he would start to feel some remorse, glance back, acknowledge his manager with a nod and indicate for him to come join him, but nothing of the sort happened, of course, Hawk never so much as gave him a tumble. When he was at last done, Hawk licked his lips loudly, trundled back and forth stoking the fire, put his cooking utensils back in the car, then disappeared into the low scrub that surrounded the clearing, only to reappear moments later with a long stick. He lowered himself again in front of the fire, pulled a jackknife from somewhere inside the recesses of his coat, and patiently began to whittle. Even after the sun had gone down and it was completely dark, he kept it up by the light of the fire, and even if Jerry hadn't been able to see him hunched over his work he would still have known Hawk was there by the slow scraping of the knife, which was the only sound to be heard save for the occasional hooting of an owl or scurrying of a small animal or hiss of a truck's airbrakes out on the highway. Once Hawk cleared his throat, and Jerry jumped.

It began to get cold. Jerry shivered a little. He was tired. He was hungry. He would have humbled himself and asked Hawk for something to eat, but he knew Hawk didn't count gestures for anything, if he had wanted to feed Jerry he would have done so, without Jerry having to ask or be bidden. And it wouldn't mean anything to Hawk one way or another if Jerry were to admit error, since Hawk never doubted himself long enough anyway to need anyone else's admission of guilt.

At last Hawk seemed to grow tired. He stifled a few yawns. Then he carefully folded up the knife and encased it somewhere within his loosely fitting garments, picked up the stick, walked over to the edge of the clearing, and with some difficulty relieved himself. The door of his old car opened with a creak, he climbed over the front seat and lay down in the back. Jerry watched it all curiously, like a spectator at the movies, and looked at his digital watch. It read 8:45. It glowed in the dark. It probably emitted "safe" amounts of radioactivity. What was he doing here?

At last after a suitable interval he got out of his car, crossed the clearing, and peered through Hawk's window. Hawk's eyes appeared to be open, but that didn't prove anything. He claimed he always slept with his eyes open in case some sidewinder (like Jerry?) ever tried to creep up on him in the middle of the night. Jerry shivered. Well, he supposed it was all right. Hawk was breathing regularly. And he didn't like to drive anywhere at night.

Jerry went back to his car, switched on the ignition, after a number of backings and fillings managed a U-turn, and headed back toward the highway. Going out didn't seem anywhere near as long as going in, with the car bottom scraping against branches and vegetation and the headlights scouring scrubby bushes. When he finally emerged onto the highway, Jerry carefully took note of landmarks, then joined the stream of traffic until he came to a truckstop diner that looked passable. Inside there was loud talk, men were eating noisily, the jukebox blared country-and-western music, and the waitress wanted to talk about her eight-year-old son Kenny. The steak was tough, the coffee plentiful, you could hear the sound of cars whooshing by on the highway outside. Civilization. When he finally brought himself to look at his watch—after having his cup filled four times and exhausting every possible avenue of conversation with the waitress—it was after eleven, and he wearily decided that he had better get back. He had no trouble finding the road and traveled confidently now over the familiar terrain until his headlights finally came to rest on the abandoned boxcar on the far side of the clearing. Everything was as he had left it. Nothing had changed. Hawk's car was still there, the fire barely flickered from time to time. He got out and threw a few sticks on the fire. From Hawk's car he heard a phlegmy clearing of the throat and knew he would get no further greeting than that. Hawk appeared to be asleep anyway, tossing and turning and making sounds, remembering no doubt some half-forgotten moment of glory, like the time he played for the queen and sang her his "new tune"—only fifty years old—"Lizzie Can Shake It." The papers had had a field day with that. Jerry tiptoed away from the car. But Hawk wasn't asleep. And he wasn't thinking of the queen either. His eyes were closed for once, but he was wide awake and alert in his thoughts. He didn't sleep much anymore, hadn't really slept well since his next-to-last wife Annie had died in '62, he didn't really know why. . . .

WELL, TIMES CHANGE. People change. World keep changing—all the time. That's what that boy don't understand—what he want with me anyway? He done got all he could get out of me. More, if the truth be known. It ain't like I'm his meal ticket, that cute little gal Lori, she the one that's gonna pay the grocery bills. Cute as a button, that gal, and if you don't hear what she putting down, then you don't got ears, boy. Too many people in this world ain't got ears, or eyes neither. They don't see nothing the way it really is, just the way they think it should be. Don't matter to 'em how a thing sounds, just whether you knowed ol' Charley Patton or Blind Lemon Jefferson—Lemon, he was one of the nicest guys in the world, give you his last drop of whiskey if it come down to it, but he couldn't sing worth a shit, didn't have no *tone*—or else they want you to remember some song that your daddy sung ninety years ago on the cotton rows. She-it, they oughta just snap to it, the boy oughta just open up his eyes and live a little, 'stead of worrying everything to death like he do.

65

I told him in the first place. First time I ever laid eyes on him, I told him, You just keep heading in the other direction, don't you go getting no fancy ideas or nothing, I'm doing fine on my own, thank you. Just keep right on passing through. Course he wouldn't listen, it was all mister this and mister that, can't remember why I even listened, seems like it was something about the world needing me. Shoot, the world don't need nobody, keep right on turning all by itself, and everybody know, only a fool need the world—ain't nothing in the world for nobody *but* a fool. Which is what we all is, I guess, at least if you listen to the preachers, who are the biggest fools of all, seem like to me.

I remember when they found Papa Eggshell, made a big deal of it at the time, wrote it up in all the papers. Shoot, anyone could have told 'em where he was right along, out behind Miz Payton's in his little shack or most likely out in some alley drunk, pissing on himself. He wasn't no good for nothing when they did find him, mind half gone, couldn't stay away from the juice, needed it so bad his hand shook when he didn't have it, couldn't even remember his own name sometimes, let alone his songs. What they want with him for? But they found him, bought him a guitar (which he promptly go out and hock, then lose the ticket, so they gotta go out and get him another), then they play him all his old records over and over so he couldn't help but remember, and they take him up north to that Newport Festival, where he excapes and lands in the hospital without even getting up to play. Shoot, now you tell me what's the sense in that? That damned old fool just confused and befuddled all the time, steal your last dime just for a drink of whiskey, that one time we went overseas, he didn't know nothing about what was going on, and still and all them overseas cats falling all over themselves to interview him. And him making up stories, because he don't re-

66

member shit and he don't care anyway. Which is why Lonnie always say, Are you another one of them damn cats wants to put crutches under my ass? She-it, they don't know. In the old days that man was *strong*. He knew his mind. Come a time when he feel like he tired of your company, he just gone, wasn't no wasting time or waiting around. When you old they ain't but one place where you fit for, and that's home. Because home they all know you for whatever you is, and they don't pay no mind. . . .

JERRY AWOKE painfully with the sun, to the sound of Hawk crashing through the bushes with all the delicacy of a water buffalo. In the pale light of day the spot held even less attraction than it had the night before. The abandoned tracks, the rusted railroad car, the tall weeds, the forgotten refuse of humanity—it seemed hard to believe that men had once populated this jungle, cooked meals, hopped trains, that this was all a living part of Hawk's memory. Jerry had seen pictures, of course, of haggard, hungry men, he had heard all the songs, he had sensed the fellowship and camaraderie—he wondered where they had all gone to.

Hawk was putting dirt on the fire by the time that Jerry emerged from the woods, having relieved himself and splashed water on his face. He felt as if he were aching in every bone of his body, and there was a foul taste in his mouth. He watched the old man meticulously put everything back in order—for what? For the next transient who came along just to cultivate his memories? Why couldn't Hawk stay in a Holiday Inn like everyone else who had made it in this great free-enterprise system that Hawk was always talking about—"God bless the United States of America," he often would say at the conclusion of his concerts, whether sincerely or sarcastically Jerry never knew for sure. "They got the only free-enterprise system in the world." Audiences were always nonplussed; Hawk never so much as cracked a smile. But what the fuck was he doing staying in a defunct hobo jungle with more than $1,500 in his pocket? What a pain in the ass the "last of the great blues singers" was!

At first his car wouldn't start, and Jerry had a moment of panic as he pictured himself abandoned in this dump, having to walk out to the highway, convince a strange mechanic that he hadn't been doing anything illegal in this godforsaken hole—he watched the dust rise up in the wake of Hawk's departure, at last the motor caught, Jerry gunned it, the car lurched forward, and he cast a single backward glance, still looking for a clue, before he abandoned the scene forever to memory.

They were just a few miles from St. Louis, and Jerry occupied himself with thinking of all the times he had read about St. Louis or written about it, in liner notes outlining the Screamin' Nighthawk's legendary travels and development as a blues singer. In St. Louis Hawk had met Little Walter, no more than twelve or thirteen, still imitating Sonny Boy Williamson, the first Sonny Boy Williamson, John Lee, playing in the marketplace. Walter had stuck with him for a couple of months, learned what he could, taken off for Chicago. Hawk's second wife —or was it his third or his fourth?—came from St. Louis, the famous vaudeville singer from the '20s, Lottie "Little Kid" Moore.

"Could she sing, boy," Hawk used to reminisce in his more tender moments. "For the last four years I was with that gal, I just about give up my music, she just naturally had me under her spell. Of course she hadn't joined the church at the beginning but

she was always *nice*, you know what I mean, we used to laugh
about all them other gals, they thought it wasn't nice, you know,
to be singing them nasty type of songs and shaking their yas-
yas-yas in front of all them peoples. But Little Kid, she didn't care
nothing about that. Man, the menfolks would just eat it up, and
the wimmins could learn something from it, too. Boy, you
wouldn't've known me in them days. She had me working regular, only time in my life except when I was a little kid and didn't
know any better—and enjoying it, too! I was working up at
Ernie's Garage, corner of Fourth and Market, greasemonkeying,
you know, fooling with them cars. And she had me going to
school nights, too, ooh wee, she musta thought she was gonna
make a preacher out of me. I was reading them books about Dick
and Jane and they dog Spot, I was doing pretty good at it, too.
Of course I forgot all that now, but I don't know what it was
come over me then, I guess that domesticated feeling just sneak
up on me before I even knowed it. Well, you know how it is,
everyone like their ham and eggs, and I guess everyone if they
had their choice likes it *regular,* but I'll tell you something true,
it's them gals that act like ladies on the outside, you get one of
those little old gals behind closed doors, just like the song say,
they liable to tear the roof off, bedslats and all. I'll tell you, boy,
sometimes I prayed that morning would come just so she'd turn
me loose. And I'll tell you something else, wasn't no prowling
going on back in them days, not for this Nighthawk, wasn't no
way, I was too tuckered out. Couldn't do no howling neither.
Just churchgoing, Wednesday evening and twice on Sunday.
Then she joined the Ladies' Sodality, man, on Tuesday nights,
and I was going to my classes on Monday and Thursday, seemed
like after a while we hardly had time for each other at all. Well,

I didn't think nothing of it until one day I got this little head cold, and of course back in the old days, out in the piney woods and levee camps and what have you, I wouldn't have paid *that* no mind, but I was getting so highfalutin and refined, I just naturally thought, Well, my dear little wife, she be worried about me working myself into a lather and me being so sick and all, so I takes off from work early, get the boss man's permission, and I comes home—and I find the preacher in my bed." Hawk would slap his knee. "And, man, don't let nobody tell you a preacher don't have a johnson just like everybody else, cause this preacher's must have been a foot long and growing!" Then Hawk might launch into his song—"Some folks say a preacher won't steal/ But I caught one in my cornfield/ Preacher talk about religion, talk about the church/ All the time he's doing his dirty work."

It was in St. Louis, too, that Hawk had surfaced for the last time before his rediscovery. He was living in a boardinghouse with Wheatstraw (who claimed to be Peetie Wheatstraw, the devil's son-in-law's son, but who was, as Hawk frequently reminded everyone, only an off cousin by marriage twice removed) and the legendary Blind Teddy Darby. They had gone into a local studio and cut an acetate and sent it around to all the record companies whose battered cards still resided in Hawk's wallet, all of whom had turned it down as old-fashioned stuff. And the acetate grew scratchier and scratchier until it was barely audible on the prized dubs which circulated among collectors at twenty-five dollars and up. The studio was still doing custom recording in 1962 when Jerry, just starting out in television in Springfield, Illinois, first got interested in the mystery of the Screamin' Nighthawk, and it was through their fragmentary records that he had gotten the address of the boardinghouse.

There he had found someone who remembered three drunken disreputable old men who played guitars and mouth harp and claimed to be recording artists, it must have been five or six years before. And there the trail went dead. Jerry hunted in bars, he checked with Welfare, he searched through old telephone books. Not a trace.

Hawk never got into St. Louis proper. He stopped in East St. Louis, bleak, desolate, a desert of urban renewal, pulled over about six feet from the curb, shut off the ignition, and sat there staring at the excavation site behind a broken link fence while the car gave up with a shudder. Then he eased out of the passenger side, carefully removed his guitar in its battered old carrying case, locked up the car, and started off down the street. Jerry pulled up behind, crunching over what seemed like an ocean of broken glass, eyed the neighborhood kids, themselves giving Hawk the once-over, with wariness, then locked up himself and at a discreet distance, feeling like Dashiell Hammett perceived, started after Hawk.

Hawk's progress was not rapid. For one thing he was weighted down with the encumbrance of the guitar. For another, even with the walking stick he had fashioned for himself, he was still uncertain in his gait, listing heavily to one side. He pulled the broad brim of his hat down over his brow. Some of the kids yelled at him and ran at him mockingly, heading straight for him and then veering off at the last minute, but Hawk never paid them any mind, just waved at them indifferently with his stick, dismissed them with a look. As they got to half-blocks of run-down little bars and corner groceries, he would stop and stare at the barred windows of every pawnshop they passed, scrutinizing it carefully as if he were attempting to memorize

71

the contents. Then at last at a sign that said "Uncle Ned's" with the familiar three balls he stopped, studied the window with the same intense concentration, and went in.

Jerry watched him through the clouded window, approaching the counter, drumming his fingers on its surface while he waited for the proprietor to materialize, at last slamming his hand down on a tarnished nickel-plated bell, the veins in his neck clearly standing out. When the man shuffled slowly out of some back room, Hawk reached inside his vest and without so much as a glance retrieved a pawn ticket that looked as if it must have resided there for at least fifteen years. The pawnbroker, a red-eyed old man with fringes of white hair and spectacles that kept slipping down on his nose, regarded the pawn ticket without surprise, said something, waited for Hawk's response, and then went shuffling back to the farthest corner of the store, where he unfolded a rickety little stepladder, climbed up on it, and took something down from the topmost shelf. He handed it to Hawk. Hawk nodded solemnly and peeled off a few bills from his wad. Then Hawk blotted the man from his field of vision, focused solely on the object itself, and at last slipped it on his wrist. When he came out of the pawnshop, he was admiring the watch, turning his hand this way and that to appreciate the effect from one angle or another.

He made a number of stops after that. Everywhere he went he had something to say, and people seemed to know him. At the arcade he stopped and had his picture taken in the booth where you get three shots for half a dollar. He didn't bother to draw the curtains, and Jerry watched as he arranged himself on the stool, unpacking his guitar from its case, holding it up with the neck above his shoulder, staring grimly into the camera as if he could stare down eternity. It was like the hundred other "publicity shots" Jerry had seen over the years. Though Hawk got older, he never seemed to change in the pictures, his grim visage always challenged the viewer uncompromisingly. It wasn't necessary, Jerry tried to explain to him, even if they needed more publicity stills there were always plenty of photographs available from the concerts, and Jerry could always arrange to shoot more. Hawk never seemed to listen, he pressed his own snapshots on well-wishers and press, as if they validated somehow that he was who he said he was despite Jerry's aesthetic remonstrations.

Hawk bought Spam and powdered milk at a small market while Jerry gazed longingly at the food from outside. He stopped to look at clothing in the window of Greenbaum's, where a somber black suit got prominent display. The signs on the privately owned store windows read Schwartz, Lipinsky, Garfinkel; the medical building was made up of Levys and Goldbergs. They were, of course, Jerry recognized uncomfortably, in Jewtown, the Jewtown that existed in every big city and gave rise to every predictable stereotype that Hawk parroted and every schwartze joke that Jerry had ever heard. No, no, it wasn't like that, Jerry tried fruitlessly to explain, but Hawk insisted he knew how it was, he didn't hold it against anyone, if anything he would have acted the same way himself. As he sang in his song, "Gonna tell you, baby, like the Dago told the Jew/ If you don't want me it's a cinch I don't want you."

The market was almost all boarded up or torn down, a sorry remnant of former glories. The colorful marketplace, which had witnessed so many closely negotiated transactions of barter or trade, where music was once played all day long and amplifier cords once hung down from second-story windows (a brisk trade

73

was done in renting electric outlets), was almost all gone now. All that was left were the pawnshops, a few radio and TV repair shops, a lone poultry man, the arcade, and stores Going Out of Business, with Slashed Price Sales, Everything Must Go!—the usual adornments of any city's streets. It didn't bear much resemblance to the stories Hawk had told him of when Memphis and Chicago and East St. Louis were all bustling, hustling centers, alive with activity and music and the exchange of ideas, when genius walked the streets. Hawk kept his head down, though, he didn't even seem to notice the current scene, he was looking for something else. At last he found it. Slumped up against the brick wall of a dilapidated professional building sat a small black man with a bandanna around his head, his back stiff against the bricks, his legs extended out in front of him in loose-fitting brown trousers cut off and billowing like pantaloons at the knee, which was where each leg abruptly ended. There was a tin cup at his side, which he rattled from time to time, and a harmonica in his mouth. Hawk, who had worked his way up to a ponderous trot, slowed down. A broad smile creased his face. The stump-legged harp player never noticed his approach but just kept playing his song, a thin reedy version of "When the Saints Go Marching In." The few pedestrians passed by without even glancing at him, and the coins in his cup made a pitifully lonely sound.

"Say, man, I thought you was dead," Hawk boomed out as he made his lumbering approach. "How come you move this time?"

The little man looked up and broke off abruptly, grinning a sly gap-toothed little grin. "Hey, man. Hey, Hawk. How you making it?" His voice was as thin as his harmonica playing, but he struggled up on his crutches, balancing himself precariously as he gripped Hawk's hand. "Man, people telled me the Screamin' Nighthawk was dead, but I didn't believe 'em. I knowed that was just a line of jive. Say, how you been? How's my gal?" Hawk shook his head. "She dead ten years now. When you move, boy? I thought you paid rent on that corner."

"Oh, you know, man, you seed what's been happening. They just about teared it all down by now. You know how it is, man. They find themselves a new politician. And the politician puts in new polices. And the polices say, You ain't got no permit, boy. Well, I told 'em about the arrangement I always had. And they said, Hey, nigger, tell that to Mr. Mayor. And they say, No —No Legs Kenny gotta go. . . . Do you know, I even showed 'em the reward I got from the city, great Godamighty it must be thirty-six years ago—it say, No Legs Kenny, you a fine man, and we give you permission to sing on the streetcorner for the rest of your natural days. You know what them motherfuckers did? They teared it up. They give me eight hundred dollars then, man, for that train that runned over my legs, would have been a thousand, but the lawyer had to get his share. It didn't mean nothing to 'em. They took that letter, looked at it backwards and forwards, and they didn't think nothing of it. Well, of course, that was a long time ago. You was making records then. Little Kid joined the church. I guess that's just the way of it. World moves on, they still jumping, it's just that they pep it up a little. But hey, man, it don't make no difference. Long as I got my Sweet Lucy. How you been making it? You don't look so good, look kind of peak-ed, where you was always black as the sun. That's how I knowed it couldn't last—even when that woman had you going to church regular as any Christian. You just too black bad, you black as any devil. But right now you looks like you be thinking about saving your soul."

75

"Oh, I be all right, man, soon as I get my health back. Damned old doctors trying to rob me of my health, make me feel like a *old* man. Hey, you still living around the corner in that old rooming house where we used to stay?"

"Naw, I done moved. They tore that down, Hawk. You remember the Palace? They tore that down, too. And Estelle, which passed, they tore down her old joint. Man, they gonna tear down this whole city, I think, just to get rid of them rats. But they don't know nothing about it—rats just go underground, they be here long after you and I is passed."

Hawk nodded sagely and leaned up against the wall. "Well, what do you say, you feel like playing something?" He began undoing the snaps of his guitar case, in clear violation of two of his most often repeated and cardinal rules: no play without pay and don't ever, on penalty of losing your professional standing, unless it was the only thing between you and starvation, beat on your box on the street. Kenny slid down on the wall, his useless stumps protruding out in front of him. He looked puzzled as he glanced over for confirmation from Hawk. "Aw, it don't make no matter," Hawk said in a different tone. "We old men now, ain't got but a little time, no sense fooling ourselves." He strummed his guitar with a resonant sweep and without further preamble launched into "Shake 'Em On Down." The battered old guitar probably hadn't been tuned in a week, and Hawk's fingers were still clumsy and uncertain on the frets. Kenny's thin, astringent harp was not in the right key in any case, but somehow they sounded commanding enough to cause passersby to turn and look and the Muslim who was hawking *Muhammad Speaks* to the little traffic that was passing by to pause for a moment in his droning patter.

Went to see the gypsy
To get my hambone done
Gypsy say, Man,
You sure need some
Well, must I holler
Or must I shake 'em on down
I'm so tired of hollerin'
I believe I'll shake 'em on down.

Hawk's voice carried through the almost deserted street. He rocked back and forth on his heels, and when the song was over he launched immediately into another, one of an endless number of variations on his theme song, "The Screamin' Nighthawk Blues."

You take a look at my woman
Make you want to scream
You see my woman
She makes you want to scream
She the meanest woman, man, I most ever seen.

She put strychnine in my coffee, iodine in my tea
Put strychine in my coffee, she pour iodine in my tea
Well, I better watch out
She put some of that poison on me.

I'm a screamin' nighthawk, I believe I better make a change
I tell all of you wimmins, I believe I better make a change
Tired of cooking on this gas stove, gonna find me a brand
*   new range.*

When they finished, they laughed and slapped hands. "Man, we really got it, didn't we?" said Hawk. Kenny just showed a silly gap-toothed grin. "Now you be sure you don't move from this spot, hear?" Hawk boomed out, as he packed up his guitar again in its case. "I don't want to have no trouble finding you next time. You tell that to your mayor." With that Hawk trudged off in the direction from which he had come, and Kenny went back to rattling his cup and playing "St. Louis Blues" in the mumbling apologetic style that he had been employing when Hawk first appeared. Jerry sidled up to the harmonica player, trying to look casual, and placed a ten-dollar bill in his cup. Underneath he saw a twenty, all crumpled up and carefully unfolded, as if it had been in someone's billfold for a long time.

He caught up with Hawk just outside of Greenbaum's, the clothing store where Hawk had hesitated earlier. There in the window was the same black suit, with the same price tag. $39.95, slashed from $119. Jerry shook off a wino who was lying in the doorway as he watched Hawk pause for a moment, devour the suit once more with his eyes, then apparently make up his mind and push his way through the door. Through the window he could watch Hawk and a gaunt white man with a tape measure wrapped around his shoulders. They regarded the suit, spoke, gesticulated, turned away from each other, resumed negotiations. Hawk slammed down a fist emphatically on the counter. The man climbed spryly into the window and tugged at the material. Hawk shook his head and must have said something rude, because the man climbed out again and stood, arms akimbo, as if he had been mortally insulted. Jerry was just about to step in—whatever happened he didn't want to see Hawk end up in jail over a matter of a few pennies—when Hawk turned on his heel and marched angrily out of the store. The man trailed him, talking all the while, finally caught up with him and touched him timidly on the shoulder. "Ain't nobody gonna jew me around like

78

that, Mr. Greenbaum," Hawk boomed out for all the street to hear. Jerry winced. Greenbaum didn't seem bothered, though. He kept talking. He made conciliatory gestures. Hawk slowed down, though he still looked angry. Then Greenbaum must have hit on the very formulation that Hawk had had in mind all along, because Hawk stopped in his tracks, a broad smile crossed his face, and he allowed Greenbaum to lead him back into the store. When he came out, he had a neat package carefully wrapped, and the black suit was gone from the window.

And that was the end of his purchases. He headed up the street limping slightly, an old man supporting himself on a crude homemade walking stick. When he got to the car he cast a contemptuous glance back at Jerry, not, Jerry came to realize, out of scorn for Jerry's person alone, but because Jerry's car had been stripped clean. The hubcaps were gone. The left front fender looked as if it had been beat on with a tire iron. The trunk was up and the spare was stolen. The radio antenna had been whipped off, but that was all right, because there was no radio anymore. Jerry stared at the wreck bleakly. His glance traveled from Hawk's dilapidated old relic, which had been untouched, to his own late-model LTD, which had had 6,200 miles on it when he had gotten it from the rental agency. How was he going to explain this to Avis? He couldn't remember if he had waved the $100 deductible. Hawk just stood there chuckling to himself.

"It's not funny," Jerry protested. Tears welled up in his eyes.

Hawk shook his head. "Ain't nobody asked you to come to this funeral," he said in a low, uncharacteristically subdued tone of voice. Then he got in his car and drove off. Jerry got in his LTD and prayed it would start and that at least they hadn't taken the battery and then that he didn't get a flat. He got another spare in Crystal City outside of St. Louis, and after that he was able to rest a little easier, still following his quarry but always at a discreet distance.

It was three more days before they reached Yola. One night they slept on the road, the next they stayed in Memphis. Hawk made the same rounds in Memphis as he had in East St. Louis, from the clothing stores and pawnshops and boarded-up clubs that were all that was left of the greatness that was Beale Street to a practically deserted W.C. Handy Park, populated only by winos and junkies, where once the music had never stopped.

"Oh, it used to be somethin' in those days," he had told interviewers again and again. "Frank Stokes, that was the medicine show man, and Dan Sains that were his brother-in-law, they played so's you would think it was one of them playing instead of two. Old Man Stokes, he had a voice that some people might not favor, but I was always partial to it, he sung in the old style with a tremble to it, you know what I'm talking about, like it really meant something. Not like some of these young fellas today, some of these Beats and Rolling Stones and whatnot, that toss it off so cool and nice and polite, like it didn't hardly mean nothing to them, except the *words*—you dig what I'm saying, Jack? Well, sure. Then there was the jug bands. On a good day you might have two or three of them, maybe more, and all them musicianers playing so loud against each other you couldn't hardly hear yourself think. Harmonicas and fiddles and jazz horns and even a tuba now and then—man, I tell you, it was really a ball. And the white folks knowed it, too. Always a gang of them hanging out, even that white boy that went to California, what's his name? Yeah, Elvis Presley, that the one—he used to come down here all the time, man, from the time he was a little bitty kid, sure I knowed him, sure did, he'd hang around just to get ideas. No, I didn't teach no guitar to Mr. Elvis Presley. He didn't need no teaching. Anyone who could make that much money knowing what he knowing, that boy don't need no education at all. Oh man, in the springtime it was like Mardi Gras, it was like the birds was coming out of the trees, y'understand? That's how much music there was in the air."

Then he might turn gruff.

"Good old days? Don't give me none of that. The competition was *heavy*, man. There was always some motherfucker to try to knock you off your corner, new sucker come to town you had to cut *haids*. Course I didn't have to play down there, cause I had my radio show in West Memphis at that time. Me and Sonny Boy and Wolf—we all sold horseshit. Yeah. Fertilizer. Grain. It didn't make no difference. I had a little song went something like this: "Good morning, everybody, tell me how do you do/ Well, we the Gold Star boys come here to welcome you." Yeah, just like King Biscuit, it was worth its weight in gold just for the publicity, man. We on every day from twelve-fifteen to twelve-thirty, lunchtime, everybody hungry for the blues, and we would tell 'em where we was playing that night. Aw, we used to play all out in the country back in them days, out at the rough joints. I mean, they was way out in the woods, dirt floors, little tar-paper shacks that you had to go cutting across the fields, I don't think them people ever even *heard* of electricity, and this was the United States of America, not no foreign land. I had me a little band back in them days. Me and Son Clark on guitars. Frenchy on drums. We had a boy they called Pink playing the can bass. And every so often we'd get us a horn player, Kid Thunder or Clarence Dawkins, the one they all call Monkey-grinder, or maybe it'd be Stormy Weather. The people all enjoyed it. I can say that truthfully. We played for the colored, and we played for the white. Oncet in a while we'd play up at the big houses for a party, somebody getting married, young girl graduating from high school, that kind of junk. You see, the young peoples just wanted to dance—it didn't make no difference to them that they was dancing to a gang of old nigger music. What did their feets know? Only their feets turned out to have second sight, ain't that the truth? First the heart, then the mind, then the pecker—excuse my language, ladies, but that's just the plain truth, you tell me if it isn't. It was just what them old buzzards was yapping about all along. Course that sort of thing had been going on under the table right along, but then it come right out in the open, didn't it? A lot of foolishness if you ask me, maybe we was better off in them holdback times, because at least you knowed what to expect from a prejudiced white man, ain't no telling what you got coming from these old jealous-hearted niggers—"

It was at this point that Jerry always tuned out. He didn't want to hear the Screamin' Nighthawk's views on racial progress, especially when the Screamin' Nighthawk was such a patent hypocrite. Though, of course, he always enjoyed the reaction he got from these pale earnest little white boys and girls, he always seemed to get a kick out of their disbelieving, apologetic, guilt-ridden response. If Jerry was there, they'd turn to him for support. And his response was simply to say, Don't believe what this old bullshitter tells you. He's just giving you his usual line of jive. Not even knowing if it was true, or if he himself believed it or not. And they would always pull up short at the idea that anything that this discriminated-against, authentic old black man was telling them could be less than the gospel truth. But it gnawed at Jerry. Could it be that everything Hawk said was tinged with this same willful distortion of the truth? Beale Street, Handy Park, the young Elvis Presley, the radio show. When they were making one of their abortive attempts to do the book together, Jerry had tried to check out some of the facts. It was true, Hawk had spent time in Memphis, he had even done a radio show at one point. It was not on from twelve-fifteen to twelve-thirty, lunchtime for the blues. It was on the air early in the morning (it was switched from five-thirty to quarter of six some time in 1948), and it evidently had lasted for scarcely a year. Jerry could just imagine Hawk and his boys strolling into the studio at that hour, after playing an all-night dance out in the country or staying up all night in some West Memphis saloon working for tips. He had even met a record collector in Memphis who remembered the Screamin' Nighthawk and His Gang performing at a high-school graduation party some time in the early '50s.

But that was all. The details were only as Hawk or a dozen other oral informants remembered them, innumerable facts, innumerable stories, all burgeoning, living, bubbling beneath the surface, lost to history. That was the trouble with the book. That was the reason there wasn't going to be any book. Everything buried in a miasma of memory, a morass of oral tradition. Hawk contradicting himself and everyone else on every occasion he was given even half a chance.

Hawk wandered around Memphis for an afternoon, seemingly looking for someone or something, and not finding it. He stayed at a little hotel off Union, where the night clerk, a one-armed piano player named Jaybird whom Jerry had met at the Memphis Blues Festival a couple of years before, told him they were full up. Jerry stayed at the Sonesta instead, putting in a wake-up call for six the next morning so as not to miss Hawk.

Not that it would have made any difference. Hawk was heading home, down Highway 61, there was no question of that, and Jerry could have given him a two-day start and still caught up. He spoke to Lori from the hotel, and she agreed to meet him in Yola the day after tomorrow. Jerry took a bath, had a steak, and for the first time in four nights slept in a comfortable bed. He had a dream that night in which Hawk came to him and confronted him balefully. "You sleeping like a white man again," Hawk said. "Now ain't you better suited to that, tell me true?" And Jerry had to admit that yes, he was better suited to it, and no, he didn't know what he wanted to bother with a mean old man like Hawk for at all. Hawk smiled grimly. "You come to dance at my funeral," he said with a sudden stab of insight, as Jerry wondered if that could in fact really be the case.

III

SO GLAD

HAWK'S WIFE, Mattie, seemed neither happy nor sorry to see him. She didn't act surprised, she just looked up, said, "Hunh!" and went on with her work, bustling about in the kitchen, attending to two or three pots that were simmering on the stove, keeping one eye on the color TV which sat beneath a rotogravure Sunday pull-out portrait of Martin Luther King and the Kennedy brothers, her other eye fixed on the baby, Rufus, who was three. Hawk in his turn barely acknowledged her presence. "You take care of my white friend, hear?" he said, with no attempt at irony, for, after all, a guest was a guest. Then he passed through the curtained partition into the bedroom, where they could hear him break wind loudly and then slump heavily on the bed.

He didn't look well, Jerry thought. He didn't look well at all. Mattie just kept on with her work, unfolding an ironing board with one hand while picking up Rufus with the other and slapping him across the knuckles for fooling with the plug to the TV set. The other children were playing in front of the house,

Martin ("Little Bo Scooter") and the girl Elyse ("Dicey"), ten and eight respectively. They, too, had barely glanced up when their father pulled in. They were swinging on a homemade swing set atilt on a scrubby tree out in the midst of all the refuse, hogslop, twisted metal, scrawny chickens, and spare automobile parts that made up Hawk's front yard. They swung higher and higher, the two of them on the single swing, bending the limb on which the rope was fastened until it looked as if they would soar off into the stratosphere on the next pump. "Be the first black astronauts if they did," Hawk had said on more than one occasion.

Hawk's house was set on a little country lane out on the edge of town. It was built, Hawk boasted, in the old country way, but so far as Jerry could tell that only meant that the workmen must have been drunk when they got it up. It was only eight or nine years old, coinciding roughly with the time of Hawk's rediscovery, but listed crazily to one side and bulged out in all kinds of unpredictable directions. Since it was put together from scrap lumber and had never been painted, it offered all kinds of richly symbolic inconsistencies for writers to mull over, and it was a poor stringer who didn't zero in on the anomaly of this jerry-built structure providing shelter for a man who had been declared "virtually a national treasure" by the New York *Times*. Several had gone so far as to implicate Jerry in this state of affairs, implying that this beaten-down old bluesman had a rapacious manager whose avarice would not permit his client to escape such filthy squalor. Jerry, of course, never entered into combat with these self-appointed saviors of the black race.

The building kept out the rain, and, padded with newspapers, it kept out the wind, too. Hawk swore it would be able to withstand any earthquake because of the reinforced bolsters at the beams. Not that there had ever been an earthquake, or that there was likely to be one in the next two hundred years. It seemed more likely in fact that if a conflagration were to come it would be set by the neighbors, a bunch of "educated fools," Hawk muttered, who drove Mustangs and Thunderbirds, got the local paper delivered to their box just to prove that they could read, and wouldn't even look twice at that low-down, no-account nigger who called himself a blues singer, nor his simpleminded wife neither, though she, poor child, didn't mean nobody no harm, she couldn't really help herself, and at least she took the children to church regular. "Those backbiting hypocrites!" Hawk rumbled. "I been seeing them all my life. Well, they can kiss my black ass, and if they don't like it—" He could think of no conclusion grand enough to finish the sentence with. It never seemed to bother Mattie, though. Nothing seemed to bother Mattie, in fact, whether because of her "slowness" or simply because she was at peace with herself, she was able always to pass through the storm, ignoring insults and acclaim alike, and emerge on the other side with the same settled smile, the same willingness to be of service. At first Jerry had thought she was simpleminded, too—for the first three years he had known her he couldn't remember her ever uttering a word of more than one syllable in his presence—but then he realized that it was fear and the fact, which he had never quite fully taken in, that she was only thirteen years old when they first met.

She was the daughter of the legendary Roebuck "Rabbit" Turner, a Yola native who had come up behind the Screamin' Nighthawk and recorded with the hastily assembled string band which Hawk had put together for Alan Lomax's Library of Congress recordings. "Some folks say she's slow," Hawk liked to boast. "They say she's dumb, you know what I'm talking about, cause she never learned to read or write, but I don't hold with any of that mess. Mattie got a sweet disposition. She know how to make a man happy. What I care if she can read and write? I *had* me a wife that could read and write, and that didn't do me no good."

Mattie was twenty-three now, bright-eyed, dark, slender, and accommodating in every way. If they did have arguments, Jerry had never witnessed one. If she had any reservations about the role that had been thrust upon her, she never voiced them in or, he suspected, out of his presence. They had been together since just before Jerry had found Hawk, when Rabbit Turner's new woman put her foot down and said she wanted that child out of the house and Rabbit gave her reluctantly to his old teacher. Some people said he would as soon have given her to the devil ("Jealous-hearted fools," replied Hawk), and it was true that despite their long years of association the two men had never gotten along. Rabbit was too much like Hawk, they were so much alike in fact some people thought he was Hawk's son (but that was ridiculous, Jerry thought, if Rabbit had been Hawk's son then Mattie would have been—). Rabbit came from the same school of music in any case, and like any child following in his father's footsteps it was bound to be rough for him. So he and Hawk had fallen out violently at times, then patched it up and come back together again, but always there was the thread of their music. And now there was Mattie. Now that Rabbit was gone—they said his woman, Minnie Stovall, had poisoned him shortly after she made him put Mattie out of doors—Mattie was all that was left. "You remember your daddy?" Hawk said to her sometimes, and she would nod. "He was a great man," Hawk pronounced judiciously. "Great man. Everything he knew he learned from me."

About the poison Hawk said to Jerry that all the talk was just horseshit. "Rabbit died from drinking moonshine, rotgut, Sterno, canned heat, anything he could get his hands on. It rotted the lining right out of his stomach, that's the plain and simple truth of it. When he died wasn't nothing left. He didn't weigh but seventy pounds," Hawk pronounced, not without a certain grim satisfaction. "I think he loved that gal more than he did his life. They was too close together, some people would say. He couldn't never understand why she stuck with me, I think he expected she come back to her daddy fore too long, Minnie Stovall or no Minnie Stovall. Say, What you doing to that little gal of mine? I think you must've hoodooed her or something, cause she don't hardly look at me no more. Shoot, when she come to me, she so scared she couldn't even stay in the same room, didn't sit down at the table with me till we been living together as man and wife for nigh onto a year. Just like a little rabbit, that's just the way she was—she was that shy, just like her daddy before her. When I first knowed him, he didn't drink nothing but Pepsi-Cola. We call him Rabbit, cause he so quick, and he didn't say nothing less'n he was spoken to. Just a kid. He had a thousand different ideas then, man, I thought he'd never run out of ideas, and he wouldn't have neither, be up there with them Beats or them Rolling Stones if whiskey hadn't taken him over. He was a nice boy, but he taken the wrong turn. Lots of bad turns in this world, and Rabbit done made most of them, but when he was younger, man he was really something."

"Can I get you something, Mr. Jerry?" Mattie's voice intruded on his thoughts.

No, no, he shook his head.

"I don't know why I been doing all this cooking and baking. I didn't know that Roosevelt be coming home. But I been cooking for three days now, you ask the kids if I ain't. It must be second sight, you know my grandmother had second sight, at least that's what my daddy say, and I can mind her holding me on her knees, and saying, child, you gonna see the world whole. That what she always used to say. You gonna see the world whole. Everybody else tried to make me talk, they thought I was a dumb child, cause I didn't say nothing till I was five, just didn't have nothing to say till then, I guess. I didn't know what she meant, she pat me on the head and say that, but then every night for the last week I been dreaming the same dream, I seen Hawk coming up over the hill, with his guitar strapped over his shoulder, and he be singing that song, you know, that I like so much, 'It been so long since I come into my mother's home,' yeah he was. And that dream keep coming back, and that was when I knowed it, and I even told the chillen they daddy's coming home, didn't I, Rufus?"

Rufus didn't say anything, but then Rufus was like his mother. Jerry, however, was amazed. He had never heard Mattie say so many words at one time before. But then, he supposed, he shouldn't be surprised. A lot of things had changed in the last few years. "You sure I can't get you anything, Mr. Jerry?"

His throat was dry, and he was dog-tired. "Maybe a glass of water."

"Show went okay? Did they like him?"

Jerry nodded.

"I sure was surprised to see you drive up," she said, bringing him the glass. "Didn't see you in my dream. You taking a little vacation?"

Jerry nodded wearily, though he knew it couldn't be very convincing.

"Well, it sure nice to see you. Roosevelt think the world of you, you know. I wonder sometimes what would have happened to us if we hadn't met up with you. You know, when I go to church, sometimes I pray for you, you don't mind, do you, Mr. Jerry? Because I hope it ain't against your religion. See, I just pray that you be well, have a nice life, get yourself a nice woman you can depend on, nothing fancy or nothing—"

"No, I wouldn't want anything fancy. Probably be too confusing."

"Reason I do, it feel like we owe you something. Course Hawk don't think so. He don't think he owe nothing to nobody. But I know we wouldn't have this nice house, we wouldn't be able to bring up the kids to go to school regular and make something of themselves or nothing like that if you and them other boys hadn't come down here in the first place. You remember that falling-down cabin out in the woods, where you first come acrost us?"

Jerry remembered, he couldn't very well have forgotten. It was all so different—not only from anything he had ever seen before but from what he looked at now with the added perspective of knowledge. He remembered his first glimpse of this town, seemingly no different from all the other flat little one-horse towns that fanned out from 61 back out into the fields and farmland, back into the bogs and swamps and piney-woods wilderness, where, it seemed, progress had stopped along about fifty years ago. He remembered his traveling companions and the expectations they had had both of each other and of their quest. He squirmed at the memory of himself, so ridiculously lost, so ridiculously hopeful.

They met on a frosty spring morning in late April of 1966 at the airport in Memphis: Ralph Thayer, a bearded poli-sci teacher from Berkeley with heavy horn-rimmed glasses, George Hartl, a long-haired freelance who had contributed one or two pieces to the *Village Voice*, and himself, recently jobless, disengaged, drifting. They had corresponded for years, though they had never met, but they knew each other immediately, being the only people in the small airport who looked anything like one another.

The trip started off on a sour note, as Hartl and Jerry suggested that they go to a barber shop before even renting a car, and Thayer was resolutely opposed. "No, no," he kept shaking his head, impervious to their arguments. It wasn't his beard so much as his principles. They, with visions of Goodman-Chaney-Schwerner, the three murdered civil-rights workers, in their heads, argued that it had nothing to do with principle, it was simply anonymity they were seeking. "So is it religious?" said Hartl, who volunteered to shave his sideburns in exchange. They stood there in the middle of that pastel, sickly-smelling lobby arguing at the top of their voices, glancing around nervously all the while to see if anyone was paying attention to these three exotic foreigners.

"No, I'm not going to be intimidated," Thayer insisted, his big Adam's apple protruding, his eyes watering behind the thick lenses, as Jerry learned they always did when he got excited. He was the oldest of them, thirty-four then, and had been involved in the exotic world of blues collecting for the longest time. He had three Charley Patton 78s in mint condition, a library of green-sleeved originals from the '20s and '30s, and a wife and children and career. He was a Marxist theoretician who would later become prominent in the Free Speech Movement, after he got tenure. Still, he seemed to Jerry irremediably self-centered and bourgeois in his protective mechanisms. "I won't be intimidated," he repeated, "by a bunch of crackers and racists."

"Look, Ralph," Hartl said in his soothing New Yorker's whine. "It isn't as if anyone is asking you to compromise your beliefs or even to cut off your beard. We're only asking you to get a little trim. I thought we all agreed we wanted to be as inconspicuous as possible—"

"I can't trim my beliefs," Thayer thundered. "Besides, my wife cut my hair before I left. My wife always cuts my hair. I don't go to barbers."

In the end they worked out a compromise solution. They rented a car at the airport unshorn. Jerry and Hartl went to the nearest barbershop, which happened to be in a mixed neighborhood. Meanwhile Thayer trimmed his own beard in a public restroom, and though they couldn't detect any difference in appearance he emerged with a fistful of jet-black hairs.

Then there was the problem of who was to drive and who would sit in the front seat. Hartl, it turned out, was absolutely hopeless at map-reading, and the map-reader, they had determined, would sit beside the driver. They could all, as far as Jerry was concerned, have squeezed into the front seat, but Thayer, a large somewhat heavy-set man, was firmly opposed to that. Hartl, not surprisingly, didn't have a driver's license, and he bitterly protested being exiled to the back. "It's not my fault," he protested, "that I'm a city-dweller. I never had any trouble reading a subway map. Besides, I get carsick, and I can't hear a word you guys are saying without leaning forward, and if I lean forward I feel like I'm going to barf." In the end Jerry sat in the back most of the time, and when he stretched out and tried to shut out the noise of their constant bickering, stood accused of having usurped the most favored place for himself.

There were a hundred other similar details in the first day alone. Where they stopped to buy gas. Where they stopped to relieve themselves. If they stopped at all. Who kept the accounts. Where they ate. What they ate. Hartl, for example, ate nothing but hamburgers medium-rare and Coke from the bottle. If he got a hamburger that was undercooked or too well done, he just pushed it away from him and went out and sat in the car. Which meant that they had to stop at the next fast-food chain down the line and try again. Thayer had a passion for chili sauce and hot spices and would have stopped at every little Bar-B-Q they passed by, but Hartl said that barbecue, whether domesticated or the real thing, only gave him the runs.

It turned out, Jerry concluded glumly on the first night as Hartl showered and Thayer nervously tested his recording equipment in the first of what was to become more than two dozen Holiday Inns listed in Thayer's *Mobil Travel Guide,* that they just didn't like each other very much. Which was a hell of a discovery to make on such short actual acquaintance, after a correspondence which ranged over five or six years and a host of subjects (politics, civil rights, the stuffiness of academics, the entrenched racism of Amerika), a shared passion, and a resolute commitment of energy and resources (they had pooled over $1,200 and set aside nearly a month for this quest) to find the Screamin' Nighthawk (a.k.a. T.R. Jefferson) or bust.

It wasn't going to happen. Once again Jerry had that sinking feeling that all was lost, even before the battle was effectively joined. They would never find Hawk, they would never even last a week like this, the whole thing was a mistake from start to finish. A roommate in college had once suggested to Jerry that he was an idealist who put too much faith in beginnings, refusing to allow things to develop at their own pace, spinning out endings which could never be realized. His roommate was talking about a girl—but Jerry had *married* the girl, the girl was Lin, they had simply marched up the steps of Ann Arbor's city hall shortly before graduation and reemerged married, in a single stroke of legal independence which left two sets of parents speechless with shock. The fact that it hadn't worked out had nothing to do with expectations, he and Lin were very different people, she wanted things he wasn't prepared to give her (furniture, respectability, children), lots of marriages didn't work out.

What *had* worked out for him, though? Jerry had thought a career in television or photojournalism would be somehow exciting. When he was at the University of Michigan, his pictures had appeared regularly in the school paper, he did several innocuous word-and-photo seasonal essays only slightly enlivened by shots of girls he might have liked to have known better—and occasionally did—and he was color commentator for football and basketball his junior and senior years, providing statistics and analysis for the drowsy Saturday afternoon broadcasts. He had majored in communications, got to know the jocks, and once in a while even got to pontificate about his newest enthusiasm, the blues, which he had discovered through records by Leadbelly and Big Bill Broonzy and which he found lent itself to every Rousseauian fantasy he had ever had about art and authenticity.

Life wasn't like that, though. After graduation their friends had dispersed, and he and Lin moved to Springfield, Illinois, where his brother-in-law, his sister's husband, then an assistant director with CBS News, had found a job for him writing ad copy for the local affiliate. For a while he maintained his free-lance ambitions, even selling a picture once to *Sports Illustrated*. His father had the picture framed (it showed a marathon runner collapsing in a fellow runner's arms with the finish line just visible behind them) and placed it behind the counter from which he dispensed prescriptions, but he refused Jerry's offer of an original print; instead he cut out the magazine page itself, even retaining the advertisement for Johnson outboards that went with it.

In the three years that they were married he and Lin moved often, and sometimes Jerry thought that he was making progress, gaining a reputation for efficiency and dependability, even if it was in a series of limited-audience, low-rating markets. By the time that he moved back in with his parents, in Brighton, after his marriage and lease had come to a virtually simultaneous end, he knew that he was mired in the same rut of "professionalism" and parochial ambition he had sought so vigorously to escape when he first rejected his father's clean white pharmacist's smock, his father's clean white innocent ambitions for his only son.

For the fourteen months that he was at home he found himself increasingly drifting into the past, a past which had never interested him in the slightest when he was growing up and all eyes were forward—away from grandparents' embarrassing accents, away from burdensome differences, toward an assimilated, progressive, *American* future which lay just over the horizon. Now he revisited the scenes of his youth, the schoolyard where a Catholic friend in second grade had said, "Are you Jewish?" and he responded, "Are you kidding?" Back to the temple from which he had escaped at fifteen with never a backward glance. He talked to the rabbi who had conducted his confirmation class but who didn't seem to understand what he was driving at now. He started reading Isaac Bashevis Singer. He pumped his father for stories about ancestors, about the old country, about his father's growing up. "What do you want to know all that stuff for?" his father would say impatiently. "Haven't you got enough problems of your own?"

It was a strange time. Jerry went to work, came home, closed the door of his room, turned on occasionally, and listened to his records—once an eclectic collection that could encompass Miles Davis, Pete Seeger, and Miriam Makeba, now blues exclusively —which more and more took up every available inch of floor-space. In the increasingly exotic sounds—so painful to his parents' ears and sensibilities that they left the television at high volume even when they weren't in the room—he caught a whiff of an acrid reality that strangely corresponded to his own. In the rarefied world of the collector he found a companionship, a sense of belonging, if only at a distance, that allowed him to share secret passions, secret obsessions, a secret language, that encouraged an exchange of views, an animated debate, an *engagement* that excluded the casual outsider. He became something of an expert, started writing for *Broadside* and a British blues magazine, interviewed Mississippi John Hurt, and began to suspect that it was his own hovering presence (perhaps now *he* was the unassimilated embarrassment) that caused his father to retire and led his parents to cut all ties, unload the pharmacy, sell the house, and move to Florida.

Jerry felt totally bereft, now his childhood was really gone. All he had were his books and records—even his papers, his first published stories, the bylines his mother had so carefully saved were carted off with baseball cards and other boyhood mementoes. He moved into a rooming house in Cambridge, then, when

97

that became too small, into a modest apartment. He still reported to work for a while; he marched in civil-rights marches, signed petitions occasionally, became known a little bit around the folk clubs and to the longhaired girls, and brooded over whether his fantasy could ever become reality. This was his fantasy: he sought to create his own life, give up his assigned identity and forge another. Setting off to rediscover some old blues singer on impulse alone was just the first step toward freedom. But now he was afraid that this, too, was going to be another dead end. . . .

By the end of the third day they weren't speaking to each other except to criticize a wrong turn taken or question Thayer's driving habits. They had stopped off in Commerce, Tunica, Austin, Senatobia, Bobo, Alligator, and Mound Bayou, following the same pattern in each little town, going to the post office, then to the general store if the two were not the same, finally to the police station, carefully explaining that they were looking for a man who used to be a singer with the idea of recording him again, attempting as scrupulously as they could to show a neutral goodwill neither hostile to the Negro they were looking for nor inimical to the white men they were asking. Originally the idea was that they would take turns as spokesman, but Jerry was soon elected representative and, dragging his feet all the while, trudged reluctantly in and out of stores, in and out of official buildings, sure that everyone was laughing at him or worse.

They found nothing. Not a single trace. No one who would admit to so much as having heard of the Screamin' Nighthawk, let alone any knowledge of his present whereabouts. It was as if the earth had swallowed him whole, but that couldn't be, Jerry thought, because his songs were still being sung, better-known bluesmen like Muddy Waters or Howlin' Wolf, who had moved to Chicago years ago, insisted that the Screamin' Nighthawk was still around, members of their bands had seen him only three or four years ago—in Mobile, Decatur, Jackson, St. Louis. Sometimes Jerry got the feeling it was perversity. More often with the few blacks he spoke to it seemed to be fear. A couple of times they would stop out in the country to ask a farmer walking behind his mule or a wizened old lady rocking inexorably on a falling-down porch. The response was inevitably suspicious, closed-off, deliberately opaque. Once Jerry thought he had found something as he idly conversed with some colored mechanics on their lunch break at Romeo's Garage. "Oh sure," they started to respond, then caught the disapproving glance of the white foreman, presumably Romeo. Jerry suggested to the others that they wait until work let out and talk to the mechanics then, but they decided it would be a waste of time, and for all Jerry knew those impassive black faces, with their impenetrable looks and impenetrable language, were only putting him on, perhaps recognized the name, very likely had nothing more to say. It was all very strange, Jerry thought, but hardly surprising. Who knew what happened to anyone in this country after they faded from the limelight?

In Cleveland they managed to stumble across the man who had engineered Hawk's last official sessions in Jackson almost fifteen years before. He was a tall stringy-looking country boy with a prominent Adam's apple who had played on some early rockabilly sides and to their surprise vividly remembered Hawk. "Sure do. Didn't leave no forwarding address. He jes' wanted his money on the table, you know, like all them people. I remember he had quite a roll, of course it might have been built up some, all ones on a cardboard backing, I've seen that once or twice in my time. Bunch of cards, too, letters, old newspaper clippings, I

remember he had a gang of 'em. Course I knowed him some before that anyways. My brother-in-law was Uncle Charley—you
maya heard of him, his real name was Charley Stewart, and he
sold tires for a living, but he was pretty well known as a radio
personality in these parts—he used to have him on his radio show
oncet in a while, I can remember one time we went out in the
country to a place he was playing. Way out in the woods—man,
you oughta seen it, you oughta seen them niggers jump. Half of
them not wearing any shoes, I ain't seen nothing like it since I
was a kid, and that old Nighthawk, he just kept frailing away on
his guitar, he could play all night and all day, like to wore me
out. That's about all I know, boys. Course you could check with
Miz Gaynor."

Their hearts leaped, and they eagerly took down whatever
information the engineer could proffer on Miz Gaynor, who
lived over near Greenville now and had owned the Jackson label
with her husband, a dentist, until a fire burned down their home
and made a widow of her. "Undependable," she started out un-
promisingly. "There was quite a few times when my husband,
Dr. Gaynor, had to go down to the city jail and talk Mr. Rogers
into letting Nighthawk out. And, of course, often I had to send
my husband or my son—that's Fred—over to one of them rough
nigger joints, I wouldn't dare go in there myself, to get him and
sober him up so we could do a session. But he could sing, I'll say
that for him. He was the best of the lot. The people really liked
him. And I suppose he was a nice enough old fellow, minded his
own business, never gave me any backtalk that I can recall, never
had much to say for himself at all as a matter of fact. Sure sorry
I couldn't help you boys any more," she said not very convincingly. Jerry didn't think she was sorry at all.

But they kept on down Highway 61 with nothing else to go

on, all because once, in a song that Hawk had recorded several times in the '30s, he had declared, "Highway 61 rolls right by my door/ Next time you see me I be heading down that old dusty road."

They were five days into their pilgrimage and just about ready to turn back. They had argued about matrix numbers, the ethnic purity of the blues and the ruinous effects of amplification upon the folk tradition, the centrality of Robert Johnson's role (assimilator or creative genius?), and the true identity of King Solomon Hill. Thayer had stopped speaking to Hartl some time the previous day when Hartl had said, "My God, if you don't shut up about the sociology of the South, I think we're all going to suffocate from the shit." Thayer, who was lying down in the back seat for a rest, demanded that Jerry stop the car.

"You heard what he said. I've taken about as much of his shit as I'm going to. I don't have to take that kind of shit from anyone." He kept poking Jerry's shoulder with increasing force, until Jerry thought he would have to stop the car or run off the road.

"Ah, Christ," said Hartl. "I'm just sick of hearing all this liberal bullshit about white oppression and how it affected the poor bush nigger in his primitive state. God, what drivel!"

"There, you heard it!" Thayer said, grabbing Jerry by the shoulder and practically jerking his head around. "It's out, you heard it, I knew it all along. Racist, colonialist rhetoric, you can't deny it. I won't go another foot with this white—*colonialist.*"

"Ah, why don't you grow up, Ralph? You act like you never got fucked before."

"I think," said Jerry, taking a deep breath, "we ought to all remember why we're here. I mean, we have committed a certain amount of time and energy and money to finding an artist who has made a significant impact on the lives of all of us. I think that impact is large enough to allow us to forget our petty differences—"

So they stopped talking to each other, and, if they had anything to say, communicated it through Jerry.

Then outside of Yola they had their first real glimmer of hope. They had already completed their rounds, tried the post office with no luck, had it politely suggested to them by the police chief that they were wasting their time and his, when Hartl, spotting a Coke machine, bright red and spanking new, in front of a run-down cafe and general store, suddenly developed an uncontrollable thirst and asked Jerry to have Thayer stop. On the porch there was an old man in a straw hat and earwarmers, rocking away. Inside the store around a potbellied stove was a group of black men, grown suddenly silent as Jerry and Thayer stretched their legs, checking out the store and examining the beat-up jukebox that sat in a corner. James Brown, Otis Redding, O.V. Wright, James Carr—Jerry saw Thayer's face wrinkle with disgust. But there in the middle of all these up-to-the-minute homogeneous offerings of a mechanized age was a handwritten card (B-4) announcing a selection of "So Glad," of which only a half-dozen copies (all of the others 78s) had ever surfaced, so far as any collector knew. Jerry could scarcely contain his excitement. He glanced at Thayer to see if he, too, had noticed, but Thayer had walked away sniffing the air, clearly oblivious. With trembling fingers he dug in his fingers for change, found a dime, pushed down the buttons, checking three times to make sure he had the right number, and waited in breathless anticipation. Nothing happened. He touched the jukebox gingerly, wanting to shake it until it burst into song, but then he noticed it wasn't plugged in. Its cord trailed off and dangled uselessly on the floor with no visible outlet or way for it to be connected.

Without saying anything to Thayer, Jerry sidled over to the counter and waited for what seemed like an interminable period until one of the old men separated himself from the rest, came around behind the counter, and said in a loud, unmodulated voice, "Something I can do for you?" Jerry explained, and the man offered him his dime back, but that was not, Jerry insisted, what he was looking for. He wanted to hear the song. Somewhat resentfully, all the while muttering to himself, the man strode across the room, retrieved an extension cord, marched back, plugged the old machine in.

The first notes were inaudible because the tubes were still warming up, but then Jerry heard it, and Thayer whirled around, hearing it too, the unmistakable sound of Nighthawk's ringing guitar, the big bass voice booming out, "So glad I be back home, see my mother's face one more time."

They were as flabbergasted as he. Even Hartl showed signs of animation and enthusiasm. They played the record again and then the other side, which none of them had even heard except on a faint tenth-generation dub. Then the questions began. Did anyone know the artist? Had anyone actually seen the Screamin' Nighthawk perform? Why no, didn't believe they had. Where had the record come from? The man behind the counter, round and unwrinkled in a dirty white apron, scratched his head. A man brought 'em by. What man? Well, shucks, he didn't know, the records all came from Jackson, he supposed, he didn't know how long they'd had that one, didn't really remember hearing it before. Did the name Theodore Roosevelt Jefferson mean anything to any of them? Well, no, they didn't believe it did. Of course they knew *Franklin* Roosevelt. He was a great man. The blank impassive black faces, calm, imperturbable, just a little bit pained at not being able to provide better answers for these nice gentlemens, slightly puzzled and embarrassed at all this fuss. Thayer and Hartl grew increasingly impatient until at last they started tugging on Jerry's sleeve. "Let's get out of here," Hartl insisted. "This is just a waste of time." But Jerry persisted. He had gotten so far as to clarify that the last name was Jefferson.

"Oh, Jefferson, Jefferson," the man who had plugged in the jukebox boomed. "Well, why didn't you say so in the first place? Yessir, there's lots of Jeffersons. There's Purvis Jefferson and Clovis Jefferson, which is the Jefferson that passed, lived over by Browns Point—used to play a little harmonica, the people would call him Boot sometimes cause his feets was so big and he used to wear them big old clodhopper boots, you know them cut-off old square-toes, you know what I mean—" Jerry nodded bleakly. Hartl regarded the man with undisguised contempt.

"Well, this Jefferson," Jerry explained, "plays the guitar. And we hope he's alive. He used to make records, and they called him the Screamin' Nighthawk. If you looked at the label, I'll bet the composer's credits would read T.R. Jefferson."

The others just stared at him blankly.

Outside Thayer had started the car. They would leave him here, Jerry sensed in a panic. They would abandon him without a moment's thought. He cast one eye toward the door and turned back one last time to the old men clustered around the stove.

"You say this fella named T.R.?" said one in an oversized checkered cap that puffed up from his head. "Well, say, this T.R., did he have a big old guitar, one of them hollow-bodied old Stellas that he plug in to a electric box?"

Jerry shrugged. For all he knew the Screamin' Nighthawk was no more than a figment of his imagination.

"Well, say, I knew a boy used to work down at Dooley's Garage, used to play a big old guitar until he joined the choich" —Jerry's spirits fell—"but naw, that was J.R., isn't that right?"

"Yeah, that's right. J.R. J.R.," a chorus of voices answered him.

"Yeah. J.R. Benwell, that the one. You want to speak to J.R. Benwell, you gwine have to speak to the warden down at Parchman first. He doing life for cutting his woman's throat. Course that woman was cheating on him every kind of way, and the poor fool didn't know it until he come home find her in bed with another woman. But the judge sent him up just the same."

They shook their heads sadly over the fate of J.R. Benwell. Jerry thought he was going to cry. They were just toying with him, he thought helplessly. Outside Thayer leaned on his horn. The old man on the porch was still rocking when Jerry came out. He didn't mean any harm; he just didn't know how to show it.

"T.R., T.R.," said the squat, heavy-set man with the big voice, standing in the doorway behind him. "Well, you know, I think that might ring a bell. Ain't he the feller lives out on the edge of the swamp, out on the old Holloway Plantation?" From within Jerry could hear a mumbled chorus of assent. "Well, say, now, that might just be your man."

"T.R. Jefferson," Jerry repeated patiently.

"Yeah, that the one. You want to know where he lives, right?"

Jerry nodded, not quite trusting his own voice.

"You think you can follow directions? Well now. You follow the old West Oak Road, turn towards the river at the first fork you come to, then you come to an old bridge, go straight on across— *don't take no turns*—after you cross that bridge you just follow the signs to the Holloway Plantation, you can't miss it, unless'n you take the wrong turn—"

Excitedly Jerry took the directions down in his little notebook, blurted out his profuse thanks, and practically fell over himself running down the steps toward the car, which was turning around on the dusty shoulder. The old mummy on the porch had scarcely moved.

They got hopelessly lost. By the time they had finally come to a bridge—and they hadn't the slightest idea if it was the right bridge—they had been driving around for nearly two hours in what was beginning to seem like trackless Arctic waste. Thayer and Hartl were yelling at him separately. "Well, that's what you get for listening to those shiftless niggers," said Hartl. "About all they're good for is singing and dancing anyway."

"God," said Thayer. "You really have led us on a wild goose chase, haven't you?"

"I mean, it's all right listening to the music, but as far as giving directions goes, they're not really worth a shit."

"The first thing we should have done," said Thayer, "was to have him show us on the map. I can't believe I have to travel all the way to Mississippi just to find another New York racist."

Was this what it was like, Jerry wondered, for Alan Lomax on his great pioneering field expeditions?

They saw an old man on a mule riding at a somnolent gait down a solitary dirt lane by the side of the road. He was wearing a broad-brimmed preacher's hat and seemed half asleep when Thayer slowed the car down and called out to him. "Excuse me," said Thayer to the old man, "we were looking for a black man named T.R. Jefferson, a blues singer. You wouldn't happen to know where he lives?"

"You on the wrong road," said the man without a moment's

hesitation. The mule proceeded at its stately pace, and Thayer kept the car even with him in herky-jerky fashion.

"This gentleman seems to be a cut above his fellows," whispered Hartl with embarrassing volume. "You can tell from his professorial mien that he's read Hegel."

"This man, Mr. Jefferson, is an old-time blues singer," Thayer explained gravely. "Professionally he has been known as the Screamin' Nighthawk."

"Hunh!"

"He used to play an old Stella," said Jerry.

"I already done tole you, you headin' in a wild goose chase if you lookin' for his house. Now you got to turn around, go back to the bridge, take your second left, road go down in between the fields, you jes' keep driving till you can't drive no more."

"And then?"

The man looked at them with some disdain. "That's Jefferson's house." When none of them said anything, he kicked the mule, which seemed to affect its gait not at all, shook his head, and muttered half to himself, "Ain't that what you said you wanted?"

They left him in the dust. Thayer, with one hand on the wheel, started fiddling with the portable tape recorder. "Will you tell him to keep his eyes on the road, for God's sake?" said Hartl. "You know, I get the impression, gentlemen, that we may be on to something. Do you suppose that jigaboo has any conception of the historic service he may have done the world?"

Jerry's hands were sweating.

"My God," said Thayer, "do you think we've really done it? Can you imagine what it will be like to have rediscovered the Screamin' Nighthawk? I can't even imagine what his reaction will be."

"What do you mean?" said Jerry.

"Well, this is almost like finding out that Robert Johnson is still alive or rediscovering Blind Willie McTell."

"But *he* knows that he's still alive," said Jerry. If he *was* still alive, if this wasn't one more joke on the part of the state of Mississippi, which seemed aligned in a common conspiracy, black and white, against them.

"But he doesn't know how important he is."

They headed down the mud-rutted road between the cotton rows, picking up speed and sending up dust. It seemed as if the low leafy cotton plants would never stop but go on forever, and Jerry was sure they were off on another wild goose chase. "Maybe we'll find Tommy McClennan off in the bushes somewhere," said Hartl. "After all, didn't he record 'Cotton Patch Blues'?"

At last the rows of cotton plants gave out, and they came to one or two pitiful little tar-paper shacks, but the road kept going, so they did, too, until finally it gave out altogether, just became a rutted wagon track which Thayer was reluctant to subject the rented car to. So they got out and walked, proceeding single-file in the direction of an isolated misshapen structure, propped up on poles beside a muddy creek, which was as far as you could go. They approached the house with trepidation, though it looked deserted. Inside there was no clear sign of recent occupancy. In the single main room there was a dirty mattress, a straw pallet, a rusty old woodburning stove with a pot of fetid water sitting on top of it, and a big brass bed. The walls were patched with newspaper and decorated with pictures of dogs of all kinds. In the yard a few chickens ran loose. It was hard to say whether the house had been left that morning by people who lived there and actually intended to return or if it had been abandoned some months before. There was no indication of who its occupants were or had been. They called out loudly, but of course no one answered, and when they went outside the children who had been playing in the fields nearby had disappeared. When they got back out to the highway, they met the old man again, seemingly no closer to his destination than he was when they first spied him. "You find T.R.'s place all right?" he asked equably.

"There wasn't anyone there."

"Naw, that's right, he ain't there," said the old man. "Wife took sick, the new one, that is, and she over there in the county hospital with her new baby. T.R. probably at the Sunset Café, leastaways that's where I left him, couldn't have been more than an hour ago."

They got directions to the Sunset Café, followed them this time without a hitch, and ended up at the same general store from which they had first started out. It was deserted now, grown almost dark in the gathering twilight. Only the jukebox and the light over the pool table brightly glowed. Sitting alone at the counter was the same squat heavy-set man who had plugged in the jukebox for them. "You young gentlemens looking for the Screamin' Nighthawk?" he said without even a chuckle. "Well, you come to the right place."

THE KIDS came in for lunch, Elyse, Little Bo, and Rufus. The television still flickered soundlessly above the refrigerator. Mattie bustled around and shushed the kids. Jerry gratefully devoured the hot dogs she set before him. "We got over five thousand dollar in the bank," said Mattie. "Imagine that."

Jerry looked around the ramshackle house and found it difficult to imagine. "What are you going to do with it?"

Mattie put her hand to her mouth as if she were embarrassed, as if the thought had never occurred to her. "Well, it
nice to have something to fall back on. You know, Roosevelt ain't
getting any younger, maybe he like to take it easy for a while.
How he get along with that Teenochie anyway, no bull?"

Jerry shrugged. "Okay, I guess. They had their differences."

"I imagine so." Mattie giggled. "I imagine so. Roosevelt
never could stand that man. He always act like he too big for his
britches. Why, I remember one time he come riding up in his
Cadillac—course it wasn't really his, finance company seen to that
soon enough—but he want Roosevelt to go out on the road with
him, you know what he want him to do? Do the cooking, do the
driving, just generally do for him like he was his chauffeur.
Roosevelt, that practically raised him from a kid and even still got
a bigger name than him to this day. But he just want to show
Roosevelt he was doing good, know what I mean? I guess that's
just the way with some folk."

"I guess so," said Jerry. "Hey, you must be in the fourth
grade now," he said to Little Bo. Bo looked up at him with the
same hooded eyes as his father. "Don't go to school no more," he
said with indifferent hostility.

"Now don't you go talking to Mr. Jerry like that. It ain't
his fault how they be doing you."

"Why? What are they doing to Scooter?" said Jerry, thinking of race, rednecks, riots.

"They tell me Scooter too slow," said Mattie. "They want us
to enroll him at a special school cause they say he got a reading
problem. If he go over there, he be riding the bus back and forth

ten, fifteen miles every day. Roosevelt say he ain't got no big problem, riding that bus give him more of a problem than anything he gonna get in school."

"Why? What's the matter with riding the bus?"

"What I want with school for anyway?"

"School's over in River View. Hawk don't want him riding to where they won't allow him to play." Mattie shrugged. "He big enough to help with the chores now, Little Bo a big help around the house, ain't you, sugar?"

"Pretty soon I'm going to go out with my daddy," said Little Bo. "He's learning me to play guitar. I figure I practice up real good, and I can second him on guitar, just like Daddy Rabbit used to do."

Mattie pursed her lips in a nervous smile. "Now you quit that kind of talk," she said, evidently pleased, embarrassed, a little bit angry, but she didn't say why. Jerry glanced over at Dicey, and she hid behind her mother's back. "I guess you've started school now, too," he said to her. She didn't say a word, but stole a look from behind her mother. Mattie yanked her by a pigtail. "Now you answer Mr. Jerry," she said.

Dicey peeked out from behind her mother. "Uh huh," she said.

"How do you like it?"

"Oh, I likes it *fine.*"

Everyone laughed. "How about you? Do you ride the bus every day?"

Dicey nodded. "She waits at the end of the lane," said Mattie. "Her brother waits with her. It just about kills me to see him standing out there waiting for that bus to come, then just waving his little sister goodbye. He just a baby—"

"I am not!"

"He ought be gitting his education, too. I gonna see if I can get Roosevelt to go down there and talk to them people. And if he don't, I'm gonna do it myself. It just ain't right, the way they doing him. I know, cause I ain't never had the chance myself. And I know he ain't dumb. I just like to see every one of my children amount to something. I think Roosevelt even agree, if he could just get hisself to admit that the white man got anything worth having sides money. Well, you know Roosevelt. He too proud to ask for a drink of water if he parched, let alone ask something of a white man. Meaning no disrespect." She smiled sweetly at Jerry, and Jerry no longer even felt uncomfortable. He enjoyed talking to Mattie, to this woman who had barely spoken a word in his presence for the first three years that he had known her, cowering under the gaze of her husband, the influence of her father, speechless with—what? Fear? Perhaps—or maybe it was just a natural discretion which allowed her to take things in for her own education.

Hawk awoke a little after one. They heard the familiar sounds of his rising, clearing his throat and sighing heavily, sitting up, the bed creaking, then hauling himself off wearily to the bathroom, where he ran the water for a few minutes and when he emerged he looked much better than he had before. Much of the color had returned to his face, and he looked more solid, more robust somehow, as if lying down in his own bed was just the restorative he had needed all along. Jerry was glad; it seemed as if they had made the right decision after all.

Hawk nodded curtly to his manager, waved at the kids, and demanded of Mattie in his deep booming voice, "How about some food?" Mattie bustled about and set a steaming plate in front of him, some indistinguishable stew which Hawk regarded for a moment with apparent distaste, then launched into with gusto.

"So you satisfied?" he said to Jerry between mouthfuls. "You figure you done your job yet? Babysit an old man all the way from Naptown. You left me in that hospital, them doctors woulda killed me by now."

Jerry nodded. There wasn't much to say.

"Can't get no rest in no hospital anyways. All them doctors poking and prodding you, and them good-looking nurses waking you up in the middle of the night, mmm hmmm. Don't make no sense. Don't know how they expect nobody to get well, when all you need is a little rest, something to put in your stomach."

Mattie lifted her eyes up cautiously. "You been sick again, Roosevelt?"

Hawk glared at her indignantly. "Wasn't nothing at all. Something I ate probably. How you been, Bo Scooter?" He took the boy's hand roughly.

"I been practicing, Daddy. I can make the F chord just like you showed me. You want me to do it now?"

"Naw. I listen to you later."

"What you bothering your daddy for when he's eating?" Scooter looked over at his mother, but Hawk concentrated on his food, shoveling it in like a steam engine, slow and steady.

"Hey, what you think of this boy?" Hawk said suddenly to Jerry. "Playing the blues like a natural man. What do you say we dress him up, call him Little Bo, the Midget from Memphis—just like Buddy Doyle. Then we tell everybody he really ninety-two years old. Then he be the biggest thing going." Hawk laughed harshly. "What do you think?"

"Mr. Jerry telling me the trip went good."

Hawk shot Jerry a funny look and patted his breast pocket.

"Went very good. Very good. Got over nine hundred for you to add to your account. And a little left over just to have some fun besides. That damn Teenochie, though. Everywhere we go he try to stick his face in front of the camera, tell all these damn lies, seem like the only thing he know how to do is fuck up. Well, he fuck up one too many times now. He had his chance, but he made a ass out of himself. So I think from now on I go back to being the Lone Nighthawk, the Screamin' Nighthawk Solo, which is how I should have did all along if it hadn't been for my manager here always looking for things to be equal, which is all right, but that ain't the way it worked out, cause that damn fool always demanding the spotlight, which ain't equal nor right at all."

"What about Wheatstraw?" said Mattie. "You always was partial to Wheatstraw's harmonica playing."

Hawk looked away, and Jerry thought he actually saw remorse on the old man's face. "Wheatstraw dead."

"Dead! What happen to him?"

"Damn fool went sailing through the air like a big black crow, landed in a cornfield, head struck a rock, must have, cause when they got him to the hospital wasn't nothing to do but cover him up."

"It was an accident," Jerry said. "That's why Hawk was in the hospital. Teenochie just got some minor bruises."

Mattie didn't say anything at first. "Who was doing the driving?" she said finally in a trembling voice.

"I was," said Hawk. "Who you think? You know I wouldn't trust Teenochie, and Wheatstraw too simple to drive a automobile."

"Did you have another one of them blackouts?"

Hawk didn't say anything, just stabbed at his food angrily.

Jerry was surprised. "Have you been having trouble before this?" he said.

Hawk just glared at Mattie. "I tole him he should have gone to see a doctor. But he too stubborn-minded, he say it nothing, his grandmother have spells like that, they just pass."

Jerry glanced sideways at Hawk, and he was surprised to see how angry Hawk was becoming. The big wen on his forehead was standing out, and his face was all twisted up with indignation. He seemed to be trying to say something, but surprisingly nothing came out. Then his head lolled to one side and he started to choke, and he regarded them helplessly, balefully, as Jerry realized he was having another seizure.

"I can't—" he managed to get out. "I don't—don't know what it is—" He spoke in a voice that sounded like his own but with a tone of wonder, a kind of puzzlement that had never entered the vocabulary of the Screamin' Nighthawk before.

The children stared in helpless fear, and Mattie gave a little cry and rushed to Hawk's side.

"Got—to—lie down. I be better when—"

Somehow Mattie and Jerry managed to support the bulky body between them and get Hawk into the bedroom. There he sprawled on the bed, his face drained of all color, his left hand trembling. Mattie started to cry. Jerry loosened Hawk's belt and said, "You better call a doctor."

"Ain't nobody on the street got their telephone yet," said Mattie. "I better send Scooter to Clark's up on the high road."

Jerry nodded. He felt as if *he* was going to cry. He didn't know what to do for Hawk, and though Hawk paid no attention to him, he just kept talking, just to make some noise in the suddenly still house. "It's gonna be all right. I'm sure it's just a little seizure. We gotta get you up and about for that European tour.

Hey, listen, you're still a young man." There wasn't a flicker of response, and finally he gave up. Mattie came back into the room, and they just sat there and waited. . . .

IT HURT. My head hurt so bad. Damn fools won't leave me alone. Just leave me sleep. Be better then. Puts me in mind of when we was hopping freights, out in the Western states, somewhere out along Utah, some such, I don't know. Sugar Boy and me. Just playing our guitars, swing from town to town. And the women—they act like they never seen a guitar player before. Oooh, Mr. Guitar Player, let me see them hands, look like you don't never work. My, but you got them nice long tapery fingers. They treated us royally in Provo. We on the radio in Salt Lake. Funny. I didn't never know there was such a thing as colored cowboys, course we didn't see none of them. Just the serving folk. Folk who worked for the white man, doing one damn thing or another, always glad to see us, always patting they hands together and reaching down into their pockets like we was preachers, always looking to have a good time, don't nobody think a thing about tomorrow. Well, they was right, tomorrow don't mean nothing anyhow if you stuck with today.

When I woke up they wanted to cut off the one leg, said, You won't never miss it oncet you get your government issue. Sugar Boy gone, must have rolled right under the wheels. Guitar gone, too. A big old flat-top Gibson, man that thing could make a racket. And I could squall like a panther back in them days, on a clear night you could hear me in five counties. At least that's what they say. Them damn doctors. I can't help but be drowsy from time to time, every time one of them start talking to me I fall off again. I think I'm dreaming till I hear one of them yapping, he saying something about taking off my leg. I thought I told you, damn, I ain't gonna be no damn cripple. I ain't gonna drag no stump around behind me like Peg Leg Sam, shit I ain't gonna do no begging. Now Mr. Jefferson, Mr. Jefferson—Mr. Jefferson, shit. I'm a man of travel, I'm a man what goes where he wants, when I feels like it I just picks up and moves. You motherfuckers ain't gonna cut off my damn leg. You come near my leg, I'm gonna slit your throat, and if you don't believe me one dark night when you don't be thinking about it I'm gonna creep up from behind and cut it just as clean as you ever cut an arm or a leg. Well, that git 'em, ain't none of 'em gonna do nothing then, and the leg get better, too, it take a while, but after a time it just about as good as new. Don't look so good, still don't look so good, all scarred and ugly, but it carry me, it carry me to this day. What they gonna do now? You can't cut off a head now, can you? And it's my head that hurt, damn, man, I can't even remember when it don't hurt. She-it, I just wish they quit their yammering. They act like somebody about to die. I seen worse'n this before. Anyway what difference it make if I do die? Mattie got some money in the bank. Kids all got some schooling, even Scooter got more than his daddy ever had. If I am his daddy. What a pretty young woman like Mattie want with a old ugly man like me? Don't make no sense hardly. Same as when I took Mattie, the first Mattie, away from Ol' Man Mose. She didn't have no business being with him no more than this Mattie does being with me. Ol' Man Mose, Chicken Neck, Stavin' Chain, Tricky Sam from Birmingham—all them funny old dudes, gone, all gone. They tell us we lived through a depression, but it wasn't no different. Wasn't nobody no more depressed than usual, less'n it was a few white folk, who was used to more. For us it was just the same. Hunt, fish, go out and trap, we eat when we hungry, we work when we get it, we ball on Saturday night and go to

church, little old country church—this was when we were kids—
all of us, every Sunday. Mama used to dress us up so nice, then
Mattie make me go later on, she always so concerned about being
respectable. Respectable! Them thieving old preachers, lying
about heaven, and shouting about hell, every one of them make
sure he get a piece of the pie. I wonder, do they really believe all
that bullshit they putting down? People sitting there on them
hard-ass seats, saying, Yes, Lawd, ain't it the truth, preacher talking mighty hot today—and singing them old songs that supposed
to raise up their souls, man they don't do a damn thing except
take their mind off conditions as they is. It just ain't for me.
Religion ain't nothing but a skin game, far as I can see. Like
them old songs got it, you may be rich, you may be poor, but
when your time comes round, you got to move. . . .

THAYER was the first to leave. When Hawk refused to go with
them, rather than spend another moment with Hartl, whom he
had taken to referring to as the Grand Wizard of the Greenwich
Village Klan, and respecting, he said, "the man's personal pri-
vacy," he flew out of Jackson that afternoon. "That's the trouble
with academics," said Hartl, even as they were saying goodbye.
"No perspective and no sense of humor—he still thinks that nigger is the Noble Savage incarnate."

At first Hawk wanted $10,000, or some equally ridiculous
sum of money, even to talk. Jerry and Hartl found a little hotel
in Vicksburg about thirty miles away and drove in every day to
see if Hawk had changed his mind about posterity, or if they
could persuade him to reconsider.

"What I want to leave this for?" Hawk said, sitting at the
counter of the Sunset Cafe, sipping whiskey through a straw

from a paper bag. Jerry looked around at the uncrowded room, the men quietly talking and eating and drinking, occasional laughter punctuating their subdued dialogue, and he couldn't understand what Hawk was talking about—back then. He had argued passionately for the advantages of fame, travel, expanding horizons, money. "What good all that gonna do me?" Hawk said, naively, he thought. "I still gotta come back here."

Once while Hartl was out hunting old 78s, Hawk drove around town with Jerry, looking for a bootlegger named Booger Jake who he said owed him money. As he drove by the movie house, the white clapboard town hall, the police chief's wisteria-covered home, he called off the name of each person they passed, colored and white, with a different kind of wave for each. "That's Miz Broom," he said of a gnarled little black woman all bent over with packages. "You see her every day walking up and down the street. Ain't nothing *in* none of them packages, but she likes to act like she just got off a big shopping spree. She always crazy, but she the only one who could read when I was a kid, so she the colored schoolteacher. Didn't do so good if you take me for a mark. Course we only went between planting-cotton time and picking-cotton time, and my daddy put me to work, that was my stepdaddy, when I was nine years old, so she didn't have much of a chance with me. That Mr. Gene setting there in the cruiser. You better slow down, boy. Mr. Gene don't like colored mixing with white. His daddy sheriff, too, and his daddy before him. I knowed Mr. Gene's daddy pretty good, because him and my mama was *good* friends. He ever pull you over you tell him I was fixing up your car for you, we was just going to get some parts. Course this Mr. Gene ain't the meanest man I ever seen. I guess that would be Sheriff Mooney over in Yazoo

County. You stay clear of him, though, he'll stay clear of you. Hey, slow down, slow down, that's Old Man Gulcher. Hey, Gulcher, what is it?"

An old man with a cowboy hat spat philosophically in the dust. "You still around, Jefferson? I thought sure you'd be gone by now. Must be getting old, you keep making them babies, you ain't never gonna get as old as me."

"What you talking about? I don't *never* want to be as old as you. Gulcher ninety-six year old," Hawk said, turning to Jerry. "He can remember practically back to slavery time."

The old man laughed, a thin high-pitched cackle, and shook his head. "Well, who gonna take care of that little old gal when you gone?"

"I guess there be somebody. Maybe you be the one to carry my business on. Sarah Mae, my aunty, staying with her and the baby now. Soon as I shake loose of these Northern boys, I gonna be gone. Crops gonna be coming in in Georgia before too long, money gonna be wearing a hole in them Georgia boys' pockets, and Hawk gonna swoop in there to catch it fore it fall. From there I figure to go on down to Florida. Florida bound to be pretty good by then, too. Then we just gonna have to see. Hey, you ought to get out that harp of yours one of these days, fore you forgets how to blow it. Bring it on down to the Sunset, fore you gets to be a *old* old man."

"Aw, I ain't got the breath no more. I got the will all right, but I just ain't got the breath."

"Well, go on and see how you feels then."

They watched the old man trudging off in the dust. Out on the edge of town beyond where the streets were paved they passed a barbershop-poolhall where the young men dressed slick.

Hawk sniffed a little contemptuously and spat out the window. "Any young blues players around here?" Jerry asked.

"You mean them? Naw, they wouldn't want to get their hair mussed. I think they spends more time in front of the mirror looking at themselves than they do looking at the girls that pass by. Back then we used to call 'em sissy men, don't know how they get along less'n they got a gang of women working for them."

Then they were out of town and in the cool magnolia-scented breeze. Big pillared mansions sat back from the road across rolling lawns. Hawk gazed at one of them. "Mr. Jack lived there until his business went bust, cause he spent all his money on a high yaller named Dorothy Mae. I played out there back in '34, when Mr. Jack's father had the place. We didn't play nothing but jigs and reels all night long, it was Mr. Jack's graduation, and all them nice young people danced up a storm. Danced up a storm, them folkses, they say we got to have you back, we got to have you at all our parties. Course they never did. But we played some other fine parties around that time, lots of 'em. Mr. Jack, he have a real craving for yallers."

Farther and farther out into the country, past the mansions, past the plantations, dotted with little tar-paper shacks, back into the swamp, where once again Hawk seemed to know every straggling face and have a word on the history or ancestry of the inhabitant of every shack they passed. They never did find Booger Jake, Jerry began to doubt that he even existed, since no one else seemed to have given any thought to him in years. Hawk, he realized, was trying to tell him something. Of course Jerry knew better, he knew what was good for Hawk. Even now Hawk spent less than half his time in this little world. Well, what if instead of going to Georgia he went to England, instead of playing some little Florida juke joint he played at Harvard? He could probably spend more time around Yola then, come home with more money, earn the respect of those slicks down at Lawson's Pool Hall and Barber Shop, maybe even retire someday to a well-earned rest. Well, in the end, Jerry thought, neither of them turned out to be completely right or wrong.

After three more days of this Hartl just disappeared one day. Jerry checked the bus depot, which doubled as Myrtle's Restaurant. Yes, a long-haired Yankee had bought a ticket to Jackson, didn't say where he was going from there, but Jerry surmised he must have flown back to New York. In any case within a month there was a story in *Time* magazine hailing the rediscovery of the legendary blues singer the Screamin' Nighthawk, mentioning the efforts of three collectors but featuring a picture of Hawk and George Hartl alone in the Sunset Cafe. Subsequently he wrote a fanciful series of articles in the *Village Voice* on their rediscovery, a series which, for all of its romantic invention, in its articulateness, generosity, irony, and compassion showed a side that Hartl had never evidenced in the flesh. Maybe, Jerry thought, that was the true Hartl, a part of him anyway; you couldn't pretend to be something you absolutely were not. But then within a year or so Hartl put out an unauthorized collection of some tapes he must have made while they were in Yola, which included snatches of songs and more complete versions of Hawk cursing out Hartl and threatening him with bodily harm if he didn't put that damn machine away. The fidelity was horrible, there couldn't have been a total of more than twenty minutes on the two sides, the sleeve was a blank white cardboard with a crude hand-stamped caricature on the cover, and Jerry, who was engaged in delicate negotiations with RCA at that point, got an injunction against him. The deal fell through anyway, probably because RCA couldn't think of a way to market Hawk regardless of what else he might have out at the time. He wasn't humble like Mississippi John Hurt nor falling apart with drink and age like Son House. He was just himself, just—Hawk. Jerry saw Hartl in court, where Hartl sneered at him that he was glad to see that Jerry was still a friend to the workingman. Since then he had not seen him again. Thayer had published his scholarly treatise in the *Journal of American Folklore* a couple of years later, complete with footnotes and cross references and a catalog of all the records that were on the jukebox in the Sunset Cafe that day.

Hartl's departure left Jerry alone, still hanging around nearly three weeks after the discovery, unable to talk the object of their search into even agreeing to be found, unable to make up his own mind to leave, unable to make up his mind to stay. Mattie was out of the hospital and looked small and scared in the big brass bed, with Scooter grabbing onto her for dear life. She didn't say anything, just stared at Jerry with big saucer eyes, as if he were some exotic white vision her husband had conjured into their lives. Which in a way was how Jerry was beginning to feel himself: conjured, bewitched, held against his will.

"What you want to hang around here for?" Hawk demanded of him, as he moped around, seemingly dogging Hawk's every step. "I be leaving soon. Peaches to be picked in Georgia, those folkses going to have money sure. What you gonna do? You wanna learn something about the road, you stick with me, boy. Ain't nothin' I can't teach you, but ain't nothin' you going to learn. What you want with me for anyway? You don't need no money, I can tell that. You ain't got the connections to make nothing of it nohow. Now Mr. Melrose—Mr. Melrose, he had the connections, dressed in a great big old derby hat, wore them fancy spats, Mr. Melrose get hold of you, he had the connections to peel off a little of that green, Jack, for hisself. I tell you the truth. You're like the boy with the cherry. I don't think you know what to do if I tell you yes. Why don't you go on home, I'm doing fine just like I am. You tell the peoples that the Screamin' Nighthawk passed, ain't nobody down here who plays that old-style music no more. Just that rock 'n' roll, like you hear them English boys playing on the radio. Let me just go on about my business, keep playing for my own people until they get too brainwashed to listen anymore."

In the end it was pride, or something like it, that got to him. Just as Jerry was prepared to leave, abandon the whole thing as a fruitless quest, and regard himself as something more of a laughingstock than he did already for being unable to persuade this old black man who had nothing that what he had to offer was any better, the article in *Time* came out, with its picture of Hawk and Hartl and an insert of Hawk some thirty years earlier. The headline read: "Legendary Blues Singer: Address Now Known," the subhead a quote from "Screamin' Nighthawk Blues" set off in italics. The story led with a description of how the search for Hawk had taken on the status of the mythological quest for the Holy Grail among blues researchers over the years. Then it described the squalid conditions under which he lived today.

"The search for long-time blues legend the Screamin' Nighthawk (real name: Theodore Roosevelt Jefferson) has led down many false paths. Most researchers were convinced that Nighthawk was dead, though the legend of his accomplishments persisted. Many bluesmen have been rediscovered in the past year and a half: Skip James, Son House, Sleepy John Estes, dimly remembered names from an almost forgotten past. None is of greater significance than the Screamin' Nighthawk, who thirty years ago spawned a searing Mississippi blues tradition, making music that was pure and personal, with a bitter contempt for all of life's injustices, in a voice which growled, moaned, shouted, screamed the blues.

"It was just a line from a song that set blues buffs George Hartl, Jerry Lipschitz, and Ralph Thayer, all under thirty, all heavily committed to careers of their own, down Highway 61, a ribbon of highway that is legendary in blues lore. It was on a narrow dirt road just off 61 that they found the Screamin' Nighthawk through a combination of sharp detective work, careful deduction, and 'just plain dumb luck,' Hartl says frankly.

"It was only when an obscure 45 (value: upward of $200) was spotted on a local jukebox that they actually knew they were on the right trail. 'We knew we had him then,' said Hartl, a slight, earnest, soft-spoken young man whose dedication to the blues goes back to his schooldays when an older brother collected Blind Lemon Jefferson and Bix Beiderbecke records. Says Hartl happily today: 'It would make a great detective novel!' Certainly it has all the elements: a shadowy, elusive hero who for undisclosed reasons is forced to operate under a disguise, false leads, scattered clues, and cases of mistaken identity. In the end the path finally led to a small backwoods saloon, where a powerful middle-aged man eyed them suspiciously as they entered. 'Then he just seemed to give up the pretense altogether,' says Hartl. ' "I'm Hawk," he said. "I hear you been looking for me." '

"The aftermath was a bit anticlimactic. At first, Hartl says, the old blues master couldn't remember his own songs at all. 'He hadn't played in I don't know how many years, there just wasn't anyone who wanted to listen.' Undaunted, Hartl and his two compatriots produced a small portable tape recorder and tapes they had made up consisting of scratchy versions of most of the Screamin' Nighthawk's old songs. 'Aw, I didn't think anyone was interested in that old stuff,' said the bemused bluesman. The intrepid researchers persuaded him, however, that there were people who *were* interested, and the hesitant Hawk set about the painful business of relearning his own songs. Progress has been good to date, though understandably slow, and Hartl reports that more than half a dozen record companies are in active competition for the tapes. No bookings are definite yet, but feelers have gone out from the Newport Folk Festival, and a European tour is a 'definite possibility.' 'I'm a screamin' nighthawk,' proclaims this grizzled veteran of the blues, 'Don't never leave no track/ I goes wherever I please/ And I may not be coming back.' Now, thanks to three young blues buffs, not only has this Hawk been tracked down after thirty years of undeserved obscurity; it looks as if he's going to be around for a while!"

"What a piece of shit," said Hawk after Jerry had finished reading it to him, going on after the first paragraph only with the greatest trepidation.

The barber stropped the razor and tilted Hawk's head back. "People really believe all that shit?"

The barber raised his eyebrows. "People believe anything you tell 'em, man," he said and quickly returned to his work.

"That's it. That's it," said Hawk. "All that bullshit, and I don't see no money. I don't hear nothing from none of these peoples. All I see is a magazine article. She-it!"

He grabbed the magazine from Jerry and stared at the picture of him with Hartl, then ripped out the page with one clean motion and stuffed it in his pocket. "The story ain't about me anyhow," he said at last. "Whole thing's about the other guy, how he track me down, how you all come after me like I'm some kind of wounded beast or something. She-it," he said, as if pondering something that he had been thinking about for a long time. "I tell you something, I'm going to do it. Let 'em see the real thing for once in their life. None of this tracking shit. Let 'em see the Hawk hisself, large as life. You tell me you with me, boy, and I'll do it. You handle all them offers that them people keep talking about. If they can pay, Hawk'll play. You just bring the money. Then, goddammit, we in business, boy."

Jerry was completely floored. He had never meant to go any further than simply finding Hawk. What was supposed to happen next he had never really considered. He found himself pumping Hawk's hand, though. And then shaking hands with the barber. He had never looked back.

>>><<<

THEY WAITED OUTSIDE while the doctor examined him. Mattie looked worried but busied herself with the dishes, shoved the kids out, pestered Jerry until he accepted another cup of coffee, and then sat at the broken old table quietly wringing her hands. "I knowed he was sick," she said in a soft voice, "but I never knowed he was sick like this."

"I'm sure he'll be all right," Jerry said, still shaken by the sight of Hawk, his face gray and drained of color, his hand helplessly shaking, his look almost quizzical, as if this could be none of his doing. "Has it been going on like this for long?"

"Not so long. Only once or twicet. I can't call the first time —oh yes, it was right after the boy's last birthday. Roosevelt had just got back from California, I think, and I put it down to being tired from all that traveling. He been working a long time now, you know, Mr. Jerry."

Jerry nodded.

"Ain't nothing you can do about it, though, I guess," Mattie concluded. "He ain't never been one just to lie down and quit."

The doctor pushed the burlap curtain out of the way and stepped into the kitchen. He was a tall, light-skinned man with wavy hair combed out into an Afro. He wore a well-cut suit and vest out of which a gold watch chain protruded.

"Your husband is a very sick man, Mrs. Jefferson," said the doctor in clipped precise tones.

Mattie fell back on her chair as if she had been struck. "Is he going to be all right, Dr. Bontemps?" she said.

"Well, I'm afraid I don't know the answer to that. He really ought to be in the hospital, where he could be looked after properly. He's had a number of incidents now, and, while he's comfortable enough at this stage, it's hard to judge the extent of neurological damage. Until we can get him in the hospital and run some tests—"

Mattie was wringing her hands. "You think we ought to get him in the hospital then, Doctor?" Jerry said, just to fill the silence.

The doctor looked through him blankly. "Well, from what you say his antipathy toward hospitalization—a trait which, I might add, is not uncharacteristic of his 'generation'—would not seem conducive to the establishment of good medical routine. Certainly he should be in the hospital, but it seems as if he would be fighting us every step of the way, and what he needs right now more than anything else is peace of mind. That plus the determination to follow certain prescribed medical routines without which all the hospital tests in the world aren't going to do him any good. Do you understand what I'm saying, Mrs. Jefferson?" Mattie nodded automatically and looked at Jerry. "He must be put on a diet which will have to be strictly adhered to. No alcohol. No fried foods. Vastly lower the intake of salt. He must exercise regularly and take off, oh, I would say, about forty pounds. If he doesn't follow the prescribed routine, he will simply keep having these attacks, no matter what the tests say, and the next one, or the one after that, could very well be the one that does the trick, that is, kills him."

Mattie gasped. Jerry glared at the doctor. He thought he was laying it on a little thick. Evidently the doctor must have thought so, too. "The reason that I say all this to you is to stress how very important it is to make Mr. Jefferson understand the absolute necessity to follow without deviation doctor's orders."

Mattie was shaking her head, still not crying. "He ain't gonna follow nobody's orders. He ain't never followed anybody's orders yet, and I just know he ain't gonna start now."

"Well, you're just going to have to help him then, Mattie," said the doctor, patting her hand. "You're just going to have to do the best you can."

They sat there, the three of them, staring off blankly into space, until at last the doctor cleared his throat and stood up. "Well, I've got to be going. I'm afraid there's no other course for him for the present. Have him get plenty of rest, don't let the kids disturb him, no whiskey, Mattie—you pour it down the drain before you let him have a drink of that rotgut. I've given him something to help him sleep, and I'll be back to check on him first thing in the morning. But if anything comes up in the meantime, you give me a call, hear?" He touched Mattie's shoulder. "Now don't you worry. I'm sure he'll be all right."

Mattie pulled her head up from the table. Her eyes were red. "It easy for you to talk," she said. "What am I gonna do without Hawk?"

Outside Jerry tried to pay the doctor. "I will send my bill at the end of the month."

"Well, send it to me," Jerry said, handing him his card. "I want to take care of it. What do you think his chances are?"

The doctor hesitated, one foot in his gleaming yellow Camaro, sitting incongruously on the muddy, tire-rutted lane. "Do you want my frank opinion?"

Jerry nodded.

"I'm afraid Mr. Jefferson's chances are slim. There's a pattern to this type of illness. Mr. Jefferson is in an advanced state of hypertension, he would seem to have a good number of other things wrong with him, he's obviously suffered incidents like this before, and my guess is that he won't follow one bit of the advice I gave to his wife."

Jerry nodded bleakly at the familiarity of it all. It was amazing, the fraternity of the medical profession—white or black, rich or poor, urban or rural, they all considered themselves somehow better than their patients, they all expressed an apparent contempt for those weak enough to become ill. "I remember when I was a boy," the doctor interjected into Jerry's thoughts, "hearing Mr. Jefferson sing. They used to call him the Screeching Nighthawk, I believe. My parents always warned us to stay away from him because he was from across the creek, he was always in some kind of trouble or other, and they said he always reeked of whiskey. My father was pastor of the New Bethel Church of the Morning Star, you see. But we children would sneak down sometimes to see him when he was playing at one of these big suppers out here in the country or at Barbour's Big House, you know it was an old plantation hall, bare dirt floors, kerosene lamps, Lord it must have burned down twenty years ago, but I can still remember the good times the people had, barefooted and raggedy as they were—we used to boost each other up and take turns peeking through the open window or pile up old Coke cartons and listen until someone caught us. He used to be a very *stirring* singer, you know."

"He still is," said Jerry, more fiercely than he really meant.

The doctor lifted his eyebrows. "Oh, I'm sure he is. I didn't mean—it's just that I haven't heard him—oh, it must be at least fifteen or twenty years ago, when I went away to college, and when I came back, you know, the dance hall had burned down and things were different."

Jerry watched him back out on to the paved road and waved weakly.

Inside Hawk lay in the darkened room. He could hear the sounds outside, children playing, a car driving off, the muffled sound of voices, Mattie's tears.

DAMN DOCTOR turn out the light. Don't that boy understand nothing? I told him, leave the damn light on, I want to see exactly what is going on. Don't understand all this damn foolishness. Why don't they send in the boy, like I asked? They know I wants to see the boy, let him show me what he done on that box of his. Shucks, don't seem so long since I was his age, just playing my diddley-bow upside the wall, trying to get all the little girls to listen. Didn't have no git-tar then. Sneak off every chance I get with my uncle's git-tar, he made it himself, him and Mose. Man, they used to make the damnedest git-tars back in those days. Made one out of a phonograph one time, took the wood off an old record player, frets made out of baling wire—

shoot, where is that boy? Wants me to hear him do that little song we was gone work up together. That boy all right, he gonna be all right, make suthin of himself, not like his daddy. He gonna have some of the advantages, but he still all right. The other boy all right, too. Course he can't play no music. He just a promoter, make money off other people's music. Which is all right, too. Don't matter how you get by, so long as they's someone'll buy what you're selling. Now he ain't nothing like that slick, the first one come to bring me up to Chicago for the Paramount Record Company. I remember Barbour promised to make me a star, said he was gonna call Chicago and get this man to come down. Course we all thought he was just woofing, but that man come down all right. Show up at the old Majestic The-ater, where they have the Saturday-morning talent contests. Come in from playing all night at a barbecue or a fish fry or some juke way out in the country, go right to the Alamo without even going to sleep or anything. Of all the acts that went on that day, I was the only one Barbour come through for. Later on the others all told me Barbour promised them the exact same thing, but I was the only one passed the audition. That man really was smooth; I call him a jitterbug, but that too good for him. He bring me up to Chicago all right, and when we all done he give me twenty-five dollars and a train ticket. Go home, boy, he say. I let you know when I need you. Before I seed that twenty-five dollars, I ain't seen nothing or heard talk of nothing either. Slept under the El at night, rode the buses all day long, just trying to pick up a little spare change by playing my box. Couldn't get no other work, because old Big Bill and all them other old jealous-hearted blues singers had the town sewed up tighter'n a twelve-year-old's snatch. Would've been all right if I'd had my boy with me, either one of them, just someone to look out after my own interests. But I was young then, kind of wild, I didn't think nothing about tomorrow, far as I was concerned the sun done rose for the last time this morning, and I's going to have a natural ball. And I did. I did. Just a country boy trying to act slick, them jitterbugs had my twenty-five dollars *and* my train ticket before I even got down to the station. So coming back I had to ride the rods with nothing in my pockets, just like always. . . .

IV

HIGH JOHN
THE CONQUEROO

LORI SHOWED UP that same afternoon without announcement. She got out of the old sway-backed taxi she had ridden all the way from Jackson. Her long blond hair streamed out behind her, she wore a short-sleeve knitted shirt and a pair of dirty white slacks. Jerry hurried out to meet her, feeling that old familiar ache. What she had been doing, whom she had been seeing, why she had been off the road so long, he deliberately declined to know. She gave him a kiss on the cheek and looked him in the eye with that same clear, frank look that always brought him back to the fact that nothing had changed, no matter how much he might have liked it to. Not about his own feelings. Not about her. He wished he could have dismissed her as just another talented kook. Maybe that was all she was, with her constant flirtation with risk and vulnerability, her seeming contempt for her own success. If that was all, though, he could never see it that way. "How's Hawk?" she said.

Jerry shook his head helplessly and tried to tell her. Up till now he had been in control the whole time, but in Lori's presence he almost broke down once or twice and there were long charitably overlooked pauses in his speech.

"But isn't there something we can do?" Lori said at last. "Surely there must be specialists—"

Jerry shrugged. "What are you going to do? Strap him down and fly him to Boston? Hawk'd just turn around when we got to the hospital and say, 'That boy there is kidnapping me. Ain't never seen him befo' in my life. Whuffo you white folks want with me?'" Lori laughed. "The doctor says if he'll just follow instructions he'll probably do okay. He left an anticoagulant that's supposed to do for a start. He ought to be in the hospital probably, but what good's that gonna do if it just gets him all agitated? Besides, who knows what kind of a hospital they've got down here? I don't know if I'm worried so much about the way they'd treat him as the way he'd act toward them. I think I'd rather see him take his chances at home."

"Let me talk to him?"

"Sure. Of course. He's out right now. I don't know how good shape he's in to talk. He wasn't able to—"

"No, I mean, he's always listened to me. You know he has."

Jerry nodded. She was right. He always had.

Inside she immediately made herself useful. She first embraced Mattie, who for her part seemed genuinely glad to see her. "Don't know how long it's been since we seed you and Mr. Jerry together. Did you see how the children growed?" Then she took Lori out behind the house to see the children and the pig

135

they were raising for slaughter and the chicken pen that Martin had built. Then she and Lori rolled up their sleeves and went to work, busying themselves with a seemingly endless assortment of domestic procedures, rearranging sleeping quarters, dusting and mopping, and cooking what looked like enough food, Jerry thought, for a two-week siege. He sat at the kitchen table listening to the hum of the old refrigerator, glancing at a week-old paper that had been used to wrap up some fish, watching the two women, warm, animated, unselfconscious, at ease with themselves, as if he were no longer in their presence.

The first concert they had played was at Harvard, and right there Jerry should have known there was something wrong, something irretrievably anomalous about the whole situation. They played at Eliot House Commons, a basement room with a stately grand piano and ornate, ponderous furniture that looked as if it had come with the king's grant. All of this had been moved to one end of the long room, and folding chairs and a makeshift stage had been set up by nervous members of the Folklore Society who had arranged for the concert. It was late November, and Hawk hadn't thought to bring an overcoat. He wore a somber black suit and tie loosely knotted at the neck. The top of his shirt was missing two buttons, and his seamed black face was expressionless and calm.

The room was packed. Although they had not had a chance to advertise the concert, news of it had spread through the classrooms and houses, and a few posters around the Square had announced that the Screamin' Nighthawk, a blues legend previously thought to be dead for many years, was actually alive, well, and performing at Eliot House.

The audience was hushed and anticipatory as Jerry nervously clumped up to the stage, nearly tripping on the small step and feeling uncomfortably that every eye was on him. He went on too long—overly flowery and overly technical—trying to place Hawk in a historical context, trying to make these kids understand, he thought at the time, just who Hawk was, who he had been. They were remarkably polite, gratifyingly attentive, as was Hawk, who sat patiently through it all with seats empty on either side of him, his leg jiggling ever so slightly. Then at last Jerry emerged from the thicket of credits (to Mose, to Hartl and Thayer, to Hawk and the concert organizers), and Hawk heavily mounted the stage, cradling his battered guitar. He sat down, fumbled in his pocket, fiddled with the cord, and then leaned over and plugged in the little Sears, Roebuck amplifier which had been sitting unobtrusively on the stage unnoticed by all or, if it was noted, discounted as a useless prop (or thought to be left over from some rock 'n' roll rehearsal perhaps). As he plugged in, the buzz from the amplifier was nothing compared to the murmur of shock and disbelief from the crowd. Hawk fiddled with the dials for a couple of minutes, and both hums only grew louder.

"Oh, dammit," said the boy beside Jerry, "we're too late."

"What do you mean?" said his companion, a long-haired Radcliffe student in purple tights. "The concert hasn't even started yet."

"I don't even know if I want to stay," said the boy, obviously distraught. "Don't you see what he's doing? He's amplified his guitar."

The combination of the amp buzzing and Hawk tuning up was deafening. A piercing whistle fed back from the mike. "Good evening, everybody," said Hawk and without further preamble launched into "Screamin' Nighthawk Blues," the ringing notes instantly identifiable, the stomping feet inviting an audience to respond with energy of its own. This audience was transfixed; silence hung over the room until at the conclusion of the song it exploded with applause. Hawk glared out balefully at the young white boys and girls, stomped his heavy-booted feet, and launched into one song after another, seemingly challenging the audience to come up with another kind of response. But the angrier he got the more respectful was the silence that greeted his efforts. There was no badinage, there were no pauses for breath, there was no ingratiating small talk, just the music itself going out in Hawk's booming voice without preface or apology. Finally, after about an hour and a half, Jerry gave a signal which Hawk either did not see or chose to ignore. So Jerry was forced to jump up on stage himself in the middle of a number and commandeer the mike at the end of the song to announce an intermission. In between sets the students all gathered around a punch bowl and Jerry went to talk to the boy who had organized the concert, leaving Hawk on stage stiff and proud, cradling his guitar, the intermittent hum of the amplifier providing inconspicuous response to all the conversation and social chatter in the room. When Jerry came back, an earnest-looking boy in horn-rimmed glasses was sitting next to Hawk, a pad of paper in his hand, pencil poised. "Do you ever do any protest songs, Mr. Jefferson?"

Hawk shook his head.

"Well, wouldn't you say the blues are the original protest songs in a way? As I understand it, they provided a kind of code language that enabled Negroes to speak to each other about the conditions under which they lived, without the white man really knowing just what they were saying—"

Hawk mumbled something.

"What? Excuse me. I don't understand."

"Back in slavery times," said Hawk, "there was a whole different kind of junk. Spirituals and such. 'I gonna be free from this burdensome world some old day.' All that kind of racket. Blues just tells the truth, don't do nothing more than that, you know."

"Yes, yes, I see, but blues goes back to slavery times—"

Hawk shook his head vehemently.

"Surely the work songs—when did blues first come into being then?"

"1904," said Hawk.

"1904?"

Jerry felt sorry for the boy.

"Did you ever write any protest songs yourself? You know, like Leadbelly or Big Bill? 'Bourgeois Blues'—that kind of thing?"

"Yeah, Leadbelly," said Hawk, eyes lighting up. "I met that gal-boy down in Angola, wouldn't let that motherfucker near me. Course I ain't saying what I was doing down there, but they had him in for some bad shit, man. Everybody knowed the white man bought his freedom, just to get hold of the rights to his songs. Leadbelly told me so hisself. Except they never were his songs anyways. Got 'em off a cat name Shorty George—you know that song he used to sing, yeah. Well, ain't that the way it always is, though? They pay you just exactly what they think you gonna take—"

The boy was obviously shaken. "Well, how about the war? It seems as if Vietnam has become a symbol to many black people—"

"Yeah, I think we ought to bomb the shit out of them

motherfuckers," said Hawk pleasantly. "Well, I better get back to work, my manager over here say I better start earning some of that money you nice white boys and girls is paying."

The second half of the concert was the same as the first, only longer. The amplifier buzzed louder than ever, and Hawk fiddled with it some but wasn't able to fix it. A few of the audience, evidently emboldened by Hawk's scrofulousness, started shouting out encouragement ("Play it a long time!" "Put it in the alley!"), which only encouraged others to shush them indignantly. In this atmosphere of warring expectations, Jerry became uncomfortably aware, people were starting to leave, discreet, on tiptoe, but leaving nonetheless. Hawk just seemed to play louder, more intensely, his eyes following the departing students, his voice booming in the silent hall, seemingly calling out after them. He went through some more of his repertoire, introducing standards like "Shake 'Em On Down" or "Bluebird" with a note that "I remember Sonny Boy when he first cut this tune" or "This one was Tommy's best," mostly in open tuning, sometimes with a slide, sometimes without, performing with a single-minded ferocity. Then without warning Hawk started talking in his rumbling raspy voice. "I want to dedicate this next song to the late President Kennedy. He was a friend to all the people, black and white, he even helped the Chinese.

"Ohhh, ohhh"—Hawk launched into yet another familiar-sounding melody in the key of D. "President Kennedy dead and gone/ Gone away and left me here to sing this song.

Well, President Kennedy, he work for the young, he
  work for the old
Peoples, we just can't let his dream go cold
Well-uh, President Kennedy dead and gone
Ain't nothing for it, just gotta sing this song.

Well, President Kennedy, he loved throughout the land
Eeh-hyah, he loved through all the land
Well, they taken him away, boy, ain't nobody raisin' sand.

Ooh-ooh, President Kennedy
Oh yeah, President Kennedy
Well, his whole life, he just work to set mankind free.

The room was silent for the longest time, then reverberated with applause. They cheered and cheered, and Hawk was induced to sing one more verse. At the end everyone in the room was on his feet wildly applauding, and the next day the *Crimson* had a piece on Hawk's triumphant debut, particularly noting the continued topicality of the blues.

In the car on the way back to Jerry's apartment on Walden Street in North Cambridge, Jerry remarked on how moved he had been. "I didn't know you wrote anything like that," he said.

Hawk stared straight ahead. "She-it," he said, "what did that sucker ever do for me? I just take the Roosevelt thing I cut back in '46, put another name to it. Mr. Melrose practically beg me to cut that record, say it gonna sell a million. Well, maybe it did, but they ain't paid me two cents for it yet."

From there they played Cornell, Gerde's Folk City, an almost empty Brooklyn Academy of Music, Hunter College, Club 47, and any number of other colleges and small rooms. It wasn't long before the novelty had worn off, and even Jerry grew tired of the uncritical adulation, the almost mindless credulity which greeted them everywhere they went. Hawk stayed the same. He scowled in the same bleak way at all the dumb questions endlessly repeated; he kept on-stage talk to a bare minimum; he just kept playing his music with the same uncompromising sternness, the same relentless fury. And yet something seemed to have changed, there was a subtle shift of attitude, and Jerry sensed that Hawk was growing somehow dispirited in an indefinable sort of way. For Jerry it was still flattering to be asked his opinion on every blues issue of the day, to be rewarded with the favors of pretty girls who suddenly found him charming, however false the pretenses. Hawk scarcely even spoke to him, though. He sat in silence the whole way down to a concert, arms folded across his chest, as the radio played Dylan, Peter, Paul, and Mary, the Rolling Stones, the Beatles. He had no interest in discussing the show on the ride back. It was culture shock, Jerry supposed. It was only to be expected.

But then Hawk, too, began to change. First he discarded the suit, wearing the black jacket and tie, then the jacket alone, finally shirtsleeves and baggy brown pants. Then he began to paw at every woman who came near him and make crude jokes at those who kept their distance. At first Jerry thought he was just loosening up, seeking some appropriate way of showing that he, too, wanted to join the festivities. Then gradually he realized that there was an element of both contempt and self-contempt in Hawk's posturing. Finally it all came to a head when Hawk showed up for a concert at Yale wearing faded overalls and an old straw hat. Jerry tried to persuade him that nothing was to be gained by this unseemly charade, but Hawk refused even to speak about it. At the concert Jerry noted that his demeanor, too, was somehow changed. He didn't seem so commanding; perhaps, Jerry thought, he was no longer so intimidated because he was more used to Hawk. When they met their hosts, though, Hawk seemed to shrink into himself rather than puff up with indignation and pride. When they encountered the eager interviewer, whose questions they had both heard a thousand times by now,

Hawk responded not with his characteristic impatience but was instead relatively meek—for Hawk—slandering only one other blues singer in the course of the conversation and not bothering to correct even the boy's most obvious misconceptions about the blues singer and the blues. Jerry made the standard introduction, laying it on if anything a little thicker than usual, and Hawk started off with the obligatory "Screamin' Nighthawk Blues." This time it was different, though. Even as he strummed the opening chords, Hawk leaned forward and murmured into the microphone, "I want to thank all you nice kind people for coming out here tonight. I only hope I can do something to merit your appreciation and deserve your applause."

Jerry almost fell out of his seat. He couldn't remember ever hearing Hawk say more than one or two words between songs, and this kind of acknowledgment was wholly uncharacteristic. When he finished the song, Hawk leaned forward again. "You know, it's quite a thrill and a honor for a country boy like me just off the farm to perform for a bunch of fine young ladies and gentlemens like yourselves. And if my speech is not so good, I hope you will kindly bear with me, because I never did have the benefit of a education like you kind peoples is lucky enough to get. Where I growed up you got your education behind a mule, and that's all I knowed until my manager, Mr. Jerry Lip—schitz, discovered me and instructed me that there was people who was waiting to *hear* from me. And so I took him at his word, and that's why I'm here in front of you all today, and I hope you will kindly accept my music in the spirit in which it is offered."

Jerry cringed. During intermission he took Hawk aside. "What are you doing?" he said in a fierce undertone.

Hawk just played dumb. "Don't know what you talking about."

"I mean all this country-boy shit. The overalls. All that talk about how you've never been off the farm. At this point you wouldn't know the front end of a mule from its hindquarters. That's what I'm talking about."

"Oh, that," said Hawk innocently, still not looking Jerry in the eye but at the well-dressed boys and girls instead. "You know, man, I didn't mean nothing—"

"No? Well, I'll tell you something," said Jerry, surprising even himself, "if you ever do anything like this again, that's it. I quit."

"No shit?" said Hawk, looking almost amused.

But evidently he took Jerry seriously, because he did bounce back, he may not have liked it, he frequently vented his spleen (he wouldn't have been Hawk if he had grown all of a sudden meek), but it seemed as if they had come to an understanding. Not that Hawk be refined, just that he be himself.

By the standards of the day Hawk was not particularly successful. He was on a par perhaps with Skip James, not as lovable as Mississippi John Hurt, not as intensely emotional as Son House. They all existed in an uneasy alliance, competing for the few openings there were for ancient bluesmen, these survivors of thirty years of historical neglect who had reemerged strangely to satisfy a new white audience that needed them. It was indeed ironic, Jerry reflected as he walked about the Newport Festival grounds with his performer's badge giving him free passage, to see convicted murderers, long-haired folksingers, Irish dancers, and Scottish bagpipers all mingling under the apparent guise of shared art and good fellowship. The night before there had been a party at the Blues House at which everyone had gotten outrageously drunk, the old men and their younger followers, and Hawk had ended up with a red-headed girl from Sarah Lawrence. That he could actually have screwed her Jerry couldn't imagine, but in the morning he was talking about "these white bitches with their milky skin and little no-account titties and slits ain't deep enough to even dip your wick in." Jerry tried to quiet him down and finally managed to get him out the door while the blues legends lay sprawled across cots and on the floor amid the clutter of bottles and debris from last night. With Hawk he walked around the festival grounds and told him about the proposed European tour.

"I ain't interested in no European countries," Hawk said emphatically, maintaining so brisk a pace that Jerry had to trot to keep up. "Man, I just want to go home. I don't want to hear no more of this racket. Just don't dust me with no broom, man, cause I ain't for it, you know what I'm talking about? All them broken-down old jitterbugs, can't even see straight no more—I ain't never heard so much caterwauling in my life before. I'll tell you the truth, man, and they say the truth may hurt but personally I don't give a shit, I'm sick and tired of you paddies."

Yes, yes, Jerry agreed, as they trotted along, past the deserted stages and concession stands, past the kids in sleeping bags and the few maintenance people who were up and about at this hour. Yes, sure, Jerry said, he understood, it was frustrating, it was humiliating, it was dumb. It was just that this was one chance in a million, the money was good, it might never come again. "You can bank it," Jerry said, "for your kids. You can piss it away if you want—"

"Oh man, you just like all the rest," Hawk said with a shrewd appraising glance. "How come this thing's so important to you?"

Jerry shrugged. "I don't know—"

"You want to go to Europe so bad?"

"It's not for me—" Jerry started to say, but Hawk just snorted, and Jerry was hurt. It wasn't for himself, it wasn't a question of going to Europe, if it was a question of going to Europe he could afford it without even blinking, couldn't he?

But what would be the point, what was the point of going anywhere with no purpose in mind, with no goal? If he went over there with Hawk, he would be working toward something, he would be working toward a greater historical good, he would be doing something for somebody. Hawk was right. His motives were entirely selfish, Jerry realized, when Hawk said, "Well, all right, if it mean so much to you." And despite himself Jerry had to admit he was disappointed that Hawk had given in.

Then they heard it. Someone playing the piano, at first it sounded as if it were far away, then Jerry realized it was coming unamplified from the main stage, tentative at first with a rhythmic subtlety but a seeming inability to fully realize all of the player's ideas, crude, out of practice, nothing exceptional, really. At first they could barely make out the voice, then it became less tentative, more distinct. The singer was a girl, the song she was singing was "Time and Again," a smoky torch song with surprising dissonances and a bluesy feel.

Time and again I get lonely
Time and again I get blue
Time and again I start smiling
Thinking of nothing but you.

Jerry glanced up at the distant figure. At her long blond hair whipping about in the morning breeze. He wanted to talk some more about Europe. But Hawk stood in his tracks seemingly transfixed. "That girl really saying something," Hawk said in a quieter tone of voice than he would ordinarily have used. They made their way up the long aisle, between the rows of empty seats. Hawk sat down in the front row, arms folded across his chest. When the song was over he applauded, bringing his palms together with heavy deliberation. The girl looked up distracted. She was thin and very pale and kept tossing her long blond hair over her shoulder with a nervous flip. Jerry couldn't stop staring at her. Even afterward he would have had to admit that it sounded ordinary to him, he missed whatever it was that Hawk heard, to him it was just a young girl trying to sound old and black on a song that turned out to be an original but original clearly based on Irma Thomas's "Wish Someone Would Care," which was itself a takeoff on an old New Orleans tradition. To Hawk none of these things mattered. "That was very nice," Hawk said.

"Thank you," said the girl, coloring.

Jerry closed his eyes, for he could imagine almost anything at this point, and the girl was so stunningly beautiful that he didn't want to imagine anything at all. That was how they met Lori.

"IT'S EMBARRASSING," Lori said.

"Why?" said Jerry, hoping to press a point by opposing it.

"She thinks we're still together."

"Well, we are in a way, aren't we?"

Lori looked at him. "Yeah, well, I mean, but not in the way that—oh, you know what I mean."

She gave him a peck on the cheek, and Jerry felt as miserable as he did every other day of his life when he was reminded of Lori, and Lori and him, and what he would have liked to be, and what he sometimes thought he could have been.

"I suppose I could get a room in a motel."

"Oh, you don't have to do that. I mean, it's just so sweet of her. It's as if she were trying to push us together, even though she knows—I mean, I'm sure she knows, in the back of her mind anyway, that it's not like that for us."

"Look, I can always sleep on the floor."

Lori tossed her hair back, catching it between her fingers and then letting it run out in a light shimmering stream. "Oh, look, Jerry, I'm sorry, it's just that I'm upset. I just never thought it would be like this for Hawk, you know? I never thought he'd get old, get sick, is this the way it's going to have to be—it's just so unfair. I just always figured that if he went he'd just go, like that, not linger on and get weaker and weaker, be dependent on doctors—oh Christ, is that the way it's going to be?"

"I don't know," said Jerry. "The doctors say if he takes care of himself—"

"Oh, that's a lot of shit, and you know it." A car approached, slowed down, and stopped to stare at this unlikely-looking couple. "Doctors . . . shit!"

"Look, Lori, what I don't understand, I mean why couldn't it work? Not as some great thing, just for what it is. Maybe we should take this as a kind of sign, I don't know, throwing us together—" He trailed off, hoping she would overlook the sense of what he was saying but be captured by its emotional under-current. If she could just feel sorry for him, he wouldn't ask for anything more than that—

"Oh, come on, please, Jerry. I don't want to talk about it. Hawk is dying, and what you're talking about—isn't—anything."

148

"It's got to be something, though—"

"Look. We had something for a while. It wasn't everything, but it was something. It isn't there anymore. I wish for your sake that it were. You know that I love you. But I can't live my life for you. Everything in your mind is totaled up in some way. It's all ordered and neat. You think you've got me figured out. Or you think you love me, but you just want to fit me into a little slot. I'm not like that. I can't figure out what's coming, I don't want to figure out what's next. Maybe you could tell me, but I don't want to know. I mean, maybe we'll even sleep together tonight, but if we do, don't make something of it other than what it is. It doesn't mean anything, none of it means anything, except that on some level we care for each other very much."

"I wouldn't think it meant anything," Jerry lied.

They had never gotten it right in the studio, Jerry thought. The music was never quite captured the way that Jerry heard it in his head or even the way he had heard it for the first time in the Sunset Cafe. On the records they made it was somehow inhibited, it didn't jump out at you, there was something stiff and businesslike about the proceedings, although the reviews were uniformly respectful and even listening to the old recordings Jerry thought he could now hear the same premeditation, the same withholding of self that you rarely got in live performance. At first he was looking for a big contract and wouldn't let Hawk record for any of the myriad of little collector labels that besieged them with requests. Hartl put out the bootleg tape on his own Jamboree label, but he only had four complete cuts and wouldn't have sold enough copies to matter even if Jerry hadn't brought suit against him. For a long time Jerry thought they were going to sign with RCA while Robbie Fielding was still following them around. They opened up a month's worth of gigs in New York City, and Fielding showed up at every one, a thin hyper kind of kid who always seemed to be up on dex or bennies or just plain manic energy. He made Hawk nervous, and Hawk hated nothing more than when he came up on the bandstand to play harp behind the old man. "He ain't got no time," Hawk argued, slamming his foot down on a bench in the little dressing room in the back of the club. "He always making the changes ahead of me, without he wait and see where I'm going. He make me look like some kind of asshole, man. Besides, he don't never listen to what key I'm in."

Jerry nodded. "Look, just see if you can tolerate him until we get the contract signed. He's the hottest new thing that RCA's got going; he's already recorded one of your songs, and he's talking about a whole bunch more. If he's behind you, it'll mean better distribution, more sales, a bigger advertising campaign, promotional tie-ins, more money—"

Hawk's face broadened in a grin. "Well, right there you just said the magic word—"

"So you think you can take him?"

"Oh, I can take him all right. I may not like him, but I can find it in my heart to overlook that."

But it wasn't long before even this new resolve was tested. Robbie Fielding was a pain in the neck, always pestering Hawk to teach him songs, always wanting Hawk to hear his latest. He wrote nearly a song a day, some explicit protest, some country, some blues (one, "The Ballad of Screamin' Nighthawk," subsequently unreleased until it was bootlegged in the '70s, celebrated a hero who "didn't take shit from no one/ He never said a mumbling word"), and he was always looking to play them for anyone who would listen and offer praise. "I don't know nothing about that," Hawk complained. "I don't want to hear none of that folderol. He always be after me to work out some new kind of song. He want to know what songs I gonna put on the album. I ain't gonna play that stuff for no one. I had too much of that stuff stolen from me in my lifetime. I keeps it locked up now, right here in my heart."

Jerry didn't believe him. He doubted that Hawk had any new material at all, but he knew Hawk's rules: no play without pay; and never, under any circumstances, whatever the temptation, tip your hand.

Then he kicked Robbie off the bandstand one night. The kids, who were now turning out in the expectation that Robbie Fielding might show, went crazy as they always did when Robbie made his way in little shambling steps up to the tiny stage. He tuned his guitar to Hawk's, fished out a harp and put it in his rack. They had scarcely gone eight bars into the song when Hawk abruptly stopped, leaving Robbie stranded in the middle of a guitar strum, his harmonica wheezing along in that asthmatic way that was peculiarly his own. Hawk glared at him until he finally came to a halt, then announced, "That's it," in his low rumbling voice. "I don't want to hear no more."

Robbie just stared at him. It was about the time his second album came out and the reviews had acclaimed him as the new Bob Dylan. After what seemed like an hour, but was really only a few shocked seconds, he shrugged and stumbled off stage, continued on out the door and never came back.

"Good," said Hawk. "If he come back before eternity, it'll be too soon."

But it cost them. It cost them plenty. First the RCA contract negotiations broke off just a few days later. Then, too, it closed off their entree to a great many clubs and concerts, because

Hawk got the reputation of being a "difficult" performer, as the Robbie Fielding story followed him everywhere. Why? Jerry kept asking himself. Why couldn't Hawk have held off a few more days, a few more weeks? But, of course, then that wouldn't have been Hawk.

After that Jerry held out for a while, but eventually he signed a nonexclusive one-time recording contract with one of the smaller companies. Then when Hawk was out in California on his own, he recorded another album without Jerry's knowledge for which he got a flat fee of $300. A college radio station recorded one of his concerts, and despite absolute promises to Jerry, somehow the end result found its way on to record. In Europe he recorded in both England and Denmark for small cash advances and negligible royalty arrangements. Soon there was a glut of Screamin' Nighthawk albums out on the market, none of them very outstanding, none particularly successful, distinguished from each other principally by the different titles assigned to familiar songs, not one capturing the sound that Jerry had carried in his head since first hearing Hawk in Yola, Mississippi.

If it hadn't been for Lori's unexpected success, in fact, Jerry doubted that Hawk would have been able to continue in the business at all. There just was not enough of a market for a cantankerous old man who couldn't decide whether to contemptuously kiss the hand that fed him or spit in his public's eye. Lori changed all that, although when they first met her no prospect could have seemed less likely. Jerry in fact had never thought that he would see her again. She was, she had told them shyly, from far-off California, had studied piano as a child for the requisite number of years, played a little guitar, knew every record that Hawk had ever made, and surprised Jerry when she called him to propose a concert at Mills College, where she was president of the newly formed Blues Society. When they finally went out there in the spring, there was scarcely anyone in attendance, and Lori looked as if she was on the brink of tears, apologizing to them over and over again, introducing Hawk to the thirty or forty girls in the room, few even with dates, in a tremulous voice that upbraided the cultural indifference of the community. Hawk shuffled up to the stage and patted her hand, then crashed out the first notes as if it didn't matter in the slightest whether he was playing for six or six hundred, this was one concert he was playing because he *wanted* to.

An English professor from UCLA sat in the front row, busily taking notes, as he would on their whole West Coast tour, for he was, he proudly confided to Jerry, cataloging the entire span of Hawk's work, not recording the songs but listing and cross-referencing them by title and noting all their little differences. In the end he came to the conclusion that Hawk knew 641 songs which differed sufficiently from one another to be considered individually as separate and independent units. Of these 318 were traditional or adaptations of traditional material, 211 were Hawk's variations on what might be considered blues standards, and 112 might be considered original compositions. "She-it," Hawk said when asked about it. "I can't even count up to 641. But if that's what the professor tells you, it must be so. It seem like a lot, don't it, though? Maybe he counted some of them twice."

At the end of the concert Hawk invited Lori up on stage. "I want you to give a nice hand to a little girl who can really sing something herself," he insisted over her protestations and blushes. At last he got her up on stage, and she sat down at the grand piano without a mike, forming a tentative chord with her left hand, playing a few treble notes with her right. Jerry couldn't understand it, really. She was no better (probably no prettier) than a thousand others, but Hawk saw something in her apparently beneath the conventional exterior. After the concert there was a reception, and Hawk stood around talking with Lori for almost an hour, quietly discussing, neither playing the fool nor disgracing himself with crudities as he often did on these occasions. Afterward Lori came up to Jerry and in a voice that was barely audible said, "I was kind of thinking of dropping out of college."

"Don't do that, you might learn something," said Jerry, who had a tendency to be flip and would have given anything now to take back that cocksure grin—but then, at the time, he must have thought he was the jumpingest cat, after all he was the one who had discovered the Screamin' Nighthawk, and, despite the reservations he was constantly expressing to Hawk and the world at large, he himself in his heart of hearts *knew* it was never going to run out. Hawk may have been the one with talent, but he was the connoisseur of art, and art was a bottomless well just waiting to be plumbed, or something like that. It was a time in his life when he might have thought the critic was more important than the song.

"Oh, I mean college doesn't mean anything to me. I just feel like there's no point," she said, biting her lip. "I mean, I already made up my mind."

Jerry nodded. He felt above it all in a way.

"I was wondering, though. Hawk said you might need a secretary. Someone to answer the phone, something like that."

Jerry looked her over, up and down coolly. Back then he pretended that she didn't take his breath away. "How old are you?" he said from the comfortable vantage point of nine or ten years.

"Nineteen," she said. "I've already told my parents. They didn't like it, but what can you expect? They want me to get a job at Disneyland. My father's a soil engineer, and he did some consulting work when they built it. He thinks he can get me a pretty good job until I decide what I want to do. But I know what I want to do—I know I want to be a musician. I haven't done much of it, really, I may not be any good, but that's what I want to do."

So she came East with them. At first Jerry didn't dare to approach her. She was like this dream that had weirdly materialized. He helped her find an apartment. He installed her in his Watertown office, tried to think up letters to dictate just to look busy, had her type up the biography as far as it went, let her talk to Hawk when he called from time to time. Nothing much was happening. Every so often a booking came through. Jerry had some publishing and was managing a couple of folk singers and a bluegrass trio that played the little coffeehouses around Boston. He was still trying to negotiate the record deal with Cascade. And he was fighting against the thought that he was falling in love with Lori, that he *could* fall in love with Lori, that if he lay back and waited for things to happen, she would just fall into his arms. The first time he kissed her he came up behind her and put his hands lightly on her shoulders. He half-closed his eyes and felt a weightless detachment, prayed that the phone wouldn't ring and she wouldn't look at him oddly, as if she had known all along that this was what it was all about and was prepared to suffer it patiently. That wasn't the way it was. He could still recall vividly just how it was. She turned around slowly, a flickering smile on her lips, touched his fingertips reassuringly, put her arms around his neck, and melted into his embrace, not yielding to some external force but not holding back anything either. She was so warm! That was what he remembered most of all. He felt as if she could heat the room with the glow from her skin.

For a while that was all there was—kissing at odd moments, in odd corners, touching each other, sharing an anticipatory secret. Then Lori invited him over to her apartment to hear some of the songs she had been writing. She played them in that touchingly clumsy fashion he had grown used to, too many changes to be called blues but too stark for rock, on a piano she had been renting for the last few weeks. They were all "personal" songs, mournful songs, "straight from the heart," as Hawk would say. Jerry was deeply moved. "They're beautiful," he said to his surprise, when he should have told her to forget it, that he alone could appreciate what she had to offer. That night for the first time they went to bed together.

They slept with each other for several months. Jerry wanted to move in, but Lori didn't want him to. "You can't be too possessive," she said, and he thought she was shy. Then when things started to go bad he began to wonder if she had some kind of secret life. Did she have other lovers? Was she as uninhibited with them as she was with him? He never found out. On her own Lori found her way to a recording contract—perhaps through some contact she made at the office, probably not, it didn't matter, not through him. The first Jerry knew of it was when Cascade called up one day. He thought it was about Hawk. Instead it was Sid, the president of the company, whom he had never been able to reach. "What are you talking about?" Jerry said when he realized it wasn't Hawk they were talking about at all.

"What, are you bullshitting me? Are you her manager, or what? She says to get in touch with you, so naturally I assume you know something about it. Look, if you're playing cute,

don't bother. You've sent this stuff all around the block, right?
Hey, I'm not playing games with you. I'm telling you straight
out, I think this chick has got it. I just want to know who's heard
her already."

Jerry tried to recover as rapidly as he could and assured Sid
that the tape hadn't traveled at all, as far as he knew. "Yeah,
yeah, well, I wanted to check with you—I got your word, right?
All the songs are original, right? *As far as you know*. Hey, hey,
just kidding. I hear an Arif Mardin arrangement behind her, only
tasteful, you know, none of this complicated shit. We'll bring in
King Curtis as session leader, give it that New York spade feel—"

Jerry just kept listening, bemused, wondering if some kind
of mistake hadn't been made. Then the man mentioned a figure
that Jerry thought he could not possibly have heard right, so he
asked him to repeat it.

"How about Hawk?" Jerry said, gulping back disbelief.

"Yeah, yeah, sure, no problem, I figured that'd be the pitch,
we can handle that okay."

"What kind of an advance—"

"Look, let's not dick around. You know as well as I do there
ain't nothing in it for us. The blues thing is dead anyway. So
what do you say we call it a thousand against royalties, one
record option, shit, it's charity, am I right? You bring the
schwartze, but I want the chick."

When he got off the phone, Jerry called Lori into the little
back room that he designated his private office. She seemed embarrassed and a little bit ashamed. "It was just, you know, I saw
the way you sent out demos all the time, and it was just so, I guess
it was the impersonality of it, I figured I'd never meet any of
these people, so what harm would it do to try?"

"But you didn't even tell me," Jerry protested, hurt, although he was not so sure whether he was hurt by her lack of candor or the simple fear of her actually achieving enough success to go out on her own. The mistake, he realized in retrospect, was in not realizing that she was on her own all along.

"Well, it wasn't anything," Lori insisted with that blank intransigence that he found so baffling, and disturbing.

"Oh shit, Lori," he started to say, then thought better of it. "Look, you can't fool around like this if you really want to have a career."

Lori seemed to stare right through him. "Look, I told them you were my manager, because I trusted you," she said. "I still trust you. But I won't go on trusting you if you talk about my 'career,' ever again. That isn't what I want. I don't know what I want, but that isn't it."

"But they really want to sign you."

"What about Hawk?"

Jerry explained the deal to her. Lori shook her head. "He's not going to sign for that kind of money."

"Lori, they're not going to pay any more."

"Then jack up my price. Or get the money out of my advance. You just make sure Hawk gets his five grand."

Jerry was bewildered. He felt as if everything had changed between them in an instant. He tried to embrace her, but she was stiff. "I'm really happy for you," he said.

"I know you are," she said in words whose import he would never fully gauge. He played them back over and over again, heard their tone exactly as it was, could never understand why one had followed the other. "That's why we can't be like we've been any more. We can be friends, can't we? Because if we can't, I want to leave right now—"

"I don't understand," said Jerry.

"I'm sorry," she said. "I know what it's like. You want everything to be exactly the way you imagine it to be, but it can't be like that, it can't ever be like that. I feel as if you'd smother me, because I'd have to be what you imagined that I really was, do you understand what I mean?"

"No." Jerry shook his head. He was still trying to puzzle it out eight years later.

They recorded at the Record Plant in New York City. It was the first time that Hawk had ever spent more than an hour or two on an album. Ordinarily he balked even at doing alternate takes, let alone more than the eleven or twelve tunes he was contracted for.

"But your bass string was out of tune," said one producer in despair.

"Then get me overtime," Hawk boomed out through the microphone. "I ought to get combat pay for what I have to put up with."

At the Record Plant there was none of that, though not, Jerry thought, because Hawk was overawed by his surroundings (he couldn't have given less of a shit that Jimi Hendrix had trod these boards or that this was state-of-the-art technology), but, of course, because of Lori's presence. Jerry could have been bitter, he reflected, that Hawk was willing to put so much more trust in Lori than in himself, but it was such a pleasure to relax with Hawk, perhaps for the first time in their long association, that he simply allowed himself to bathe in the experience, as if he, too, were an innocent onlooker privileged to witness this primitive ritual.

"This is a very basic music," said Eddie, the engineer, fiddling with the dials. "And that's just what these musicians are —very basic."

Russ Levine, the producer, was deferential to the point of contempt. Somehow none of it mattered.

"What was the first song you ever heard?" said Lori, as the playback of the last song died out, and Hawk looked lost and mystified in the dimly lighted studio amidst baffles and electronic equipment left over from someone's rock session.

"I was a last-born baby," offered Hawk. "Didn't hear nothing but my daddy and his daddy making music, fiddle music, jigs, reels, all that kind of trash. Wasn't nothing like the blues then —oh, there might have been one or two tunes that was close, but the first blues song that I can recall, an old feller in our town, he wasn't nothing but a bum, really, and people all called him Turkey, I never did find out his last name, he sung a song about 'Devil jump a black man, run him a solid mile/ You know he caught that nigger, and he cry like a natural child.' Of course peoples today don't want to hear that kind of junk, they don't want to hear about no devil or about no black man either, but that was all that we was hearing when we was just kids coming up." And then he sang it.

There was a stunned silence when he was through. Russ Levine and Eddie knocked on the window and signaled thumbs up, but Hawk just looked phlegmatic, as always.

"Some of these old-timers," said Russ, shaking his head, as Jerry felt that small feeling in the pit of his stomach that he identified with pleasure but might equally well have identified with fear that the pleasure would stop.

Lori kept pressing him to remember the songs he had first

heard and played, no great feat since Jerry doubted that Hawk had ever forgotten anything, he claimed he still remembered the feel of his mother's womb; the trick was in getting him to acknowledge it. The sessions went on for three or four days, with Lori always expressing the desire to hear one more tale, to try to improve a song with just one more take. Finally he just declared that enough was enough, packed up his guitar, invited Lori to come down to Yola before too long, and disappeared into the night.

The two-record set that was released got a Grammy nomination and won the *downbeat* critics' poll for 1969, but it didn't sell any better than any of the others and Hawk was disgusted when they put together a third record from the outtakes. "I knowed I should have quit when I was ahead," he insisted angrily to Jerry. "Then if they wanted another record, they would have had to come up with some cash, Jack, none of these silly-ass awards."

Around six o'clock Hawk sat up in bed. He rubbed his head with his recalcitrant left hand, then held it out in front of him and watched it respond clumsily to the brain's commands. He shook his head disgustedly. An old man. He was an old man. He remembered the contempt he had once felt for Ole Man Mose when Mose had gotten too feeble-brained to do for himself. It was funny how life had a habit of catching up with you. On the one hand he felt no different than he had forty years ago, fifty years ago. Old?—don't know nothing about old. Tired was something else. He was the same, it was just his body that was tired. He spat through his few good teeth on to the floor. "Mattie!" he called in a voice barely audible even to himself. "Mattie!" He was hungry.

Mattie poked her head through the curtain. "You got a visitor, Roosevelt," she said. A visitor. He didn't want no visitors.

PROBABLY THE PREACHER, that lowdown scalawag Reverend Other Williams. Be hovering over the bedside, say, You better pray for your soul now, like I done tole you so many times before, the Lord he finally catched up with you, and maybe he's right. Call me Brother Roosevelt all the time—Brother Roosevelt, we's worried about your soul—like I was the president or something. I suppose it don't matter none—never did like my name, though. From the time I was a little bitty boy. Grandma used to call me Punkin, then it was Punk for short. Big fellows, little bit older than myself, they used to call me Feets, cause they think it so comical the way my toes always be sticking out of Daddy's cut-off brogans. Then for a while it was Little Mose cause, really, that was who I patterned myself behind, I come up behind him just like ol' Sonny House come up behind that little yellow squirt, Charley Patton. Friend say, Man, you play that box just like Mose. You know, I be slipping across the field with my old gal, Sal, and I couldn't tell the difference between the two. Aww, get off with your racket—that's what I say, but I was so swelled up inside, man, I thought that was it, just like these kids today, they grunt and groan till they sound like that little Jimmy Brown, don't understand, that's just the starting point. From there you got to git your own. Dog Man say to me one time, Man, will you play that "Riverbed Blues," just this oncet like Ole Man Mose. Say, man, I wouldn't bother with you, but I got a thing with ol' Ella Mae Trimble, and if that moon slip behind a cloud I want to see if I can't slip her out the back door without her husband knowing that she gone. See, that's where that song come in. He so crazy about that song the way that Mose do it, he say he can listen all night long. So I play it, Doggy give me two bits, and I tell him for two bits I play the song one time, play it twice for four, play it all night long if you like, just slip me a dollar. Shoot, I didn't know no better, neither did Doggy and Ella Mae. That fool listen to me sing, it start him to thinking *about* Ella Mae, when he can't find her he go get his shotgun, and if Doggy couldn't outrun a hound, he be so full of buckshot he be spoiled. Don't know what happen to Ella Mae, but we didn't see her at no *dances* for a while. But that was just the way it was in those days—play all night for a fish sandwich and glad to get it, too. Shoot, we thought we was doing good. Play those blues, Nighthawk, they used to say. And I could play 'em, too. Little old shanties set way back in the country, nothing but dirt floors and kerosene lanterns and the chairs flying—my, my. Come on, Hawk, make that box talk, all right, all right, aww, Mr. Hawk, you don't know what your music do to me—

"HAWK? HAWK? Say, Hawk—" A girl's voice. Pale-blond hair, sitting there—where she go? Lori, Lori, that Lori girl. Hawk's big laugh rumbled in his throat. "Hey, girl, what you doing? What you doing down here?"

Lori touched his hand. Hand felt warm. "You all right, Hawk? I didn't mean to wake you. Mattie said—"

"Oh sure, sure." His voice came out in a hoarse whisper that wasn't him ("Oh babe, I don't know myself"). "I been awake a long time. How you doing, baby?"

"I'm doing good, Hawk." Lori looked as if she was about to cry. What you gonna cry for, gal? You think this old man's gonna die? Shoot, no, this old man's too mean to die. He started to laugh but only spluttered until he began to cough.

"Well, that's good," Hawk said. "I'm glad somebody doing something. All them doctors getting at me, telling me I can't do nothing, gotta take it easy, rest—"

Lori's eyes lit up impishly. "Yeah, well, you better get some rest if you gonna do all these things you been boasting about. People keep telling me how this dirty old man keeps promising to fix my business for me, but don't look like you ready to fix nobody's business just yet."

Hawk laughed loudly. "Lookahere, gal, you just crawl in betwixt these sheets, and you see if I can't still be doing it. Only thing is, you're gonna have to con-trol yourself, cause Mattie ain't gonna stand for no screaming or crying—"

Out in the kitchen they could hear Mattie's voice. Lori smiled, came closer to Hawk, flung her arms around him, and received his hug in return. "You're gonna be all right, Hawk," she said. "I know you are. Ain't anything can keep a tough old buzzard like you down—you're too mean to die."

Hawk shook his head solemnly. "Ain't nobody too mean to die. But I ain't prepared just yet. Hey, Mattie fixing me something to eat?"

Lori grinned. "Mattie's *always* fixing you something to eat— even when you ain't got no appetite. I think you just like to boss her around sometimes, just to make sure she's still gonna jump. What you gonna do when she says to fix your own self something to eat?"

Hawk shrugged. "By then I guess I be too old for the orphans' home."

"How are you, really, though? Do you feel all right?"

"Oh, I don't know, I've felt better—"

"I guess."

"But then I felt worse, too. Can't rightly recall when. Maybe the time I drunk that poison whiskey. Let me tell you something, don't never fool around with no bootlegger's wife. I didn't think he knowed nothing about it. It was the perfect setup, too. Him off in the woods all the time, making corn. Annie Mae just so fat and contented with her backdoor man—that's me. Sam coming home all wore out and not having to be pestered by no hungry wife—you know what I'm talking about. Only thing I didn't figure on was nosy neighbors and just generally jealous-hearted people. That and the poison whiskey. I thought that sucker was my friend. To your health, he says, and I drinks it down. I just about didn't have no more health after that—I never did feel so twisted up inside. But I tell you the truth, my records would've been worth a sight more money if that whiskey *had* rubbed me out. Just like that boy, that Johnson boy, shoot, if he lived as long as I did, he'd be scuffling, too. Some day, I'm gonna tell some white kid, Yeah, I knowed Robert Johnson. Matter of fact, I seen him just the other day. That kid's eyes gonna poke out like he was a goggle-eyed perch. Course he ain't gonna believe me at first, but the suspicion gonna sneak up on him, this nigger just might know. So he's gonna say, cool and cautious-like, What? Where? Wha-wha-when? And I'm gonna stand there just as sure as I'm born and tell him, I seen Robert just last year, he joined the church, Holiness church, he ain't touched his git-tar in years, and he's working as a bartender in Milwaukee." Hawk started to chuckle. "That'd really get 'em, wouldn't it?"

Lori laughed. She laughed so hard the tears came into her eyes. She wondered if it was that funny or if she wasn't just looking for some excuse, if she wasn't overreacting. "Oh, you're such a lot of talk," she said. "You know I'm going to put out a book that says the Screamin' Nighthawk behaved like a perfect gentleman at all times, he was true to his music, he was true to his wife—"

"Don't you do it, girl. You gonna put me out of business."

"I hear the doctor thinks you should be in the hospital," Lori said. "He says you should be some place where they can take proper care of you—"

"I ain't going to no hospital. Them doctors all doing their best to kill me. I already excaped from one of them places, ain't going back no more. If I'm gonna die, let me die at home, in my own bed, with my own people."

"How come you're giving Jerry such a hard time?"

Hawk put on a pained expression. "Aw, I ain't never done nothing to cause him grief. That boy always complaining about someone mistreating him; ain't no one mistreated him more than he has mistreated hisself." When he saw that this wasn't working, he tried another tack. "I know he mean well, but you tell that boy to stop jawing at me. You know, if he'd just leave me be, wouldn't be no problem. Oncet he knowed I was coming home, what's he gonna stay on my tail for all the time like he did, why not just let me be? I taken care of myself for seventy-eight years, I imagine I can do all right on my own by now."

"He was just worried about you."

"Well, I know that. He always worried about me or you or some damned body. He be better off if he worry about hisself."

Lori couldn't help smiling.

"Well, it's true. You know just as well as I do that it's the God's honest truth. It's not that that boy don't care about hisself all of the time. It's just that he don't never speak up, just look at you with them big sad eyes, like how come you treating him like this and him just begging for more all the time."

Lori laughed. "Well, you certainly hit the nail on the head, didn't you? Ah, shit, how come you know so much and you still so dumb?"

"My mama," said Hawk with a proud grin, "didn't raise no dumb babies."

"I wish I could've met your mama."

"Yeah," said Hawk reflectively. "You would have liked her. She was a little bitty thing, come up no higher than your shoulder, I outgrowed her when I was eleven years old. Didn't never talk much, never told me what to do and what not to do, said, what's the sense of that, you gonna do it anyway? So she told me what to do after I done what I wasn't supposed to do. It was just after slavery time when she was borned, and she never got off the plantation, but everybody liked her, didn't matter if they was white or black, everybody had a kind word to say about Miz Jefferson, Auntie Ruth. She lived to be ninety-three years old, you know, a old old woman, died just about when I met the boy—well, hell, you knowed that. Never did nothing big, never went no further than Memphis—and that was only oncet, to see Roseamanda married—but she never quit neither, never just curl up and die, used to go around with a fruit basket, little special things she cooked for the old ladies. By the time she passed, she was fifteen, twenty-five years older than some of them old ladies she was visitin'. Some folks got the spirit of life inside 'em, and she was one. Whenever I come home she was always there, and that what I be thinking of still when I come over that hill, that little rise, you know, where you can see the creek and the hollow, thinking about how she loved to hear me sing my songs. You see, she didn't never give up, not even when she was crippled and bent over with the arthritis, she still work up there in the white folks' house, they like to treat her like a doggone queen. They respect her, see, cause she respect herself, thass what I'm talking about. Long as I'm suckin' in air, I'm gonna be the Screamin' Nighthawk. Can't be the Screamin' Nighthawk no more, might as well hang it up, you know what I'm talking about, gal?"

Lori nodded, as Hawk came out of his reverie.

"Trash, that's what I'm talking."

The bottom dropped out of the blues market. For a few years it had actually paid off, and Hawk could make a living off the coffeehouses, European tours, SNCC benefits, Vietnam teach-ins, and college concerts. His records for Cascade sold no more than an average of a couple of thousand copies apiece, but they garnered good reviews and opened the door to more and better bookings. Hawk bought a new car (a '61 Chevy) and a color TV. It was a comfortable enough living.

Then one by one they dropped out of sight, decimated by death, illness, personal problems, or a combination of all three. Skip James, Son House, Mississippi John Hurt, Bukka White— all of whose discoveries were heralded with such self-righteous fanfare—were one by one forgotten as their audience grew bored with *lèse majesté*. But Hawk wouldn't go away. He was too real, too ugly, he said, too demanding to be taken up by a small coterie, too self-contained to be cast aside. He was angry when Cascade didn't pick up his option. He called up Sid, somehow got through to him, and cursed him out in no uncertain terms. Then he started calling around the country to all the little labels whose numbers he had accumulated in the course of his recent travels, shouting into the mouthpiece with that staccato, rapid-fire delivery that left everyone baffled as to what he was saying. Finally Jerry negotiated a deal with Pharaoh, a little label in St.

Louis that specialized in blues records. He kept going for the next few years with a myriad of small-label deals—he would spend no more than a couple of hours on the record itself, offering new titles but familiar tunes recycled for each session—plus the few bookings Jerry could get for him, blues festivals, and the rare occasion when he might consent to open for Lori and pick up a couple of thousand bucks.

He survived. He survived, Jerry realized, just as he had been surviving in the world Jerry had been so intent on rescuing him from, only now he was no longer suited to that world either. It didn't really matter anyway. Whether it was Sweden or the Florida Panhandle, always he headed back for Yola, always he headed down to the barbershop or to the Sunset Cafe, always you could spot him swaying, almost lurching down the street, weighted to one side by the big battered guitar whose equally battered case was covered with stickers from all the places that Hawk had been. There were the same old men sitting around, chewing tobacco, eager for the latest word, playing dominoes and pitty-pat. There was always an old man in a Stetson slowly rocking along on his mule. There was always an old lady dozing drowsily on a porch. There was always Hawk, dominating the conversation, spinning out his monologues, sitting back, hands folded across his stomach, and lecturing his audience as if they were schoolchildren listening attentively to fairy tales. "Them European countries is different, man," he would sometimes begin. "Don't know nothing about color, they treat you like royalty over there. I mean, they really *appreciates* the blues, got them little white boys come running around, say, Mr. Hawk, Mr. Hawk, can you teach me what the blues is all about? She-it." His audience all laughed. "Next time, I telled 'em, I'm gonna take y'all over there with me, so they can see what some real niggers look like, see if they can appreciate some gen-u-ine funk—"

Jerry never knew if they really believed him. Hawk showed them the clippings. He showed them the homburg he had bought in London, and of course they knew he had been away. But he had always been going away, and if he came back with a homburg for all they knew that was what people were wearing in Oklahoma City this year. Once a BBC crew came down to film Hawk for a British documentary. It seemed as if everyone in town turned up for the filming out at Hawk's house, as the director and his assistant and cameraman all were transfixed by the mass of black faces peering up at Hawk on his front porch. "This here's my house, and my wife, and my kids," he said, introducing them one by one. "Them people over there is my neighbors, who is a bunch of no-account niggers who ain't had nothing to do with me since the day I moved in, cause they too high-class and got their nose up their ass." There was a murmuring in the crowd, and some of them started to go home. "These here, they my friends from the Sunset Cafe."

The television crew followed him down to the barbershop and the Sunset Cafe and out into the country, where they surveyed the charred remains of Paul Barbour's juke joint, the Big House. "Used to be some fine times out here," said Hawk. "Me and Elmo and Muddy Waters used to play all night sometimes, people would come from five counties when they knowed someone big like us was going to be playing. White folks burned it down. Don't really know why, but I reckon Mr. Barbour just wasn't paying his taxes or something—he was mixed up in a whole heap of things, Barbour was."

Jerry followed the crew all around town, embarrassed by the

director's unabashed appreciation of even the most prosaic sights. "Beautiful," he said as he saw an old lady who looked as if she had never set foot in town hike up her dress in drunken glee as Hawk rocked the joint at the Sunset Cafe. People were shouting and laughing and screaming, just as they always did; it was in fact just as it had always been, awkward, unforced, with no one but Jerry aware of, or concerned with, this intrusive presence, the camera, which somehow made everything seem so different, while nothing that you could put your finger on actually had changed.

"It's marvelous, just like Wales," said the director, sighting Hawk through the viewfinder. "I've never seen such poverty before. That's right, that's right," he said, as a big fat woman thrust her belly jovially in front of Hawk's face. "They really can't help being themselves, can they? I believe you've got a national treasure in Hawk. It's just marvelous that we're able to capture him in his native surroundings like this."

Jerry made the requisite sounds of agreement and worried that he had somehow betrayed a trust.

V

THE SCREAMIN'
NIGHTHAWK:
LAST OF THE
LEGENDARY BLUESMEN

AN INTRODUCTORY NOTE

Why a biography of yet another blues singer (*Jerry had written*)? This is a question I ask myself as we see the proliferation of literature on a music that is basically unconcerned with the test of literacy, that started out in fact as a substitute for formal communication. For blues originated in the fields, a kind of shorthand communication among fieldworkers who to begin with had neither a language nor a musical instrument other than the one they brought from Africa (*the skin is the drum—look up Zora Neale Hurston*) in their enslaved state. The first blues can truly be said to have been hatched when the first slave, perhaps to lessen his almost unblankable burden (*shit!*), perhaps to reaffirm that he was not alone, called out to another in song, "Well, the work, it sure go hard," and his friend answered back, "Sure beats working in the boss man's yard." (*Something like that? Check Odum and Johnson. Is this total bullshit?*) It was the true birth of the blues.

Why another book on this subject, though? Why more words on what is essentially an emotive offering, one which demands not a sociological but a *soulful* response? Well, it is precisely for that reason that I want to avoid most of the conventions (*strictures?*) of this form. Over the last few years I have had the rare opportunity to be associated with one of the great blues legends, a man I think I can call my friend. We have lived together, worked together, traveled together, cursed each other out, and fallen into each other's arms (*figuratively speaking? God, what bullshit*) when we got the news that Hawk had won the 1969 *downbeat* award for his historic double album *A Man And His Roots*. We've had good times and we've had bad times together. I've witnessed Hawk paying his dues, playing the little clubs and back-country juke joints where his appreciative audience has numbered no more than twenty or thirty day laborers. We've been through a lot together. I've even seen Hawk recognized in his own home town (how many times does a prophet live to enjoy that kind of acclaim?), as December 27, 1972, was declared Screamin' Nighthawk Day in the drowsy little town of Yola, Mississippi, and the mayor presented this last of the itinerant blues singers with a key to the city in which he had grown up and lived most of his long life. (*How could he have lived there if he was traveling all the time? Rephrase.*) It's been a long journey for Hawk, from a backwoods cabin to the modest home he has been able to build in the last few years on the basis of royalties and concert fees; from the rough, no-holds-barred world in which he grew up to the polite applause of the college campus. I think that's why it occurred to me, as it occurred to Hawk, too, as more and more of this world is dying off—not only the men and women who remember it, but the world itself, disrupted by interstates and television and all the creature comforts of twentieth-century progress—it occurred to us that the true story of this world has never been told. The brutal day-to-day existence which the blues singer of necessity has always led, the almost existential acceptance of the vicissitudes brought on by fate and character (*oh shit, merde, Meurseult, God, more fucking existentialism*) . . . In short, my aim in these pages is to do something no one else has done, to communicate the plain unvarnished truth about the blues singer's life simply in terms of one individual. This is oral history, and you must remember it is all dependent on the memory of one man, now past seventy. An effort has been made to check facts and provide documentation, but, as in so many memoirs of this sort, you run up against the impenetrable wall of conflicting memories, vaguely recollected scenes (due to either real or selective memory gaps), and a haze of names (phonetically spelled out, with no written records to check against), dates, places that have forever retreated into the miasma past. With these qualifications, then, herein begins the unlikely collaboration of an amateur historian (who didn't know what he was getting into) and one of the great repositories of the oral culture of our time, as well as one of the most remarkable men I have ever met, the Screamin' Nighthawk.

MISSISSIPPI ROOTS

The Screamin' Nighthawk was born Theodore Roosevelt Jefferson on December 27, 1902 (1901? draft card says 1907), in Issaquena County on the Holloway Plantation just outside of Yola, Mississippi, to William "Ollie" Jefferson and his common-law wife, Ruth Mae Johnson. Ollie was a sharecropper who had been born on the Holloway Plantation to parents who had worked the fields as slaves—

RIGHT THERE you got two things wrong (*Hawk's voice intrudes rudely on the first of several dozen reels of tape*). My draft card say 1907, but that was just so's they could take me for the Big War. Shit, they didn't have no records on me at all till they made them up, how many times I got to tell you that? Fact is, I was born in 1899, reason I know, that was the year they all talking about Teddy Roosevelt gonna be president or some shit like that. But that wasn't why my mama named me no Theodore Roosevelt, it was because that dude run his troops up San Juan Hill, a-whooping and a-hollering, with a colored man in the lead. I even made up a blues about it, but you don't want to hear that sucker, cause it ain't got nothing to do with nothing.

Other thing you got wrong, my daddy wasn't no sharecropper. Course you could call him a sharecropper, that's what old man Holloway thought he was, but my daddy just lay up in the bed all day, didn't do no work at all, leastaways that's what my mama told me. Say, he bad, he bad like Jesse James. He was a bootlegger, he was a gambler, he was a musician—can't get no worse than that. If he'd just been one or the other, might have been all right, but it was the combination, see, that finally caused him to leave. I wasn't no more than five or six, there was just the three of us, everybody else grown up and moved out, me, my big sister Lavalle, and Little Ollie—we called him Pigmeat, or Hambone sometimes—that was my daddy's from his outside woman, but we treated him just like one of our'n, wasn't no different, every Saturday he go to see his mama, every Sunday we'd all see her in church. My mama and his mama—that was Miss Ida Bee Tarrant that was, later on she married the deacon, Mr. Lacy—everybody call him ol' Gatemouth cause he get his jaw to flapping all the time, but she wouldn't tolerate none of that foolishness, "You call him Mr. Lacy," she say, she get herself so stuck up in the air she didn't even notice Pigmeat no more, and he was a sad little creature, always needing to be told what to do. "Wipe your nose, Pigmeat." "Don't play with no Tarwaters." Tell him he was just as good as anybody else, but he didn't believe it, and then he up and died in the influenza epidemic of 1918. You know, Ham and me was down in New Orleans then, man it was a fearful sight to see, women screaming and crying, grown men, too, they carried the bodies out and piled 'em up in the streets for the wagons to come. Preachers standing in the corner claiming it was the second coming, day of the judgment, sinners flinging themselves forward saying, "Have mercy, Lawd. Oh Lawd, save me." Me and Ham call each other Deacon This and Brother That, singing nothing but them way-back raggedy old hymns and the people just throwing their nickels and dimes at us, didn't mean nothing, they figured they wasn't going to need no money where they was going, and they was right. Churches and sporting houses doing a full business, me and Pig was just working the streets by day, well, Pig blowed a little harp and he could sing some, too, even though his voice wasn't never too strong. One night these two sisters, they offer to go home with us—well, they look like they about sixty, and kind of scurvy, too. So Pigmeat go home with them, but I stay out on the streets playing. Well, Pigmeat was the one they wrote the song about—if he didn't have bad luck, wouldn't have no luck at all? Wouldn't you know that them two sisters had the influenza—carried them off, carried him off, too, in three or four days. Well, you see, he really didn't have no luck! (*Hawk laughs—chortle of fiction or chortle of fact? But your father, he is reminded.*)

Oh yeah, well, my daddy was a gambling fool. He bet on anything. He bet on the weather. He bet on the sunrise. He bet on whether you open your eyes one at a time when you wakes up, and if you do which one you opens first.

But one time he got in deeper than he meant to. See, he bet this big buck nigger he could drink any three men under the table, didn't matter who they was, get anybody he like. So this Big Nigger—that what they called him, only other name I knowed him by was Hooks—he get these two friends of his, even bigger than him, and they all set up in a row while my daddy go and get him three or four jugs of that old moonshine. Well, the first nigger that took a pop, he just stare at my daddy until his eyes bug out and then he fall down to the ground, not dead, just passed out like. Well, next fella, naturally he don't want to take a drink, but Big Nigger, he stand over him till that fool just naturally have to swallow it down, and *he* fall over. Well, Hooks looking at my daddy mighty suspicious now, and my daddy talking fast, trying to get him to go along with it, but Hooks, he may be big, but he ain't stupid, and he say, Lookahere, Jeff, you go ahead and take your drink out of the same bottle, ain't no need to stand on politeness, I let you go first. And anybody could see, he didn't want to do that, he trying to act like it nothing but nerves, but finally he take a drink, and then Hooks make him take another and another, and when he seed that my daddy ain't gonna take any more he poured the rest of it down his throat. So, regardless, he won his bet, but poison whiskey, that's what got him in the end. (*Hawk laughs again, a big chortling laugh, and Jerry wonders how this squares with the coroner's report—if indeed there was a coroner's report—on the death of Ollie Jefferson.*)

Only thing that was left after the funeral was his git-tar. When he was living home, my daddy never even allowed me to touch it—that's how jealous-minded he was of that box, I think he loved it more than he did my mama, I know he did. Course I would sneak off anyway late at night when my daddy too drunk to notice, and I creep across the fields down to the creek all among the crickets and frogs making their noises, and I be plunking away and they be plunking away—man, we was all making a racket. Naw, this wasn't the first git-tar I had. First git-tar I had was a piece of baling wire I strung up side the wall, pull it tight so it be just right, make all kinds of different sounds on that wire, sound like a cat screaming when little boys start to pull it apart —she-it, yes, I think everybody make their start somehow or nother like that. See, I had the feel for music from a baby on, didn't never need nobody to tell me nothing, didn't make no difference if you give me a tune, cause I could make up my own, didn't matter what kind of music it was, I liked it all.

My daddy didn't play no blues songs, really, didn't really pick no git-tar, just frailed on it, old-time songs like "Working on the Railroad," "She'll Be Coming Round the Mountain," "Bicycle Built for Two"—oh, all that kind of junk. Course he play anything you pay him to play, don't make no difference, if he don't know it he try it anyway. Like I said my daddy was a gambler. And my uncles all played, too, they played git-tar some, and my Uncle Roebuck he play banjo, my Uncle Ferris play the fiddle, and together with my daddy they make up a string band that was known far and wide, far and wide, man, play jigs, play reels, sing them old-time story songs, oh oncet in a while they might have did a blues.

That's why it so peculiar in a fashion, I mean it wasn't nothing I was brought up to, my mama just want me to sing church songs, and my daddy, he just an entertainer like Sammy Davis Jr. or somebody, but for me first time I heard that man, they call him Alabama Red, don't know why, cause he was from around Greenville, sing the blues down by the railroad track—oh my, people standing around throwing money at him—well, I tell you, the blues turn me every way but loose. Couldn't have been more than six or seven years old, and I knowed that was what I wanted to play.

Well, of course, it's Ol' Man Mose that everybody connected up with me, and really he the one that done it if the truth be told —Alabama Red the first, but Ol' Man Mose the man when it come to the blues. Shit, yeah, he even git the chickens to dancing, my mama say he could just about make a preacher lay his Bible down, that's how powerful Ole Man Mose was. In his prime, I'm talking about, not later on after the whiskey got him. Moses Chatman—I believe he an off cousin to old Sam and Bo that used to play that old "Sittin' On Top of the World"—well, anyways, Mose played with a bottleneck, and he made that git-tar sing. Lawd have mercy—that's what that git-tar be saying, Lawd have mercy—he could play so sweet, and he could play hard, too, and I be pestering him, jawing at him all the time so's he could show me how to do, cause he was like a god to me to start off with, even though he wasn't no more than fifteen or so years older than me probably.

Well, it seem like finally he start to show me a few things just to get me off his back, keep me from pestering him all the time. Course by then he was courting my mother, I suspect, leastaways that's what I think now, but at the time, ten-year-old kid, I never thought nothing about it. He just give me a chord to play, and he say, Youngster, you go off and practice, and I go off by myself for two, three hours, don't come back till I got that sucker right, say, Lookahere, Mose, I got it now, and he say, Naw, you don't, gotta go and practice it up some more. So that was just the way it goes, although it never struck me what was going on at the time, see, I was just a kid, really, I did a grown man's work, but I don't think I even knew what a pecker was for. Course I found out a little later on when I started in with Mattie, Mose's wife, that I run away with to St. Louis. And I thought about it some at that time—sure did.

Well, Mose wasn't no nice man. Shit, might as well be honest about it, he was a motherfucker, just as soon cut you as look at you, and that's the truth. No, you can't get me to say nothing nice about him. Course he was a good blues singer, till the whiskey drag him down, towards the end he was just a sorry-ass feebleminded old man, and he wasn't no more than fifty years old when he died in '32. But he was always mean. Never let nobody else play on his set. Take you out to a gig sometimes, and if he feeling real good he let you second him on guitar—maybe!— but just so you don't get any ideas he mess you up so you look foolish, change the time, or make a change that you ain't expecting, just deliberately fuck you up and then point it out to the peoples, saying, Well, I tried to train this boy right, but how's a body gonna play when he laying down all this racket behind me? Well, get him off then, they say, and I slink off that stage —well, it wasn't hardly a stage, most of the time we just standing at one end of the room, pushed over in a corner like, little cabin, chimney smoking, people dancing in their bare feet, all that kind of stuff, and me feeling like I'm the worst piece of shit in the world, I feel like I really made a disgrace. I tell you, boy, it was an education, but I wouldn't do that kind of shit to nobody, cause I know, that's just the way I came up, and it wasn't no good way.

But anyways, well, you know, there was lots of musicianers played just like him back then, only trouble with them they was dumb in the ways of the world. Long time after, after Mose got records out, the scouts'd come down, say, What you got for us, Mose? And he say, Oh sure, boss, I got something good, mmm-hmm, and he parade out some of the most raggedy-ass country clowns, some broken-down old man who couldn't even sit up straight let alone hit a good lick, and Mose say, Yesssir, Mr. Boss Man, this the best we have. And them old whiteys look at each other, say, That the best he got. So naturally wasn't nobody get to make records *but* Ole Man Mose. Not until Barbour gets in the scouting business hisself, and by that time I was thirty years old. Man just listen to two verses of my song, cut me off, I thought, oh boy, that's the end of it, Ol' Mose right maybe, ain't nobody know nothing about making records but him. But the man say, Boy, we ain't never heard nothing like this before, you even better than Mose. You sure you ain't got your name on no other contract? I say, No, sir. Well, they say, put your mark right here, cause I tell you, boy, you done made a hit. After that I guess Mose seen he better make the best of it, and he tole them, Oh sure, I teached that boy, he was like a baby to me, which is how I guess all them stories got started. But I never did have no more trouble from Mose until the day he died—which, as it happened, was not very long.

Course I was a full-growed man by then, had kids of my own somewheres. I'd been a rambler and a gambler, worked up the turpentine camps, chopped cotton, worked on the railroad, too, got into a little scrape down around Minden, done just about everything a man could think of and then some, but I always stuck pretty close to home and I always kept my git-tar by my side. Oncet the records started to coming out, though, I was gone, me and that boy they call Wheatstraw, course his real name was Whittacomb, something like that, he just called himself after Peetie Wheatstraw, we jumped all up through Illinois and New Jersey and all up into Canada. Played right out on the streets, people throwed money at us, some of them people had never seen a colored man before. One place, I remember, they had lots of cow farmers up there, I don't know, might've been Wisconsin, them farmers gathered around, and they didn't even want us to play nothing, just touch our heads and feel our skin, and all the time jabbering away at each other in some foreign language. Other times I just be whomping away on my box, and Wheatstraw blowing harp and popping his eyes out like all get-out and the people laughing and dancing like they never heard nothing like that before.

And sometimes I come home, my mama would have a new man, but most of the time she alone, just waiting on me to return, cause I was always her favorite—and her hair beginning to turn gray, and she just look at me and shake her head and say, Roosevelt, you just look at yourself. Ain't you never gonna settle down? You just like your daddy, God rest his soul. And then I play her favorite song for her, which she always like to hear me sing till her grave, "So Glad That I Be Back Home," and the tears come streaming down her cheeks, and she pat me on the head, and she say, You know, you a good boy at heart, but you just ain't got no Ruler over you. When you all going to quit your foolishness and come home to the church? And I didn't tell her then, and I ain't told her yet, that that day ain't *never* gonna come.

JERRY SURVEYED the material, he went over it again and again in dismay. Trying to sort it out. Trying to make some sense out of it. Trying to determine what was true and what was not. He spoke to Hawk's sister, Lavalle, an old lady living in a little cabin in Mound Ridge with her daughter. She adjusted the wig she had insisted on putting on before allowing herself to be interviewed. She moistened her lips and poked her mouth around as if she had a set of loosely fitting false teeth, but in truth she had no teeth at all. She cleared her throat and spat out a wad of chewing tobacco, so the tobacco juice dribbled down her chin. Her daughter, Olympia, who looked nearly as old as her mother but was stout where the mother was lean, seemed to have no recollection of Hawk at all. "Of course I wasn't no more than a baby when he left home, and look at me now." She laughed a dry old lady's laugh and sat with her legs comfortably spread under her long gingham dress. "Mama could probably tell you a whole lot about her baby brother, but she don't remember so good anymore, do you, Mama?" The old lady just smiled. "She remember how her daddy died, though, don't you?"

"Kilt in a fire. Drove right into a oil truck stopped for a train. They was all burned to a crisp. You could see the smoke for miles, yessir."

"This was Hawk's father?" said Jerry. "The gambler?"

"I don't know nothing about no gambler," said Olympia. "Oh, he might have played a game of poker or pitty-pat. He just a farmer like everyone else, though, the way I hear tell it. His daddy left him twenty acres, and Mama give it away. To her first husband, y'understand."

The old lady giggled. "He never gived me no trouble."

"Y'see, her mind wanders. Sometimes she don't remember nothing, and sometimes she be clear as a bell. She could tell you a whole lot about them days, if you just catched her right. You know, Mama's had a hard row to hoe. A hard row to hoe," said Olympia, shaking her head. "She was such a pretty little thing, too, wasn't you, Mama? You seen her picture?"

Jerry didn't even answer before Olympia had waddled inside and come back with two gilt-edged pictures. One showed a lady with flashing eyes, her hair piled up imperially on her head, and a lace mantilla draped across her shoulders. "Well, that my mama's mama," she said triumphantly. "Hawk's mother?" Olympia nodded. "And this here Mama with her brother Junie, he pass, oh let me see, about '55, I think it was." A young man in a sailor's uniform stared into the camera straight ahead, hair clipped short, eyes clear and expectant, shoulders squared. The woman beside him was fine-boned and delicate, with a demure scoop-necked dress and a rose in her impeccably waved hair.

"You think Hawk can pick that git-tar, you should've heard Junie. Just ask any of the people hereabouts. Course he wouldn't play nothing but church songs, didn't think nothing of Hawk nor his music neither. Mama the only one with a soft spot in her heart for her brother, and that because she practically raised him by herself. Everybody else, when he come around they just say, Oh, oh, look like trouble, money, women, something go wrong, somebody after him. Mama just say, he gonna be all right, that boy gonna be all right some day."

"He meant well," the old lady suddenly interjected. Jerry nodded encouragingly. "You couldn't count on him for nothing, though."

Jerry waited, but nothing else was forthcoming. Well, he supposed she was right, you still couldn't count on him for much. "Do you ever see him any more?"

"Oncet in a while. We seen him just last month. Didn't we, Mama?"

The old lady cackled. "He a bad weed, the cows gonna cut him down."

Jerry confronted Hawk with the discrepancies. They didn't seem to bother him.

"Olympia don't know doodly-squat," he insisted. "Junie poison her mind against me. I got no quarrel with Lavalle, but Junie had a hairy ass. I don't even like to think of him, I don't never mention his name. I swear, he could play the git-tar like it was a charm. He never did nothing with it, though. And he never did a honest day's work in his life, always getting the other niggers to do his work for him, just like a preacher, so smooth and fat and putting on that hincty smile, tell the truth I never did like to admit that he was my brother—course he might've said the same. Might've been cause we wasn't natural brothers, but I don't think so. I seen natural brothers that couldn't get along for nothing and stepchildren that was as close as white is on rice. I think he was just naturally jealous-hearted cause I was always Mama's favorite. She wouldn't hear nothing bad about me. Lavalle tell you anything?"

"Not much," Jerry admitted.

"Well, then," said Hawk.

He talked to Mattie Mae, though, Mose's wife, who had run off to St. Louis with her husband's young protégé and then either deserted or been deserted by him there. She was a light-skinned old lady with liver spots on her hands whom he found in a gigantic project in Cleveland. She showed him into a genteel apartment filled to overflowing with bulky plastic-covered furniture, moving with a slow arthritic shuffle while leaning on a cane. She seemed neither pleased nor displeased at this visit, just nodded when he explained that it was through Hawk (actually it was through the Cleveland Housing Authority) that he had gotten her address in the hope that she could tell him something about the old days. From the wall above a padded red leatherette chair pictures of Jesus (light-brown) and Martin Luther King (the same) looked down. On a low table beside the plastic-covered sofa were pictures of three girls—at a graduation ceremony, at a wedding, and on some other formal occasion—and a snapshot of Mattie Mae in a sparkling white nurse's uniform.

"Well, yes, I suppose it was the way Hawk tells it," she murmured as she listened to Jerry's brief account of their tempestuous affair. "I guess he wasn't no more than fourteen, though he was big for his age. Course I ain't saying how old I was, that's a woman's right, isn't it?" She smiled coquettishly. "But I was a little older than him, and I had been married to Mr. Chatman for three or four years at that time. But, you know, we women do make mistakes of the heart. I was married to that Mose for no more than six months when I knowed I made a mistake. That Mose was a mean old man. Why, he beat me and whipped me and did things I can't ever tell another living soul about." She raised her eyebrows. "And, you know, I was just a little slip of a thing. Not like I am now, all broad and stout, but I had a light-hearted attitude and a girlish figure that I received not a small number of compliments on, if I do say so myself. And of course I loved a good time, that was how I met Mose, and that was how I met Hawk. If it hadn't been for my willful nature, I would have grown up to be the girl my mama and daddy wanted me to be, but whatever I did I did with my eyes open. See, I used to sneak off to them Saturday-night dances by myself, I always enjoyed a good barbecue or fish fry, I didn't care if it was rowdy like my mama said or if the people was cutting up all night long. Even after I was married, Mr. Chatman didn't want me attending none of them parties, cause he said they was too rough for a young woman of my refinement. Shoot, I guess he just wanted to keep me to himself, well, I knowed that, and he didn't want me running into none of his outside women neither. Course I went anyway, and I guess I seen some things back then that a young girl shouldn't never see. But, you know, somehow it seemed different being out in the country and all, everybody knowed everybody else, if some child acting bad his parents gonna know about it, not like here. Of course all kinds of terrible things went on, but somehow it just never seemed to bother me. So when Mr. Chatman asked me if I could slip off with him and tie the knot, well my goodness I considered that an honor and a privilege, I imagined that I'd be envied by women in four counties. Little did I know. Mose may have been the best musicianer around, but he sure wasn't no Loving Dan." The old lady's laugh crackled dryly. "Well, see, he'd been to Jackson, he'd been to Natchez, he say he even been as far as Chicago, Illinois, everywhere he go people know who Ol' Man Mose was. So to me, well, I don't really know how to explain this, it seem foolish to an old woman, but you can't explain nothing to a young girl who's got her mind made up, so there wasn't nothing that would have stopped me, even if I'd known then what I know now.

"Well, I found out my mistake soon enough. Almost too soon. If I could've just taken two steps back—but you ain't never privileged to do that. Not in this life anyhow, and maybe not in the next either. So I suffered along, I bided my time, I went to my mama, but she said, Baby, you done made your bed, now lie in it. And my papa wouldn't hardly speak to me at all, it just about break my heart, cause he *knew*. And I didn't have no money, no more good times, uh-uh, Mose practically kept me prisoner, locked the door behind him when he went off to play, cause he had seen what happens by him being what they call a backdoor man—you can hear him going out the back every time that front door slam. Well, that was Mose. I guess you might say that's just about every musicianer, I was to find out to my sorrow.

"But anyways, I started to notice that there was this young boy coming around, always pestering at Mose to learn him to play git-tar. And he bother Mose and bother Mose so, sometimes Mose just show him something just so's he can get shut of him, it seemed to me. Anyway he kept coming around and coming around, and then one day I noticed that he was looking at me kind of funny while Mose was showing him a chord. And I didn't think nothing of it. But one day he came back when Mose wasn't there at all. And he bang on the door. And I say in my manner, I'm sorry, I can't let you in, cause Mose took the key. Well, that ain't gonna stop a young man like Hawk was, so he say, I just be a minute. So he goes around to the rear of the cabin, where there's a little window just to let in the air, and somehow he squeezed through where no full-grown man could have gone. But he was full-grown, oh my yes, and I knew right then and there that this was the agent of my deliverance. That's where Mose got the story of the twelve-year-old boy that Elmore stole from him and made such a hit with. Course Hawk wasn't no twelve years old, but then again I don't believe he had made fourteen.

"Well, I harped at him and harped at him, and he thought the world of me, but he thought the world of Mose, too, as a blues musician anyway, so it was me, really, leading him on all the time, cause I think he would have been satisfied just to keep squeezing in through that little window, until finally we run off together to St. Louis. We didn't do much—Lord, it wasn't for too long—but we was *happy.*

"But eventually we drifted apart, like so many young folks do. Because truthfully I was in love with the city, paved streets and streetcar rides, and folks dressing up fancy, and I had it in mind that I wanted to better myself, which is how I came to be a nurse at a later time. But Hawk, I don't know, I think he got to getting homesick, after all he was just a young boy, and he always say he want to feel that dirt under his feet—I don't know. Oh my, we was young and foolish then, but I wouldn't give up my memories for anything in this world."

I only saw Mose one more time, when I was visiting friends in Chicago, and somebody from down home told me Mose was there to do some recording, so I sniffed around a little, looking for him, and finally somebody say, 'Look, he over there,' and I look under the railroad El and there was a bunch of old men, winos, fighting over a bottle, and I didn't go no closer, just said to myself, Thank you very much, Mr. Chatman, but I believe I'll leave it right where it is."

Jerry thanked the old lady and went back to his hotel in the Loop, where he tried to square the conflicts among the various stories. Had Mose been paying court to Hawk's mother before marrying Mattie, and was that how Hawk had met his first love? Or was Mose running around with Hawk's mother while actually married to Mattie at the time? Perhaps both were the case, or then again neither—maybe Hawk had just made up the story to excuse his own fooling around with Mose's wife and then over the years come to believe it. Or not believe it. Perhaps Hawk had confused his mother with Mattie, and Mose had really been trying to stop him from hanging around Mattie, or—each variation added new complications. Mose and Mattie and Hawk and Lavalle and their mother—he had a cast of characters. Now if he could only figure out what to do with them!

DR. CLARENCE LEWIS' MEDICINE SHOW

The medicine shows were an important part of the blues singer's educational process. Not only did they provide him with the opportunity for travel, they expanded his musical horizons as well and offered him the ideal forum to perfect his entertaining skills. The medicine shows were a rough apprenticeship. Working under the most primitive conditions, but for the most discriminating of audiences (the black audience, as any student of popular culture will know, has always been in the vanguard of popular taste), the singer's task was not only to put his song across but to sell his sponsor's patent medicine as well. Sometimes this gave rise to the most risible of situations (*rise/risible—delete one*), as prominent recording artists were drafted to deliver, and sometimes even to record, their sponsor's theme song as a commercial blues (Sonny Boy Williamson's "King Biscuit Stomp" is only the most prominent example). Quite naturally recording artists and vaudeville stars were preferred, though at the time the Screamin' Nighthawk first went on the road, the first so-called country blues had yet to be recorded. Mamie Smith's "Crazy Blues" was waxed in 1919 some time after Hawk seems to have joined Dr. Clarence Lewis' Traveling Caravan and Medicine Show. There are few surviving accounts, and so far as I know no one has ever interviewed white medicine-show operators themselves (though for a good account of a prior period and a parallel area of development, see Robert Toll's *Blacking Up*, Oxford University Press), so we must rely on subjective accounts by artists and audience alike to get some of the flavor of those heady days. Even without any real newspaper coverage, however, there was no difficulty in getting the word out when the show came to town, and of course many of the performers had strong local reputations. "They all knowed me around Yazoo City," says Hawk, for example. "Whenever we come into that town you can bet that everyone and his brother turn out." When he started with the medicine show, Hawk was still known in some quarters as Little Mose, despite his unfortunate falling-out with his mentor. By the time that he had served out his apprenticeship, he had a style and a repertoire of his own.

When Hawk returned home to Yola, however, around 1918 (*1915? earlier? later?*), his personal life was in disarray. The woman that he loved, Mattie Mae Turner, had abandoned him for the city (*plausible resolution?*), which had proved far from hospitable to a country boy "just off the farm," and Hawk came home in his works "a nervous wreck. Ol' Man Mose was fixing to light a firecracker under my ass. Mr. Holloway was just about ready to skin my hide, cause Mattie Mae was his best cook, raised up with his own chillen. Also I believe he kind of fancied her himself." (*Libelous?*) It is no wonder then that he seized the first opportunity that came along to leave home again, for there was nothing for Hawk at this time in his little home town. "Truthfully," he says today, "I didn't know what I got. Course a young man never does. You get to be old, you know, but you can't do nothing about it. . . ."

It is surprising how many shows of this sort actually came through all the little Mississippi hamlets at this time, but then it was the populace's principal form of entertainment. There was no radio, no television, there were for all practical purposes no phonographs (a decade would change that). Dr. Stokey, Dr. Benson, and Dr. C.E. Hankenson, in Gus Cannon's neat phrase, were the entertainment order of the day.

("Aww, Gus Cannon, that old yardbird, popping his gums all the time. We call him Mushmouth cause of the way he sing. Couldn't never understand why everybody making all this racket about Gus Cannon this, Gus Cannon that. I heard them records they cut on him when he was a old man, ain't no telling how old he actually was cause I hear tell from some that he actually go back to slavery time. But they cut him anyway. Him and his goddamn banjo. Couldn't play worth nothing then, and can't play nothing now, that's for damn sure. . . .")

Cannon, an inveterate follower of the medicine-show circuit, was, with Furry Lewis, Jim Jackson, Frank Stokes, and the white blues singer Jimmie Rodgers, among the most prominent recorded graduates of this circuit. The show that young T.R. Jefferson left town with Dr. Lewis' Traveling Caravan and Medicine Show.

Dr. Lewis, by all accounts, was an imposing silver-haired

gentleman from Muncie, Indiana, who every spring went out on the road first with his white minstrel show and then—because he would never trust any underling to oversee it himself—with his second-string "nigger entertainment." The "elixir" which he sold was worthless, of course, but to the poor whites and blacks who formed his twin audiences it was a relatively harmless nostrum which apparently served as a very effective diuretic and purgative. The troupe was a small one and traveled in a number of touring cars with an open flat-bed truck which doubled as equipment van and stage. There was a blues singer, a woman blues singer (Natchez Ma Rainey), a blackface comedian (Negro), a couple of dancers ("They was always high brown and pleasing-featured"), a comedian or two, and the impassive "Indian" who served as straight man and foil to the comedians and master of ceremonies.

Dr. Lewis sat in his private touring car with the shades all drawn until the entertainment was over, then Son Ford, a tapdancer-comedian who later recorded a few sides for the short-lived Bullet label, tapped tentatively on the window and Dr. Lewis capped his bottle of whiskey (apparently he was an inveterate drinker, though none of the entertainers can remember seeing him drunk), stretched out his long legs (he was as tall as six and a half feet according to the recollections of some, though Hawk says, "He wasn't no damn giant, like some of these people be saying"), and was introduced to the crowd, to heartfelt cheers, as "the kind gentleman who brought you this fine entertainment."

Members of the cast, including young T.R. Jefferson, then circulated among the audience, each with a case of the magic elixir, as the silver-haired doctor beamed down upon his "little brown brothers" and Peg Leg Markham, the debonair MC, later to become famous as a comedian on the chitlin circuit (though his cousin, Pigmeat, perhaps because he did not suffer the debilitating loss of limb which gave Peg Leg his rather common nickname, gained both the greater fame and greater reward, a source of unending sorrow to the less fortunate cousin), gave the pitch for the medicine, a combination of patter, toasts, and sly material hinting that the man or woman who drank this stuff would see an immeasurable improvement in sexual performance, if improvement was needed, and a sustaining success if success was already at hand.

By all accounts this pitch was extremely successful, so much so that occasionally the salesmen would run out of bottles of elixir and the good doctor would have to repair to his touring car to mix up a fresh batch with whatever materials were at hand. Sales were not hurt by the antics of the shills, some of whom were not altogether open about acknowledging their condition of employment. One man in the crowd, perhaps a friend of one of the entertainers with whom arrangements had been made beforehand, perhaps one of the roustabouts or entertainers themselves, might take a swig and simply let out a blood-curdling yell. Sometimes, according to reliable sources, a man or woman would throw away the crutches on which (s)he was supporting himself (*on which they were supporting themselves?*). Little Mose always had to remember to retrieve the crutches afterward. "That was just part of my job, man. You know, I didn't bring those crutches back, it got took out of my pay. What do you expect? Sometimes I think I want to ram them crutches up ol' Doc Lewis' ass."

At first Hawk only got to sing one or two songs, but soon he was fronting the show. He became quite a popular entertainer over the next few years, but, more important, he developed a style of his own.

I DIDN'T sign on as no singer. I sign on as a roustabout, jack of all work, do just about anything there is to do. Sometimes I be the one that swallow down that elixir, but them poor dumb country niggers never catch on. One time some farmer in overhauls say, Ain't that the same little booger just stood up there and sung that song so bad? Dr. Lewis step forward and he say, Sir, you are mistaken, I ain't never seen this little motherfucker before in my life, and besides that other little motherfucker is out there in my private car right now, where he is laying out a new suit of clothes, in case I perspire on this hot July day. Of course he didn't talk like that in public, out there in front of all them dumb old country clowns, he act just oh so dignified in his morning coat, with them tails that he got to pluck up before he sit down. But Daisy, she tell me—she one of the yellow-skin gals that dance around and shake their ass and just generally cut up—she say, Ooh-wee, you ought to hear that Doc Lewis when he get going, when he get all worked up and stuff, and he didn't need no medicine neither, cause he always was partial to the high yallers and teasin' browns.

Well, that man wasn't nothing but trouble. Said he was a doctor, but he wasn't no more doctor than I am. Come to find out, he done some time in Cummins for cutting some poor little gal up, he fix her so she wouldn't never grin no more cause she wouldn't do none of his specialties. Course he didn't think nothing of it cause she was just another yaller, but what he didn't know was she was a yaller the sheriff was plugging on the side. When he found out what the doc had done—course I didn't see none of this, this was before my time, understand—he say he gonna cut that peckerwood's balls off, he don't care what happen to him cause he love that little gal more dearly than he did his own wife. Anyways it didn't come to nothing, six months maybe —but we didn't never go to Arkansas neither, I noticed. Even so the little gals gathered around that bright-yellow car of his, they running their fingers on it, Ooh, Doc Lewis, I just want to feel the paint, ooh, Doc, you got such a nice finish on it, and everywhere we go, he take his pick, some of them no more than pickaninnies with their hair tied up in braids. Well, ol' Doc Lewis, he really like them little gals when they just starting to bud, just starting to get hair on them tight little cracks, sometimes he practically kidnapped them little gals out of them little small villages and towns, say, Boys, we got another dancer to go along. I surprised they didn't get him on no Mann Act, like they got to protect them young gals against mens just coming in and stealing them away from their mamas and daddies. But ol' Doc Lewis, he really know how to get his pole greased—so maybe the medicine do something for him after all.

Anyways I go along and go along, learn to stay away from Daisy and any of the other gals the doc lay his eyes on, come to pass in time I come to be the blues singer on the show. This is how it happen. Already had a blues singer when I joined up, name of Blind Arthur Bell, you probably never heard of him, cause he didn't make no records that I know about, he was too early for records, but he was a powerful singer, from Florida somewheres to begin with. And besides being such a powerful singer he could play the git-tar in any key that you care to hear, any way that you like. Sometimes he sing the old spiritual songs, make you want to cry, it make you feel so bad sometimes, when he sing about going home and someday all my troubles gonna pass and all such stuff as that. Sometimes the doc come out of his car, tell him don't sing no more of that shit, boy, cause you getting

everyone so downhearted and blue. He say, Goddammit, Blind
Arthur, you quit that racket, I gonna have to dismiss you if you
don't. You just cut out all this foolishness, cause you ruining
everybody's good times. Then Blind Arthur look at him, he wasn't
no blind man, of course, he may not have seed too good, but he
seen plenty of what was going on, and he say, Dr. Lewis, you
tend to your doctoring, and I'll just stick to my business as well.
Don't I always give you a good show? And he was right! He give
a good show all the time, sing that "Crazy Blues" and "Downhearted Blues" that was just coming out on the victrola, do his
minstrel stuff, you know, "Nigger and the white man playing
seven-up, nigger won the money, scared to pick it up," oh, the
colored love to hear all that kind of stuff.

But it were his stubbornness that done him in all the same.
One time the sheriff poking around for something to stick his
nose into, little old country sheriff, he gotta get his share, just
like everyone else, just like the policeman on his beat, and for
some reason ol' Doc Lewis ain't coming across, I don't know,
maybe he got something on the sheriff. But he poking around
for something, and he hit on Blind Arthur, say, That nigger ain't
blind. And the doc, he say, Oh yes, he is. You just fixing to deceive the people. Well, Arthur, he ain't gonna stand for that, so
he just say, Oh yassuh, I been blind from birth, and maybe you
want to see my certificate from blind school to prove it. Well, the
sheriff, he just a mean man, and he say, Well, sir, if this nigger's
blind, we're just gonna prove it. If he blind, ain't nothing going
to bother him. And he take this lighted torch, metal poker actually, and he bring it closer and closer. But Blind Arthur don't
never blink, just keep staring straight ahead. Until finally he
bring it so close that Blind Arthur don't have no chance but to
turn away or cry out. But Blind Arthur didn't never cry out, not

even when the poker went into his eye. So that's how Blind Arthur really become blind, and he didn't know naturally how to get along. So we had to leave him there in Senatobia. But that sheriff didn't never find out what he done to Blind Arthur, cause that nigger too contrary to give him the satisfaction.

That's how I come to be the blues singer on the show, wasn't no big deal like the books say. Didn't teach me nothing neither, except don't stick with a story too long. Sing a few songs, tell a few jokes, me and Chief Thunderbird, who wasn't no more Indian than I was myself, except he begun to believe it, wearing them feathers and shit all the time. Chief Thunderbird say to me: We been friends a long time, ain't we, Hawk? And I say to him: That's right, Chief. Friends to the end. And he say: How about lending me a dollar, man? And I say: That's the end. Been going on long enough now. All that kind of stuff. Simple country people, they couldn't never get enough. They could hear the same old jokes a hundred times over, and they still couldn't figure 'em out. Then I sing a song about the 'lixir.

Lewis lixir fix you right up
Lewis lixir, you drink it from the cup
Tell all your neighbors, tell all your friends
You drink it once, you'll drink it again.

Stupid-ass song. Yeah, I made it up. Then maybe I sing a blues—you know, "St. Louis Blues," "Yellow Dog Blues," "Mr. Crump Don't Like It," one of them old-time kind of songs—and then Dr. Lewis' girls come out to do a dance. They had a piano player play along, man who wore red suspenders, I can't call his name no more, I think he was a schoolteacher, just went out in the summertime—well, you see, that wasn't where I met Teenochie, but that was the kind of thing Teenochie do, play for the shake dancers, which is why I always call him a honky-tonk piano player, which for some reason he don't like—Teenochie always want to put on airs, that fool don't care to remember, you know what I'm talking about, when he the one that wear that derby on his head, snap them suspenders and pretend he don't notice nothing when them girls come over and hang all over him while he tickling them keys. Shee-it, them broads just shake their asses in your face, course you wouldn't even notice it now with the costumes they wear out in the streets, them little bitty skirts that don't even cover them up front or back, but back then it was really something! You can look, but you better not touch—cause they Dr. Lewis'.

JERRY FOUND IT ALL fairly difficult to believe, but what was he to do? He knew those were colorful times, violent times, it was a different world. And it was a world that was all but gone, vanished, disappeared. He had seen a medicine show once, a moth-eaten, woebegone sort of an affair owned by an Indian and featuring a peg-legged harmonica player who traded jokes with a suspicious-looking Chinaman, all the while pitching some kind of snake oil as an all-purpose cure for warts, fleas, worms, and crabs, not to mention its usefulness as a venereal charm. It had attracted a motley crowd, but even the few who were present were turning away in disbelief when the police came along to disperse the show. It wasn't anything like that, he knew. At least he didn't think it was.

He went back through some of the little country newspapers for advertisements and references. He tried to get a feel for the period, to imagine an era in which there was no television, no radio, no precise idea even of what was going on in the next town let alone halfway around the world. Hawk even had a picture, which for some inexplicable reason had survived all the moves and changes of circumstance and vagaries of a lifetime and showed the automobiles, the black comics in blackface, the doctor looking benign and paternal, and a young, slender Theodore Roosevelt Jefferson staring blankly into the camera. That was in fact the only thing that identified this visage from another age as Hawk, that unwavering, unsmiling, inscrutable stare. He stood there with his sleeves rolled up, galluses holding up sagging pants, the veins in his powerful forearms just barely showing in the faded photograph.

"What were you thinking when they took the picture?" said Jerry, trying a new tack.

"What was I thinking? I wasn't thinking nothing. I was thinking how many days to payday. I was thinking, I been hauled around by this phony-ass doctor too long—" He spat disgustedly. "How the fuck do I know what I was thinking?"

"Who took the pictures?" Jerry tried helplessly.

Hawk just stared at him.

There was no one else to turn to. Jerry found a few other survivors of the medicine shows, and they all had similar memories. The crowd. The pitch. The chorus girls. Parading through town to draw a crowd. Putting up a tent, if there was one. That didn't tell him anything he didn't know already. He tried to track down anyone who might have been with the Dr. Clarence Lewis Show. Dead. All dead, or disappeared. It must have been a traveling mortuary, he thought, almost beginning to doubt its very existence, though he had the clippings and the single photograph. Until he finally managed to locate a sister of Dr. Lewis, a Mrs. Hugh Pennington, in Elyria, Ohio. He spoke to her on the phone, and one time when Hawk was playing a gig at Oberlin he made it his business to seek her out. She lived in an old tree-lined section of town that probably hadn't changed since Booth Tarkington wrote *Penrod and Sam*. Screened-in porches. Fanned-out elms. A girl on a swing. Automobiles moving at a leisurely pace. All benign and complacent and impossibly inviting. Mrs. Pennington was an old lady with a long pinched face, rimless glasses, and thin white hair that straggled out from under a knitted bonnet. The maid showed him in to a dark, slipcovered parlor, and Mrs. Pennington pursed her lips with a soft smacking sound as she took his measure. Nothing seemed to escape her notice.

"Clarence was a friend to the colored," she said. "I don't know what it was. Very early in life he got the notion that he wanted to help his fellow man. Mother and Father would have liked it if he had gone into the ministry, but I suppose that's why he became a doctor."

"Was he, uh, a medical doctor?"

"Well, of course he was a medical doctor. What other kind is there? He attended the Oxford School of Osteopathy right out of high school. Clarence was always advanced for his years. But restless. He never married, you know. I could never understand it myself. I often asked him, 'Clarence, why don't you settle down, start a family, you aren't getting any younger, you know.' My late husband, Mr. Pennington, was a little older than Clarence, naturally, and he'd sit him down for heart-to-heart talks—man-to-man, I should say—well, Clarence would never disagree, he was too polite for that. But he would say, 'It wouldn't be fair to a wife, to a family.' He was a very scrupulous man. I suppose that's why he started up with his traveling. He wanted to do something for somebody, and then he came in possession of the elixir formula.

"He didn't invent it, you know. Oh, no. The way it came about, he noticed an old colored man who was familiar to all of us on sight taking a drink from a bottle one day—only it was not an ordinary whiskey bottle, not that sort of thing at all. So he went up to this man and said, 'Say, Bub'—Clarence would call everyone Bub, white and colored alike, it brings me back sometimes when I hear them use the word on television occasionally —'what's that you've got there?' The colored man offered him a drink, and just to be polite Clarence sipped a bit. 'Edith,' he told me afterwards, 'it was the damnedest sensation I ever felt in my life, excuse my language. It snapped my head back like I had been shot out of a cannon.' Naturally he inquired from the colored man just what the ingredients were, but that poor man didn't know. It was a home remedy that he made for himself, and as he said to Clarence, 'Sometimes it come out good; others I just don't know.'

"Clarence offered him five dollars for the bottle, but he wouldn't take but two. Then Clarence took it down to the lab to be chemically analyzed. Even they couldn't be certain of some of the ingredients. So Clarence began his experiments, he worked night and day—I've never seen a man so excited—until finally he thought he had duplicated the taste of that original home remedy. Not duplicated, really, improved. He left it to me, you know, the patent. Of course it's worthless since the government stepped in. There's too damn much government, if you ask me. But I attribute my good health to daily ingestion of Arthur's elixir—I'm ninety-two, you know, and I have a cellar full of the bottles, it never goes bad, you know. Would you like some?" She rang for the maid, who came back shortly with a brown stubby little bottle. "And yet I feel somehow as if I've let Clarence down. He wanted me to continue with the elixir. Those were practically his dying words. At least that's what I've heard were his dying words.

Clarence died on the road, you know, in 1959. I suppose that it was fated to be."

"Did you ever hear of a singer called Little Mose or the Screamin' Nighthawk?" Jerry said. "I think he performed on your brother's show."

The old lady squinted at him. "Oh my, no. I imagine you're referring to the colored show? That was where Clarence's heart really was, though I never understood why. In the end he sold the other—the white minstrel show—to a man named Claxton. I'm afraid I never saw either one. I may have been a bit of a snob, but I was always urging Clarence to put together a higher-class entertainment, something he could put on in Xenia. Like the circus. Oh my, I remember the excitement there used to be when the circus came to town. You don't get that kind of excitement anymore, I don't imagine. Everyone sitting in front of their own TV. Clarence wasn't interested. He said the colored should get a little pleasure in their lives, too. My brother was a saint. Some folks called him a nigger lover, you know—"

Jerry pondered that one for a while. He even thought to tell Hawk, just to see if Hawk would get a laugh out of it. But for all he knew, it would just prompt Hawk to embark upon a new explosion of stories that were both unusable and unverifiable.

He made one more attempt. He found a woman who remembered Blind Arthur Bell. She had a cousin who thought she remembered Blind Arthur's daughter had moved to Buffalo or somewhere like that. "Last I seen of her, she had married a man name of Walter Jackson, I think it was. Something like that. Leastaways they said they was going to get married and move to Buffalo or maybe Baltimore. That was her second husband, poor child, her first got tore up in the saw mill."

It wasn't much, but it was something. Jerry looked up the name in the phonebook when he got to Cleveland. He tried every permutation he could think of. Finally he found a W. L. Jaxon, tried the number, and got a suspicious-sounding voice at the other end of the line.

"What you want with him for?" Jerry gave the reason. "Well, he dead. He been dead these four years."

"I wonder if I might speak to his widow, Mrs. Jaxon?"

"Yeah?"

"Could I speak to her?"

"This is her."

Jerry explained what he was calling about.

"You got money from my daddy?" said the woman. "Am I gonna get money from my daddy?"

"Well, no—" Jerry explained that basically all he wanted was a little information. Was her father always blind? There was a cold pause at the other end. "Of course my daddy blind. What you think they call him Blind Arthur for?"

"No, but I mean, was he born blind, was he always blind, as far as you know?"

"He blind from the day he come into this world." There was the sound of the phone slamming down. Jerry scratched his beard. What would a sheriff be doing with a red-hot poker in the middle of July anyway?

MAKING RECORDS

The Screamin' Nighthawk was recorded again on November 27, 1936, after the famous Paramount dates. He was in his early thirties, and while it might seem that his career had gone nowhere up to this time, his style was by now fully formed. He recorded in a hotel room "someplace in the Texas panhandle," he remembers, and the dates of the session coincide with the end of Robert Johnson's first landmark recording date in San Antonio. When pressed on the matter, Hawk professes to remember virtually nothing about the near-legendary Johnson. "I heard tell about him. They say he died of the black arts, down on his knees and barking like a dog. Of course I don't believe none of that shit."

It is in any case a rather common, if fanciful, tale, and Hawk's uncharacteristic memory lapse may very well stem from a kind of professional jealousy. "Robert Johnson, Robert Johnson, everybody woofing about Robert Johnson," Hawk will mutter on occasion. Many times I have seen him confronted with the supposed similarity between his own "Hellhound on My Trail" and Johnson's. Did he get the song from the great King of the Delta Blues Singers? eager students will inquire. Did he know Johnson personally? His response to this sort of question is to turn the tables on the questioner. "How you know Robert Johnson didn't get it from me? Was you there, boy?" He was, of course, considerably older than Johnson, the heir to a very similar tradition, so perhaps he has a point. It is indeed possible that Nighthawk preceded Johnson, as we have found in so many parallel cases where the better-known bluesman is in fact carrying on the more obscure artist's style (Blind Boy Fuller, for example, who took many of his most characteristic licks from Willie Walker and Reverend Gary Davis). Whatever the case, they were, of course, very diffe·ent bluesmen.

How he came to record at all at this point has been a matter of some conjecture. According to Hawk, "I was just traveling through Texas. Passing through, you understand, had a little trouble with them Moore boys [these would appear to be the famous Moore brothers, of whom Lightnin' Hopkins has sung so bitingly], spent a little time down in Huntsville, well it wasn't actually Huntsville, they give me over to a farmer, we did chores and such, didn't wear no ball and chain. That was where I met this fellow, Texas Alexander, had a great big voice, but he couldn't play a lick. Well, he was in, don't know how long he was in for, but he tole me to go up to San Antone—them Mexicans love to hear the blues, he said. So I done what he told me, least I was heading in that direction, when I run into the man from the Vocalion Record Company, Ernie. He say, Hey, boy, I been looking all over for you. I say, You have? Well, I been here the whole time. I say, Why didn't you let me know you was looking for me, bo, you shoulda just sent out an invitation. Just joking around, you know, but he was a big broad-shouldered man, and them shoulders start to shake, and he say, I can tell I'm gonna like you already, boy. Then he take me to this hotel room, big room, high ceiling, they hung blankets from the wall to deaden the sound, set up the microphone away from the window so you wouldn't hear no traffic noise. Man just sit there with his earphones on his ears, wasn't behind no glass wall like they do nowadays, and he say, You ready? Well, I didn't waste no time, didn't waste none of that man's money neither, I just cut loose, wasn't no second takes, just did it right off the top of my head. Cause they was all tunes I was familiar with, they was the songs I was known for, you might say. Got seventy-five dollars a side, six sides, I believe, and the man promise me more if the records actually sell. I be in touch, he say to me. We gonna make some more of these wham-bam records some day. She-it, I thought I was really going places then, but I ain't heard from that man to this day. Reckon the records didn't sell, maybe a car run him over, shoot, I don't know. But the next man talk to me about making records was Mr. Melrose from Chicago, and that was a whole different story."

The records which he cut that day remain classics of the genre, the cornerstone on which the Screamin' Nighthawk's reputation is firmly based. "Screamin' Nighthawk Blues." "Loving You All the Time." "President Roosevelt Help the Poor." "Travelin' This Old Highway All the Years of My Life (Highway Blues)." "What's the Matter with This World (We in a Terrible Mess)." Just Hawk and his guitar, each number featuring shimmering bottleneck playing, each number without question identifiably part of the Mississippi tradition but also demonstrably original and rich in associations.

It's hard to say why this session, too, turned out to be something of a dead end. Certainly Hawk was one of the most talented blues singers of his generation. He was also, it was swiftly becoming apparent, one of the most *determined,* a fact which is borne out not only by the number of recordings he was able to make over the years but the number of different *connections* he made solely on the basis of his own persistence. It is scarcely ironic, for example, that the Screamin' Nighthawk should still have been looking for a recording contract in the early 1960s, peddling worn demos and battered testimonials from office to office while a host of folklorists were anxiously seeking for any clue to his existence. (*Surely a little exaggerated?*)

And yet the records didn't sell, the $450 which he received for the recording session was soon gone ("My mama was having a terrible time at home, and the little girls was pestering at me all the time, so that money just burned right out"), and the Vocalion representative for whatever reason (for all we know he was never able to locate the peripatetic Hawk again) never fulfilled his promise to be in touch. Perhaps it was simply that this kind of primitive musical style was an anachronism by now, a thing of the past. Like Bukka White's celebrated 1940 sessions (also for Vocalion), Hawk's recordings may well have represented one last fling in the grand manner. Certainly Hawk's heavy voice and ringing bottleneck guitar were reminiscent of an earlier era, at a time when people generally were looking for a lighter, more "swinging" sound (this is perhaps the principal distinction between Robert Johnson's "Hellhound" on which Johnson sang in a pinched, clear, slightly nasal tone, while Hawk boomed out the same message in his characteristically chesty bass—there was no existential hesitation or compromise in that voice). In addition, Hawk may well have been difficult to record. Contrary to his own claims, according to the Vocalion logbook of the time, every song in fact required at least five or six takes, sometimes more. Having been present at many subsequent Screamin' Nighthawk sessions (I am, of course, speaking of the Screamin' Nighthawk of the '6os and '7os), I can safely say that Hawk is indeed a perfectionist when it comes to recording, but on the other hand I have never seen him require more than one or two takes on any one song. Indeed he sometimes will flatly refuse to repeat himself, unless he receives extra payment for his effort. Perhaps this original session is the genesis for that attitude. It would appear that this is one of those vexed questions, the answer to which we shall never know.

(*Skip Lester Melrose Chicago sessions for time being.*)

The next time he would record was for the Library of

Congress in 1942. The war was on, and Hawk, nearly forty now, was working as a tractor driver at the time. ("Practically living in bondage, man, we wasn't no better than the beasts of the field. They wouldn't let us off the farm for nothing. Mr. Holloway, he was fit to be tied when he found out I'd gone and enlisted. Tried to get it reversed, but he couldn't, cause I'd already filled out my questionnary. Y'see, it was just a racket to them, keep colored down on the farm. They didn't pay us nothing, said it was necessary for the war effort. Necessary, shit. It wasn't necessary for old man Holloway to cut his patriotic profits. And we was raising peanuts then, man. Peanuts!") When John Fairchild, a tall, bespectacled and distinguished-looking man with a bowler hat and a British accent, came into the Delta seeking to preserve yet another endangered species in the unsullied Afro-American tradition (*Plant? Animal? African violet?*), the purebred Mississippi blues. Fairchild, who retains the slightly aristocratic air of the Shropshire countryside where he grew up, remembered the occasion well when he included a long pseudonymous account in his landmark of field research, *Roots and Branches: On the Trail of the Vanishing Folk Song.*

"We had been in the area for some time, recording harmonica players, colorful folk preachers who chanted out their 'sermons' to the equally vivid response of an aroused congregation, string bands, work gangs, and the like, when word came to us that there was in the vicinity a commercial blues singer whose name and legend were on the tip of every ethnomusicologist's tongue. It was difficult to believe for, so far as we knew, the Rootin' Groundhog, as I shall call him here (the name, like all others in this volume, has been changed to protect certain confidentialities), had vanished, been "done in" or poisoned by a jealous woman after his last Chicago recording sessions. It had even been speculated by many otherwise well-informed sources that the Rootin' Groundhog was merely another name variant for the even more mysterious Robert Johnson, who, it was theorized, wishing to disappear and escape his doomed legacy, had roughened his voice, taken on another name, even duplicated his own recordings—though in an altogether different style—all to no avail. For we knew, of course, that Johnson was dead, a fact which had hideously assaulted us over and over again in the pursuit of our current field research. So it was with great trepidation that we approached a burly-looking man in overalls and straw hat, momentarily 'taking a breather' behind old Bessie at the plow, an altogether imposing and slightly menacing figure who was obviously displeased to be 'caught napping.' He eyed us as we approached him across the furrowed rows. 'I understand that you gentlemens are looking for a blues singer,' he said with simplicity."

THAT MAN couldn't tell the truth plain if it jumped out and squatted on his face (*Hawk grumbled*). I was driving a tractor, not no doggone mule. Little colored fellow name of Perdue in spats and a derby hat come walking out across that field, getting his feet all covered with shit. Mr. Fairchild, he sit in the car. 1941 Olds, it was. Bright yellow. I never will forget that car. Perdue I never did like, he was a sneaky little devil, going around all the time with his mouth poked out, looking like some kind of a golliwog. And, see, he was connected up with Mr. Fairchild. Got him some kind of a bounty for every nigger he brung in. See, he'd been to a year or two of college at that time, and he was already putting on airs, I believe he a professor at one of them

Northern schools today. Well, he'd talked to me several times already about making some records for Mr. Fairchild, but I told him I didn't want to have nothing to do with it. I knowed you didn't get nothing for it. Nothing but a bottle of corn whiskey and a chance to be remembered, that little weasel Perdue say to me. Remembered, shit; let 'em forget, I just wants my money, I told Perdue. Anyways he stand there jabbering away, and I didn't hear nothing about it, cause I can't hear a word that fool be saying, with the tractor running and all. And finally he reach over and cut the engine. And I say, What you do that for? Because, you see, that tractor wasn't no easy thing to start up again, it as *stubborn* as a mule. And he say, I been telling you, nigger, Mr. Fairchild want to speak to you, cause he could get down just like the rest of them when he loosen his little tie. Say, Listen here, you pig-ass motherfucker, Mr. Calloway gonna give you the afternoon off if you cooperates, and I ain't gonna tell you what he gonna do if you don't. Well, somehow that Mr. Fairchild must've got on the good side of old Calloway, though I don't know as he had a good side, truthfully speaking, and I should've knowed that. But anyways I goes over to the car, and Mr. Fairchild just sitting there just as pretty as you please—he was what we called a pretty boy back in them days, all dolled up and neat as a pin, talked funny, too, with one of them funny accents—naw, I don't just mean he from across the water, tell you the truth, I always wondered what him and Perdue was up to, cause that Perdue, he do anything to get ahead. So he sitting there, and he say, I understand you are a *blues* singer. Well, that seem like a pretty dumb thing to say. We all *knows* I'm a blues singer, otherwise what the fuck is he doing here in the first place? And he say, I have recorded Mayfield Brown and I have recorded Little Eddie Simson. And Sugar Bear Wylie. And I making a complete record of the Mississippi Delta blues. And if you don't record for me, we just gonna wipe your name off the history book.

Well, that didn't make much of a stir with me. And I believe he knowed that. And Perdue, he knowed that. Professor—he always used to refer to hisself as Professor. Even when he was a little kid, it was Professor do this and Professor do that, like he was some kind of visitor from outer space or something. Only ones that liked him was white folks, and I think that was because he talk so much all the time, they don't know how rat-ass sneaky that little squealer could be. Anyways, he whisper something to this Fairchild and Fairchild, he nod, and Perdue say, Not only have Mr. Fairchild gotten Mr. Calloway to agree to let you have the rest of the day off, but he has generously agreed to pay you for it, too. Like I was supposed to fall down and drop dead or something, for the two dollars wartime wages we was getting paid.

Mushmouth smile. I don't say nothing. Furthermore, Mr. Fairchild have agreed to pay you eight dollars besides, he go on, which is more than he have paid to any other nigger, he say under his breath. Still I don't say nothing. And Mushmouth whisper in Fairchild's ear, and then he nod again and say like he coming up with their final offer, And Mr. Calloway have agreed besides to give you an extra day off, with pay, to recover from the *hard work* of recording. He say it real sarcastic-like, and then he add like as if I still don't understand, The recording don't take but a few hours if you cooperates. That mean you got another forty-eight to carouse or have yourself a ball or even go into Jackson when the stores and places of business are open.

You see, he knowed I wanted to enlist, that had been in my mind ever since I go back on the farm with that old redneck Calloway. And, see, I could never get to the recruiting station when they was open, cause we was working six days a week, no time off except Sundays. And Calloway, that scalawag, practically keeps us in bondage. So that done it, I say, Yes, suh, Mr. Fairchild, I plays you whatsoever you want to hear. . . .

The titles which he recorded that day were somewhat uncharacteristic of the generally known repertoire of the Screamin' Nighthawk. For the most part they were not the conventional blues fare but topical blues, and patriotic numbers, both original and familiar ("Yankee Doodle Dandy" is just one of the unlikely titles that come to mind). There were in addition a multitude of recollections, most, I'm sorry to say, undoubtedly apocryphal, reprises of old unrecorded pre-blues numbers, and even one solo excursion on mouth harp. Although one suspects that this material had to be coaxed from Hawk (*dragged out of him, might be the better description*), it is nonetheless of invaluable documentary importance (and John Fairchild deserves our undying gratitude and praise for his singular pioneering efforts) both for the light it sheds on Hawk's fertile creative process and for the wealth of allusive material it clearly shows to have been at the blues singer's beck and call. . . .

THIS WAS WHERE JERRY broke off. That was the end of the ill-fated attempt at biography. Three chapters begun, all sunk in a bottomless morass of indifferent memory and provocative tale-telling. He was no longer able (if he ever had been) to separate the wheat from the chaff; he despaired of ever making a coherent progression out of what was obviously a trackless waste. It was the music, after all, that was going to preserve Hawk's reputation, Jerry decided; his life would just have to be given up as a bad business.

VI

MOON
GOIN' DOWN

THEY WERE JUST finishing up supper when Hawk came in, leaning heavily on his stick and still seemingly lurching to one side.
"Aww, no, Hawk," said Mattie, half rising, but Hawk dismissed
her with a wave of his hand. "Feel pretty good," he said, sinking
into the heavy padded chair that he reserved for himself. "Need
a change of scene." With that he lapsed into a glowering silence,
as the TV blared, the baby dozed in front of it, and Lori continued to regale them with tales of hoodoo and New Orleans.
Jerry watched her carefully for signs, he distrusted what she was
getting herself into, but she seemed neither high nor desperate,
her nose wasn't running and her eyes were burning no more or
less brightly than ever, so he began to dismiss some of the stories
he had heard or imagined—for the time being.

"I used to know a feller played boogie-woogie piano in all the
best sporting houses in town," said Hawk. "This fella so smart

they call him Dr. Rhythm, cause what he was playing wasn't even in most people's *minds*. He could rock the joint, and he could speak three languages, too—English, French, and I think a little guinea Spanish, and in the summer when it get too hot for him he go up to Canada or maybe New England to take his vacation. Man, he was something to listen to, there ain't nobody like that no more. Sometimes late at night he get to playing classical, you know Chopin or Lieberstram, all that kind of junk. The girls that wasn't occupied, they just come out and listen, and everything get real quiet-like and nobody say a word. Then he stomp right into a boogie-woogie, cause nobody likes it when the girls gets all quiet and ain't full of fun, it ain't good for *business*. But that boy could play. Never did hear what happen to him. He travel up and down that Gulf Coast, and people knowed him near and far, even down to Cuba, they probably dig him because they was half-breeds, too—you know what I mean, too dark to go in the front door but too proud to go around the back."

"Hush, Roosevelt," said Mattie. "You sure you don't want nothing to eat?"

Hawk shook his head. "Just water." He held the glass steady in his right hand, Jerry noticed, but his fingers closed around it only with some difficulty. Jerry glanced over at the children. Only Little Bo was still awake, and he was watching his father, not the television. "Well, you know it's good to be just sitting around talking again," he said to Lori. "It's been too long, baby."

"Well, it sure is in my mind, it's just this bug here keeps me working all the time, and when I'm not working I'm recording, and when I'm not recording I just feel like I've got to get away from everything and everyone, from *him* mostly," she said laughingly, indicating Jerry. "Man, you know when I went into this business, that's just what I didn't want it to become—a business.

I thought I'd play when I wanted to and where I wanted to and only when I felt like I wanted to. But I found out that to do that you've really got to pay your dues, and by the time you finish paying, it may be that you don't want what you set out to buy in the first place."

"Ain't it the truth, baby?"

"But that isn't the way it is with you, Hawk—"

Hawk didn't say anything, just nodded his head.

"Hey, it hasn't been so bad, has it?" said Jerry, feeling a little guilty. He always agonized over Lori's bookings, sometimes he felt as if he treated her *too* circumspectly, but then, he reflected, he wasn't the one who had to go out there and deliver.

"Hush up, let the child eat," said Mattie.

"You know, sometimes I feel like a whore. No, I really do. To go out there in front of all those people and have them expect something of me that I'm supposed to give every night, even when I don't feel like giving. And then, you know, you have to fake it. Or you get stoned just to pretend it isn't there. Do you know what I mean?" She turned imploringly to Hawk.

"Sure, honey, sure I know what you mean. But that's why you got to always sing what's in your heart. That way, you don't have no problem choosing. You feel evil, you *sings* evil. You feel good, why that's the way it come across. You can't go making no distinctions between you and your music. You sing what's in you, and it can't be wrong, cause it's in you for a purpose."

"You really believe that, don't you?"

"Leave that child alone, can't you?"

"I better. It's what's carried me through my whole life."

IT STARTING ALREADY. They treating me like I'm sick, like I'm a old man. Well, they ain't far wrong. Just an old man, don't

216

bother no one, speak when spoken to, thinking his thoughts, that's about it. Half them thoughts about things that happen fifty years ago when we was kids and old folks clucking and shaking their heads at us, preacher shouting from the pulpit, saying, Won't they ever learn, Lord? Naw, they won't never learn. How can you learn a little kid to act like a old man? Just like you can't teach nothing to an old man neither. His body tell him he done for. His mind tell him, Slow down. But his spirit say, Shut up, fool, I gonna get it one more time. Young people can't understand, they take one look at you and they *know* you past it. Just like I knowed Ol' Man Mose had his day and his day was past and gone. But he didn't know that, how was his spirit just gonna lay down and die? Young fella ask me, I believe it was this very one, say, Don't you have no regrets? Well, I think about that one. Regrets? I regret that I didn't do better. And I regrets that my mama couldn't see me when I sang for the queen. But ain't you glad that you been discovered by all these nice young white peoples? Well, to tell you the truth, if they was going to discover me, I just wish they could've done it when I was younger and could put out more. I didn't never get tired then, the ideas just come so fast they just all jumble up together. Not like now, when they come stumbling along, seem like they gonna trip up before they even gets to me. Shit, I ain't grateful, if that's what you mean, but it don't matter anyhow. Act nice, don't say nothing to nobody—shit, don't none of it matter, a man's just got to be treated with respect. They don't know, they look like they about to bust out crying, but I surprise 'em all yet. I ain't nothing if I ain't Hawk. . . .

AFTER the dishes were done they joined him on the screened-in porch, watching as he puffed on a barely lit cigar, the glow winking and dying out again in the deep country darkness. The house next door, a modified trailer up on blocks, showed no light, inside there was only the dull glow of the television set. There were no streetlights, and no car passed. Hawk drew reflectively on the foul-smelling cigar. "You got any more bookings for me?" he said at last.

Jerry shook his head. "Well, you know that was the last. Kurt's talking about another European tour, and I'm sure we can pick up some other gigs as soon as you're feeling better."

"Feeling better? I'm feeling better already," Hawk boomed almost convincingly.

There was a light knock at the screen door. A skinny-looking old man in a puffed-up cap poked his head in. "Hey there," said Hawk with a gracious little wave, as the man hesitated in the doorway. "Get the door shut before the whole woods is in here with us. Thought you was dead a long time ago."

"Can't. Can't kill me," said the old bald-headed man, sweeping off his cap as he slithered past, nodding deferentially to Jerry. "How you being, anyhow? I heared Doc Bontemps, Will LeBow's boy, was out to see you this afternoon."

"Just getting old, is all. His daddy be proud of him now. All that nigger want is for his boy to get educated, but for hisself he ain't learned a damned thing."

The two old men cackled. "I hear you lost Lottie." Cap nodded. "Still living back out in the woods in that old cabin all by yourself?"

"Me and Blue. Blue getting old, too. Can't see good no more. You remember when Blue could outrun any hound in the county, man he used to lead the rabbit he just so joyous to get out, run circles around them little bunnies like he was just frolicking. Now he just like the rest of us, don't see nothing, don't hear nothing, and he smell bad most all the time."

"He miss Lottie."

"Yeah, he miss Lottie. I declare that's a fact. Sometimes I think he miss her more than I do, get to sniffing around wondering when she gonna come back, and I tell him, Too bad, old fellow, ain't never gonna happen in this world. She was a good old girl. Got carried off by the lard. Doctor told her she eat too much of the fatty stuff, gonna choke off her blood supply, and that's what it did. One night she wake in the early-morning hours, she didn't hardly make a sound, just put her hand to her throat like as if she was choking. Couldn't say nothing." He shook his head. "Heart stopped."

"You still moonshining?"

"Doing better than ever," Cap said proudly. "Some fool done complained to the county, sheriff come up and he bust up my old still. I give him a few bottles, and he don't say nothing, just take a ax to that old broken-down thing we give up on fifteen years ago, said, There, I guess we got 'em, don't we, Cap? I say, Yassuh, captain, you sho did, you jes' put ol' Cap right out of business. He always treated me fair, that boy. Some folks say they don't like him, but I say you always know where you stand with him."

"That's right. Not like some of these young fellers. Ain't nothing worse than a jealous nigger, I don't care what you say. I'd rather have a white man's prejudice any day of the week."

"Young nig-groes always fixing to stir up trouble. Now they want to bus the kids to school, take 'em across the highway, plunk 'em in with all these damned peckerwoods, stir up I don't know what all kind of mess—"

"Surely they're not just trying to stir up trouble," said Jerry, sorry he had said anything almost before the words were out of his mouth.

Cap's eyes flashed on him. "Ain't nothing else *but* trouble," he said. "White folks against niggers. Niggers against niggers," he muttered mysteriously.

"That's right," said Hawk.

"But in the end it'll be better, won't it?" said Lori.

"Ain't none of us gonna be around for the end. Less'n they hurry it."

"But your children—"

"My children be better off if they just leave us damn well alone."

Lori didn't say anything more, and Jerry kept his mouth shut.

"You hear who's come back home?" the old man said to Hawk.

"Who?"

"Little Mose."

"Little Mose!" Hawk rumbled. "He dead."

"Naw, not him. His *boy*, that didn't never know his daddy. He getting along about thirty-two, thirty now. His mama took him up to Chicago when he was just a kid, said when he come back he gonna be big-time. He go by the name of Edwards, he taken his mother's name." Hawk nodded. "You know, they say sometimes it skips. His daddy was a worthless fool, couldn't play for nothing neither, about the only way he put peoples in mind of Ol' Man Mose was the way he drunk himself to death, just like his daddy, only quicker. But they say this boy got records out, he come back in a brand-new 88, with a long coat, fox-fur collar, and his hair all nappy like he was some kind of overgrown pickaninny. He playing down at the Sunset tonight, at least that's what they say."

"Hunh," said Hawk indifferently.

"You been down there yet? Cats been asking about you. Wondering when you coming back from Europe or California or wherever you all been."

"Ain't been nowhere, ain't gonna play no more of these gigs that don't pay no money, ain't that right? That boy there gonna see to that."

Cap looked at Jerry suspiciously. Jerry inwardly shrugged; it was just one more thinly veiled insult to ignore. "Well, I better be going now," said the old man apologetically. "I just stop by to say hello."

"Hunh," said Hawk again. "Just don't you never say goodbye."

They tried to stop him when he said he was going down to the cafe, just to look around. "Look, why don't you just wait a few days?" Jerry said, thinking of his grandfather, who had died in a snowstorm when no one had been able to talk him out of leaving the house for Symphony.

"It's late," said Lori. "Let me go down to the cafe and talk to Little Mose, see if he'll be around for a few days, he'll probably want to come back here and see you—"

"Aww, Hawk," remonstrated Mattie. "You heard what that doctor boy said. Don't you think he know what he talking about? He say you should be in bed. It ain't right, Roosevelt," she said, putting a restraining hand on his shoulder.

He sat there staring straight ahead, seemingly too weak to

shake her off. At last she took her hand from him with a helpless shrug, and Hawk struggled to his feet. "Don't you think I know nothing?" he rumbled.

Mattie was practically in tears.

"Why not wait a few days?" Lori said. "Take it easy, rest up, get your strength back?"

But Hawk shook his head and reached for his big broad-brimmed hat. "Ain't nobody going with me?" he said.

Down at the Sunset the evening was already well under way. The dancers were energetically working out, while the band (guitar, bass, drums, sax, and keyboards, with another guitar propped up on the crowded stand) was playing something that sounded like "Cool Jerk." The Sunset had prospered since Jerry first came to Yola. It had added on a whole new wing in imitation knotty pine for entertainment, the parking lot (which had scarcely existed ten years ago) was paved and boasted a wooden sign announcing "Entertainment Tonite" with "Moses Edward" scrawled out on a piece of cardboard tacked up underneath. The Budweiser clock on the wall now illuminated a small stage and dance floor with a younger, better-dressed class of clientele. Even the old wing with jukebox, bar, and potbellied stove seemed somehow transformed by the tinsel decorations left over from someone's birthday celebration perhaps, and Jerry was not sure he recognized anyone from the days when he thought Hawk had a proprietary interest in the place.

Hawk nodded to one or two older couples, Cap came over to their table to say that he was just leaving, Mattie and Lori excused themselves, and Jerry struggled to get his bearings. On stage the band ran through an assortment of ten-year-old soul instrumentals ("Soul Serenade," "Soul Twist," "Green Onions," "The Stumble") and up-to-the-minute funk. They were dressed in matching outfits with short jackets of sequined blue and occasionally glanced at the scuffed music stands monogrammed SB but more often scanned the crowd for diversions. A waitress came over for their order, and Jerry paid for it, getting a Coke for Scooter, while Hawk was still fumbling in his pocket.

"Which one of them's Little Mose?" said Hawk angrily in a voice that cut through all the noise and clatter.

"I don't think he's on yet," said Jerry at precisely the moment that the bass player took the mike, while the band vamped in the background, and announced:

"And now, direct from Chicago, the man you've all been waiting to hear, he'll Cry a Tear For You, Won't Let Go Till It's Gone, he'll Love You Hard and still leave you Screaming for More. The man who don't want no Spiders in His Stew, you don't look out he'll Follow You to the Ends of Time, he's an Easy Lover, don't never Leave No Trace. So let's put your hands together, ladies and gentlemen, and give a nice home-town welcome to the Master of the Stratocaster, the Crown Prince of Gen-u-ine Funk, the Señor from South America—what's that? Oh, you'll have to excuse me, I thought Mississippi *was* South America. Let's have a warm welcome for one of the few good things that come out of Yola, Mississippi—and he come a long way, baby, Moses Edwards, Little Mose and the Bros."

The crowd laughed and applauded good-naturedly as a small dapper man with a close-cropped Afro and tight-fitting blue jumpsuit bounded up to the stage and without so much as a moment's pause stamped his feet, let out a little scream, and launched into a fast-paced, no-holds-barred version of "Try a Little Tenderness." By the middle of the song Little Mose's face was bathed in sweat, he loosened one button, then another of his snug suit until his chest was bare and glistening, then he unscrewed the mike from its stand, tiptoeing forward in little steps to the edge of the stage, striding back and forth like a proud bantam.

It was all pretty standard, Jerry thought, as Little Mose segued into "In the Midnight Hour"—the band, the showmanship, the entertainer's calculation—but he had the crowd in the palm of his hand, as they answered his "Good Gods!" and "Tell the truths" with their own "That's right," "I hear you," and "Tell me about it." "Have mercies" with their own deep-throated murmurs of assent.

He supposed the singer must be in his mid-thirties, though it was hard to tell from the smooth-skinned, light-brown face, the squint of his close-set eyes, and the sardonic, slightly amused cast to the features, which effectively distanced performer from performance, making it impossible to gauge just what were the singer's own emotions. The next song evidently was one of his own, to which he applied the full treatment, falling to his knees, grasping at the hand of a lady in the front row, milking his audience for everything it was worth.

"He's not bad, is he?" said Lori. "You ever hear of him before?"

Jerry shook his head and signaled to the waitress for more drinks. His face was bathed in perspiration, as if he were the one who was getting the workout.

"I guess he must be on some little Chicago label?" said Lori. "You think Hawk knew about him?"

Jerry shook his head again. He was watching Hawk, who was staring intently at the stage, never taking his eyes off the singer—what was he seeing? Jerry wondered. Was it Ol' Man Mose he saw, reliving memory, or did he see something altogether different through artist's eyes?

Hawk caught him looking. "What you think of all this foolishness?" that big voice boomed out. "All this jumping around and carrying on and all that shit. Seem like just a lot of jive to me. Course I don't know."

"Kind of loud," said Lori, shouting into Hawk's ear.

Hawk grunted, as Little Mose screamed and launched into an impassioned version of "I Feel Good." "Too much noise," Hawk pronounced. "Course I don't mind, but that's where he making his mistake." He poked Scooter in the ribs. "See, out in the country we used to listen to the crickets, think they was making some kind of song. Once you get used to this kind of racket, you ain't never gonna hear them crickets no more."

Scooter nodded, and Jerry gulped down his drink. He supposed maybe it was true. Hawk wasn't talking about hearing loss, he was talking about something else. And yet he had himself amplified his guitar so he could be heard above the din in the joints where he played. Lori touched his elbow, as if to say go easy, but tonight he really didn't care, he didn't give a shit if he got drunk or not. He signaled for more.

"Hey look," he heard Hawk's voice boom out, "that gal ain't wearing no underdrawers." Jerry looked disbelievingly in the direction that Hawk was pointing, and sure enough there was a young girl in a saffron-colored dress scrunched down on the floor and wearing no underpants at all.

He looked away embarrassed and caught Lori looking at him and reddened. "I'm not wearing any underdrawers either," he thought she whispered in his ear, but it was hard to hear and besides she was wearing jeans.

An old man with spiky white hair came over and asked Mattie to dance. She smiled and got up, placing her hand decorously on his shoulder, but by the time she got out on the floor she was shaking her ass in his face and doing the bump just like anyone else. Jerry had scarcely had time to adjust to that when a mountainous woman with a black Medusa wig piled high on top of her head came over and asked if he would like to dance.

"Oh, no, really," he said demurely, thinking if she ever sat on him he would be crushed.

"Oh, come on," said Lori.

"Sure. Come on, sugar," said the woman in a small, sweet voice. "You know, you only live once!"

Jerry was still shaking his head as Lori pushed him up from the table, and before he knew it he was out on the dance floor himself, carrying himself stiffly in response to the fat woman's graceful swoops and dips. "My name's Claudia," said his partner.

"Jerry," he said, intoxicated with her graceful movements, the smell of the dance floor, and the blue haze of cigarette smoke.

"Well, gotta get back to work, Jerry," she said at the end of the number, jingling the waitress' change apron that he had failed to notice earlier.

"You want to dance?" he said to Lori.

Little Mose was singing "Here I Am (Come and Take Me)," and Lori folded herself into his arms. He sniffed her hair —he could have gulped her down. "You know, I forget sometimes—" he started to say.

"You forget a lot. You know, you're drunk."

"No, I mean, I forget how much fun—"

"You think Hawk's gonna be all right?"

"Hawk? No, I mean you and me—"

"You think he's going to be all right?"

When they got back to the table, Hawk was remonstrating with Mattie about something. "Now the boy don't have to go home. His sister can take care of the baby." Mattie started to get up from her seat, and Hawk put his hand on her shoulder.

"I don't want to hear no more of that," he said angrily.

Scooter asked if he could have another Coke, and Jerry gulped down his own drink, so he could join him.

"I never knowed that boy to be such a serious drinker," said Hawk to Lori, eyeing Jerry with surprise.

The singer was doing another one of his originals, a kind of disco ballad with a long spoken rap that concluded, "Be true to your dream, or your dream won't be true to you." Jerry snorted. He had never heard such shit before in his life. How was your *dream* going to betray you? Be true to your dream, and your dream will be true to you? He laughed out loud and turned to Hawk, but Hawk was preoccupied with a bunch of people who had come over to say hello. He turned to Lori to see if she might like to dance again, but she was dancing with the same woolly-headed old man who had been dancing with Mattie before. Like himself, Jerry noticed with some triumph, she was tight and con-stricted in her movements, for all her apparent spontaneity she seemed stiff and self-conscious in her response to the old man's lithe and courtly steps. They said you could tell a lot about a girl from the way she danced. They said you could tell how a girl fucked from the way she danced.

"What do you think?" he said to Little Bo.

"It's kind of old-fashioned," said Scooter shortly.

"Hunh!" laughed Hawk.

The rising level of conversation, the clink of glasses and bustling clatter of tables being cleared, pretty girls lifting up their arms in celebration of—*nothing*—

Jerry wanted to ask Hawk if this was the way it was in the

old days, if this was the way it had been. Did everybody fall into bed at the end of the night, did everybody fuck in the end? He thought some sociologist should take a poll. A poll with your pole.

"You like to dance?" said a voice close by. Looking up, he saw that it was the heavy-set waitress, Claudia, again.

"You think you can get me a drink when we're done?"

"You don't need no more to drink, sugar," she said shyly.

"Goddammit," Jerry exploded. "Everybody's telling me what I need, and what I don't need. Why doesn't everybody just leave me alone?" It seemed as if for a moment the music stopped and every eye in the hot, crowded room was on him. He thought he heard murmurs of disapproval—but, of course, that was ridiculous. "I'm sorry," he said. "I don't know, I don't know why I—"

Claudia's feet moved with a delicacy and swiftness surprising in so large a woman, as she executed intricate little steps that made Jerry feel as if *he* were fat and clumsy. "Don't worry about it, sugar," she said kindly and put her hand on his shoulder as a slow number started up and gathered him in to her. He felt crushed against her bosom, wishing he could lose himself in the generous folds of flesh. Looking over, he saw Lori dancing with Scooter and Mattie sipping decorously on her drink. His head was buzzing, the music filled his brain, driving out any stray thoughts he might have had, he clung to Claudia for dear life. He was drunk. She patted his back understandingly. "Thanks, sugar. Gotta get back to work."

Just then the band went into its riff, the bass player grabbed the mike and declared, "Now let's hear it. Let's hear it for Moses Edward, Little Mose and the Bros. Put your hands together, ladies and gentlemen, I want you to let the man *hear* it. Well, right now, ladies and gents, we gonna take five to stay alive, we might take ten, my friend, but we'll be back again. Any re-questses, you just let us know and we do our best to satisfy you. We *always* do our best, and we always satisfy—you know we do, sugar, that's right. So y'all be sure and stick around, don't be a clown and put us down or be a square and walk out and go somewhere. There's plenty more where this come from, y'hear?" Looking bored, the band finished out their number and put their instruments down. The horn player and keyboard man lit up cigarettes. Jerry stood out on the dance floor until it was practically deserted and only then stumbled back to the table.

They were talking about him. They were acting as if he wasn't even there. "We gonna have to carry that boy home," Hawk laughed. "I don't know what's got into him."

"Roosevelt, will you just leave him be?"

"Are you all right?" said Lori, giggling, as he seated himself unsteadily.

"I just wish you would all leave me alone," he said, muster-ing one last attempt at dignity.

Now that the dance floor was clear, a number of people noticed Hawk for the first time and there started to be a steady procession over to the table. It was like old home week, as Hawk greeted each one in turn with "How you been? How you doing, man?" extending his hand, never rising from his seat, accepting their well-wishes with a deference that let everyone know he was only taking it as his due.

"Hey, you met Little Mose yet?" said one of the men whom Jerry thought he recognized from earlier times. Hawk shook his head. "Hey, man, that ain't right. That boy dying to meet you. Just a minute. Let me go get him."

A few minutes later he brought back Mose, who, far from giving the impression that he was dying to meet the older man, appeared sullen and a little resentful to have been dragged to the table. Despite the heat he was wearing a floor-length coat and smoking a thin cigar, while a lithe young woman with long curly hair that appeared to be her own clung to his arm. Up close Mose looked even more bored and worldly-wise than he did on stage, his hooded eyes giving a slightly sardonic edge to a smooth-skinned face which could have been anywhere between twenty and fifty, so effective was its owner in masking any trace of emotion, in warding off any betrayal of commitment from its somewhat pinched features.

"I knew your daddy," Hawk said at last, after a silence that seemed as if it might go on all night.

"I never did," said Mose.

"No, I guess you wouldn't. Your mama must have taken you away when you was three, four years old."

"That's right."

"Never been back?"

"Come back one time, after my first record was out." Hawk nodded. "I didn't have no gig. Just wanted to see where I was from. Roots!" he spat out with a harsh little laugh. "That's what everyone be talking about, ain't it? I come down here, Mr. Charlie say, Bend over, boy, I'll show you your roots."

"You ain't lying neither," said Hawk. He stared at the younger man, but Mose said nothing else. His companion drummed her painted fingernails on his shoulder.

"This here's my manager," Hawk said. "Mr. Jerry Lipschitz." Jerry half rose and reached across the table to shake hands. He barely felt the grip of Mose's limp fingers. "And I'm sure you've heard of Lori Peebles."

"Oh yeah?" For a moment a look of interest penetrated the

impervious features. "Yeah, I seen you once, I think we might've played on the same bill—"

"I'm sorry, I don't remember—"

"Oh yeah, it was a big benefit thing up in Chicago. For Reverend Jesse, you know what I'm talking about?"

"Out at the baseball park?"

"That's right."

"Oh, that was beautiful," said Lori.

"That's right."

"I just got back from Europe, you know," said Hawk. "Them European cats just eat up all this kind of shit. You ever been over there yourself?"

"No, man, I been planning to make it over one of these days. I mean, I been *asked,* but the way I figure it, I gotta get *paid,* you know what I'm talking about? What I want to go over there for if I ain't gonna get paid?"

"That's right. That's right. Ain't no sense in going just for the glory. You should talk to this boy here about setting you up a tour. He knows all them big-time cats."

"Yeah, maybe I have my manager talk to him."

Jerry looked from one to the other, like a spectator at a Ping-Pong match.

"The people go crazy when they find out who your kinfolks are."

"Oh yeah?" said Mose, half interested. "You think so, man?"

"Shit, to them Ol' Man Mose is like a fucking god."

The young man laughed a short tight laugh. "To my mama he was like the devil hisself. I never even knowed my grandaddy was a musician till I started hanging around the clubs—you know, trying to be a bad boy. Up till then the only place I sung was in the choir. But when my mama seen I had my mind set on singing *my* music, that's when she said, Well, I guess it's in your blood, ain't nothing I can do about it. She didn't want to have nothing to do with me, but I promised I'd buy her a home someday, I'm still gonna do it, man, that day still gonna come."

"Sure it is," said Hawk. "You say hello to your mama from me the next time you see her, y'hear? Tell her I didn't even know she was still up there, else I would have looked her up myself."

Mose appeared to be embarrassed, as if he had been lulled into making a revelation. "Oh yeah, sure. Mama still stay in touch with down home. Practically her whole congregation from down home."

"Yeah," said Hawk. "That's right."

The bass player was getting the rest of the band together on the bandstand. "Well, look like I gotta be getting back to work," said Mose without any hint of emotion in his voice. "You take care of yourself, hear?" He clapped Hawk on the back. "Nice meeting you folks," he said with an entertainer's broad grin and a little wink besides. He walked off with his girl, their arms loosely entwined.

Hawk looked after them. "I couldn't remember his mama's name," he said, shaking his head sadly. "You remember his mama, baby?"

"Now how could I remember his mama—"

"Oh yeah, shoot, you wasn't even born yet when she left home. She was a little bitty thing, meek and mild, never could figure how she got mixed up with his daddy. His daddy worse than Ol' Man Mose, and now he's the third. She-it." He put his arm around Little Bo. "Well, that's all right, we beat 'em anyway with just a old man and a little boy—"

"I ain't no little boy."

"Well, sure you ain't."

Jerry kept on drinking. The music all blended together. You don't miss your water, he heard, until your well run dry. It's hard, but it's fair, I'm in love with my best friend's girl. Don't make your children pay for your mistakes. Try a little tenderness. All undeniable home truths. All somehow hitting home tonight. He looked over to Hawk for guidance, but Hawk was seemingly preoccupied, nodding in time to the music, a benign, almost dreamy smile on his face.

"You think this guy's any good?" he said thickly to Lori.

"Ssh," she said, touching his hand.

Then he was dancing with the overweight waitress again, babbling on about something, he didn't know what and he didn't know why. "You know, I likes talking to you," she said. "I don't understand a word you saying, but I likes hearing your voice saying it." Jerry supposed he should take that as a compliment.

Some time during the set Little Mose shushed the band. "I want to introduce someone we got out there here in the audience tonight," he said into the microphone. "A great singer, a fine entertainer, we had the pleasure of working with her once in Chicago, Miss Lori Peebles, let's give her a nice welcome, y'all, a great singer and a beautiful lady. Well, she come in with her manager here tonight just to catch our act. We got another old friend of ours in her party, I'm sure y'all remember him, the Screamin' Nighthawk. Yeah, stand up, Hawk, and take a bow. Come on, man, stand up."

The drummer played a roll, and Hawk stood up, leaning heavily on the table, glaring out into the darkness, thinking only he knew what thoughts. He sat down again, and Mattie took his hand. "I knowed his *grand*father," said Hawk, "for the lying sonofabitch he was."

"Hush," said Mattie. "Hush."

I TIRED. And I sick. And I old. Ain't nothing for it, ain't no cure ever been invented. It seem so different sometime, and yet it ain't no different at all. They was eight of us all told, with Sister's kids and Pigpen and Mama and Daddy before he left. And we all work in the fields. I can remember Daddy showing me how to pick that cotton, say start at the bottom, son, move up like this, that way you don't miss nothing, see all the bolls as you move up. When I was a kid, I just wanted to pick five hundred pounds, thought that was what make a man, I heard tell some cat pick a thousand pounds, just a story, man I thought that was really something. See, back then that's what I thought that song "John Henry" all about. Foolishness. Didn't realize then there wasn't no way you could beat that steam drill down, that steam drill gonna kill you sure, just like it kill John Henry. Well, early on I made up my mind, said, It ain't gonna kill me. Just like the words of the song. It kill John Henry, but it won't kill me.

Man, we come out of the fields at the end of the day, come home to that little tar-paper shack, wind just whistle right through them walls was so thin, wasn't nothing else to do *but* sing. What the fuck else were you gonna do? Watch television? Didn't know nothing about little girls—leastaways not till I was ten, eleven years old. So we get together on the porch, sing them old songs, till we sick of 'em. Then on Saturday afternoons we go to the picnics sometimes—everybody go way back in the woods, bring chicken and that good smoked ham and the bands be playing, you could hear them fife-and-drum sets for miles, man, let *everybody* know what was going on. Sometimes they have a ballgame out in one of them big old muddy fields, stumps sticking up, and ball ain't gonna roll nowhere, you get a home run if they lose it in the high grass. Didn't have no gloves back in them days neither, and the ball all wound around with yarn that turn black. I can remember Daddy ranging all over that outfield, oh he was a good country ballplayer, and Mama shouting out at him, C'mon, Will, don't nothing get by my Will. And that ball go sailing out over the fielders' heads, and Daddy run like the wind and pull that little black thing down, just pull it in so nice and gentle like it go slap against his palm. And afterwards the wimmins all gets together and talks about their husbands and their kids, and trade stories, and the mens all throwing dice and getting hot and drinking corn and trading stories, too. And the git-tar pickers just keeps on playing, whether folkses is dancing or not, if one get tired there's always another to take his place, sitting so close they could practically breathe for each other, and the sound go ringing out, carry in the night air. Seem like things was never gonna change to a kid, but they did. Daddy didn't stay with Mama, niggers didn't stay with cotton, even the white man didn't stay with what he knowed then. I just wish Mama and Daddy could have seed me now. . . .

THEY TRIED to dissuade him. Jerry did everything but hold him down. It wasn't the proper time, it wasn't the proper place, let him at least wait until he had his own guitar, until he was feeling better and got his strength back. But it was like talking to a wall. After all their entreaties Hawk stood up, tapped Little Bo on the shoulder, and looking to neither left nor right lurched heavily to the stage, which was presently unoccupied.

At first the bass player tried to stop them. "Hey, man, you can't use that ax," he started to say, as Hawk clumsily strapped on an electric guitar and Little Bo picked up Mose's Stratocaster and fiddled uncertainly with the amplifier dials. Hawk just glared at the musician, who stroked his barbershop mustache and at last looked over to Mose for guidance.

"Hey, man, it's cool," said Mose, who looked as if he had gotten high between sets. "Sure, let the old man have his chance, maybe they like him better than they like us."

Hawk touched the strings tentatively. The sound seemed to jump from the Fender amp, and Mose laughed harshly. Bo looked small and frightened on stage but never took his eyes off his father and drew a chair up next to him. Hawk adjusted the mike, and Lori took Jerry's hand.

"It'll probably be all right," said Jerry uncertainly.

"That damned old fool," said Mattie, her eyes filling up with tears. "What he have to go and make a damned fool of himself for?"

"It'll be all right," said Jerry, thinking if only they could get through the next half hour, if he could simply project ahead, shoot forward in time, and *know* how it all came out—why did things always have to complicate themselves, unnecessarily, so that what you had prepared yourself for was altered or erased and you just wished yourself back at a point you had never been happy with to start off with? That was how it had been with Lori and him—if he just could have accepted what he had, if he had just been able to peek ahead at the future and comprehend the *risk*, if he only knew now that Hawk would simply survive—

"Hey, I love you," he said out loud and was immediately chagrined—why chagrined, that was what he felt, wasn't it? Lori squeezed his hand. Did it mean anything? There was no telling.

"Ladies and gentlemens," Hawk announced, "I'd like your

attention please. Our first number that we gonna sing for you, the very first number that I ever recorded—"

Jerry panicked. There was something wrong. He wasn't playing some genteel college—was he forgetting where he was? I have stripped him of his protective coloration, Jerry thought, like a damned ecologist.

Then Hawk struck a chord, Little Bo fell in manfully behind him, and his voice filled the room, made bigger somehow by the unrelenting hum of conversation, the rising tide of good times and better expectations.

I'm a screamin' nighthawk, baby,
And I don't want you to deny my name . . .

Jerry was uplifted all over again by the sound of his voice, amazed at the thrill he still felt at its majesty and presence, but he didn't dare to look around. When he did, *they were dancing!* It wasn't anything. It wasn't anything, he knew. It was just in the normal order of things, but they were dancing! Hawk finished the first number, and with no preamble launched into the next.

Went to the gypsy, get my fortune done
Gypsy say, Hawk, you sure need some
Well, must I holler, or must I . . . shake 'em on down . . .

One after another they ran down the old songs, the strain evidently telling on Hawk, for his face was pouring sweat. Bo studied his father intently, hunched over the Stratocaster's elongated neck, doing his best to follow the irregular patterns of the music, his knees so close to Hawk's they were practically locked.

Jerry took Mattie's hand. "You see, there wasn't anything to worry about," he said, as much to reassure himself as to reassure her. He hadn't robbed Hawk of anything, or, if he had, he had scrupulously replaced it with something else. The world was changing, dammit. Even the Sunset Cafe had seen demonstrable changes which Jerry had done nothing to bring about. He was no grave-robber! Lori looked at him peculiarly. He hadn't spoken, had he? "It's not so bad, is it?" he said again. But Mattie didn't look convinced. Her lips were pursed tight as she watched father and son, old man and little boy, struggling to recapture a past— or was it to prevent the present from becoming past? Stemming the tide? Plugging the leak? Jerry's head was spinning. Hawk and Rabbit Turner, Mattie's father. Hawk and Ol' Man Mose. History was repeating itself, but history was obliterated, and Hawk alone remained to tell the tale.

"I'm drunk," Jerry said to Lori.

"I know."

"You want to dance?"

"You'd probably just fall down."

Jerry giggled. Shit. He loved her. "I know." He reached for her, but she was holding Mattie's hand, saying something. Hawk was stomping his feet and inviting everyone to "Play with Your Poodle."

"Hey," said a voice beside him. He looked up, and it was Little Mose. A hand was extended, a soft contemptuous handshake, didn't mean anything one way or another, why should it? "Old man ain't bad," said Mose. Jerry shook his head, as if to clear it. "I mean, he can get *down*. Shit, will you look at them niggers jump." He laughed and immediately broke off, whether because he had revealed himself to a stranger or was ashamed of the emotion he really felt. "You folks doing anything after the show?" he said, looking only at Lori, who seemed scarcely aware of his presence. "Reason I ask, we having a little party back at the motel, get some folks together, relax, and I promise you, looks like we're going to have a good time." His thin lips formed a smile.

Lori looked at Jerry. "No," she said, "I don't think so. I'm kind of tired."

"We got some good shit, mama," said Mose meaningfully.

Jerry, half asleep, was snapped into wakefulness. Could Mose have heard something about Lori? he wondered. Was the word out on her all over? She loved spades, she was strung out on—what? He tried to steady his gaze and stare into Mose's hard little eyes, but he could read nothing in the other's expression.

"No, I don't think so. Not really."

"I understand we got mutual acquaintances," said Mose even more meaningfully.

Was it his imagination, or had Mose suddenly taken on a more sinister cast? Lori seemed agitated. As if to further disturb him, she turned her face away from his inquiring gaze. "Why don't you and Mattie just, uh, dance?" she said. "I'll be all right. Really."

He wasn't going to move, he wasn't going to leave this table, but Mattie took his hand and he followed docilely. He had never been much good at defending Lori from anything anyway.

Well, I rolled and I tumbled
I cried the whole night long . . .

Hawk and Little Bo were going at it fast and furious. The music speeded up, even as the good times got better and everyone was lifted higher and higher.

"You think she'll be all right?" he said thickly to Mattie.

"What you talking about?" said Mattie indignantly. "That gal always going to be all right. When you going to make up your mind to that? The minute you start to trust her, you know that when she gonna come home."

"What?" He was not sure he had understood what she meant, or even heard. What did she know of him and Lori?

When I woke up this morning
All I had was gone.

Was that the secret of her marriage to Hawk? Did you have to make yourself purposefully dumb? He wondered if she had ever fucked around on the side. His imagination writhed as he thought of Hawk finding them in bed together. But had Hawk ever fucked Lori?

"What's the matter, Jerry? You feeling all right?" Without realizing it, he had winced, as if struck. But that was not the point. That was the point. It had nothing to do with that.

"Yeah, I'm all right." *Trust. Trust.* Trust in other people's *wholeness.* Don't try to make them over. Love her for what she is. Forget what she ain't. An old joke Hawk had told him. He thought that was the punch line, but what was the joke?

Mattie clung to him. "I think he gonna be all right," she whispered in his ear.

"Oh yeah, sure, I guess so."

Well, Vicksburg on a high hill
Natchez on down below . . .

The words soared past, earmarked for some dark and mysterious grotto behind his consciousness. The rush of the music, Little Bo not just hitting the chords now but picking against Hawk's lead, Hawk's fingers still clumsy, not quite used to the action of the electric guitar but making music nonetheless. A discriminating ear would throw it all out. Call for a second take, then a third take, then complain the later takes didn't match the feeling of earlier ones. But nothing was ever exactly the same as anything else, that was the whole point, wasn't it, you just gave in to the moment, *other people* gave in to the moment, you just reacted instinctively, you didn't judge *instinct*.

I could see my peoples
They ain't coming back no more . . .

When they returned to the table, Mose was gone. "What did he want?" Jerry said suspiciously.
"Oh, nothing."
"You're not going to the party afterwards?"
"Of course not."
"Oh. You want to dance?" he said. "I didn't fall down."
"Sure," said Lori cheerfully. "Why not?"
The dance floor was packed, and Hawk was doing a slow number, one of his favorites.

People are talking, all over town
They all saying, you gonna put the old man down
Well, baby, don't deceive me
Please don't leave me
Baby, please don't go.

Jerry just let it wash over him, he wanted to bathe in the sensation the way Hawk lost himself in the verse, repeating the simple words over and over with countless variations of tone and phrasing and a passion that increased with each repetition. Lori wrapped both arms around him and clung tightly, he felt her softness, he felt her breasts, he imagined her wet until he got a hard-on and closed his eyes. He loved her. I love you, you know. Didn't that count for anything? Of course it did.

241

"I love you," he said into her hair.

"Don't," she said, shaking her head. "That tickles."

"You know, that tickles me," said Hawk in imagination, "to think of how you loves her, how you been loving her all these years and afraid to speak your mind." He had never said that. He had never talked to Hawk about Lori. He never would. She felt soft and pliant and open, like a flower about to bud. He cupped both hands around her ass and squeezed her gently. She squirmed. He imagined his finger entering her through her clothes. Tonight he knew he would fuck her. He felt sure of it now. He would sleep with her, and in the morning her hair would be fanned out on the pillow and she would be radiant in sleep. He would fuck her tonight and she wouldn't care how much noise she made or who she waked in the little cabin. He would fuck her, and it wouldn't mean a thing. But that didn't mean anything either. He could almost taste the salty brine. He could almost ache with anticipation.

Up on the small stage Hawk was getting tired. Like a phonograph winding down, he thought. Words coming out harder, everything slowing down. He looked over at Little Bo and gave him a nod. Time to wind it up—phonograph couldn't get wound up no more, needle was broke, wasn't no more lead in the pencil. Hunh! The dancers politely applauded, what the fuck did they care, they just wanted to go on about their own business. The boy done good, have to tell him that afterwards, he worked hard while I was gone, and it *paid off*. "Thank you, ladies and gentlemens," and then something caught him up, a little gust of wind maybe, maybe they were *too* quick or he just wanted to give them something to think about, Little Bo was already setting the guitar down when he hit the opening notes, watched the music go right through them, it wasn't the electricity, it was the music, Little Bo picked it up, good kid, nice boy, he thought he could smell the smell of a fish fry, somewhere they was having a fish fry, miles away out in the country, smell come drifting in soft as memory, if he closed his eyes he could picture it—*Don't!* Don't close your eyes, something told him. His head buzzed—or maybe that was the amp. His head hurt. Don't let yourself sink under. Finish the song. Don't quit now. Don't quit *never.* Just keep it going. It be over soon enough.

> *Well, that moon going down*
> *Sun refuse to, sun refuse to shine*
> *Well, that moon going down*
> *Sun refuse to shine*
> *Well, that no good motherfuck*
> * stole that gal of mine.*

Was it his imagination, or was the room rocking? Flames licking at the windows. Don't sink, don't sink. He forcibly lifted his eyes up—people laughing and joking, jiving each other, having a *good* time. Whoo-ee. Just like it always been. Just like it always be. Till the end of time. Till the world gonna end.

> *Well, that smokestack black*
> *And the bell it shine like,*
> *Bell it shine like . . .*
> GOLD!
> *Well, that smokestack black*
> *And the bell it shine like gold*
> *Well, I ain't gonna stop walking*
> *Till I get in pretty mama's door . . .*

Oh, now we got it, now we got it, that's it, we got 'em jumping like a champ. Bell, it shine like, bell it shine like GOLD—

that's just what it like. That bell, it shine like—but, you know, it ain't easy. It ain't easy. It hard. What the other words? I can't remember the words so good anymore. Bell, it shine like GOLD. They tells me I never was no good at words, but that ain't true, and it don't matter neither. It's the feeling *behind* the words. Ain't nobody ever said I don't have the feeling. Bell, it shine like GOLD.

Oh man, oh man, I don't feel so good. People still out there? You make yourself look them in the eye like a man, just like your mama tole you. Yeah, they there. They *still* laughing and joking, world hasn't ended yet, won't end till tomorrow morning, when they wake up beside somebody else's wife or husband, or else somebody shoot out the lights. Bell, it shine like *gold*. I ain't gonna let go. I ain't never gonna let go. That boy don't understand. If you got it, you *can't* let go, else otherwise it let you go somehow. Can't see nothing. Can't hear nothing but the music. Open your eyes, you damn fool. Open your eyes. Yeah, I open my eyes, they be putting their hands together. I touch myself, and I can feel the sweat pouring down. I didn't die! This is what I really want.